RANGER'S APPRENTICE

THE ROYAL RANGER BOOK 4

THE MISSING PRINCE

RANGER'S APPRENTICE

THE ROYAL RANGER BOOK 4

THE MISSING PRINCE

JOHN FLANAGAN

PHILOMEL BOOKS

PHILOMEL BOOKS
An imprint of Penguin Random House LLC, New York

Copyright © 2020 by John Flanagan.
Published in Australia by Penguin Random House Australia in 2020.
Published in the United States of America by Philomel Books,
an imprint of Penguin Random House LLC, 2020.

Philomel Books is a registered trademark of Penguin Random House LLC.

Visit us online at penguinrandomhouse.com.

Library of Congress Cataloging-in-Publication Data is available.

Jacket printed in the USA; book printed in Canada.

ISBN 9780593113455

1 3 5 7 9 10 8 6 4 2

US edition edited by Kelsey Murphy.
US edition designed by Ellice M. Lee.
Text set in Adobe Jenson Pro.

To the memory of my brother,
Peter Flanagan, 1940–2019

1

THE SICKLE MOON HAD JUST SLIPPED BELOW THE WESTERN horizon when the file of mounted men emerged from the trees. There were ten of them in all and they pushed forward a few paces until they crested the ridge looking down to Castle Araluen. The rider at the center of the line held one hand in the air in the universal sign to halt, and the line of riders drew rein, watching the castle. The horses snuffled impatiently. They sensed that the massive building meant shelter and water and feed, and they were impatient for all three.

The rider to the right of the man who had signaled leaned forward attentively in his saddle, studying the open ground before them. It sloped down initially from the ridge, then began to rise again toward the castle, dotted here and there with clumps of trees and shady arbors. For the most part, the ground was open and a rider crossing it would be within full view, if anyone were watching.

And the likelihood was, someone was always watching. But now the open parkland looked deserted. Any potential watchers would be within the castle itself, and that was where the small party of armed and mail-clad riders was expected.

Most of the castle's windows were in darkness—as would be usual at this late hour. There were beacon fires in braziers set at regular intervals along the walls, and two torches flickered at either side of the gate, which was now closed and locked against intruders.

"It all looks normal, my lord," the rider said quietly.

The man beside him nodded. "I'd expect it to—even if it's not."

Both men spoke in Gallic. As they hesitated, a yellow lantern was exposed on the walls above the huge gate and drawbridge, spilling its light down the granite walls of the entryway.

"And there's the signal," the leader said. He turned to a rider on his other side. "Jules, make the reply."

The man he had addressed had flint and tinder ready, and a lantern hung from his saddle bow. It took him a few moments to light a handful of tinder, then to press the resulting flame to the wick of the lantern. As the tiny flame took, he closed the front of the lantern, which was made from blue glass. He held the light high, letting the blue gleam spread out over the small group.

A few seconds later, the light on the castle walls moved slowly from left to right, then back again, repeating the action three times.

"That's the all clear," the leader said, nudging his spurs into the side of the horse he rode and moving forward. The line of riders followed him, dropping into two files as they went, with the leader and the first knight who had spoken at the front.

They moved at a slow trot, their horses' hooves making little sound on the soft ground. As they reached the bottom of the first slope and began to climb toward the castle, the horses naturally slowed a little and the riders urged them on to greater speed. They heard the massive clanking of a large engine, and a slit of light showed at the top of the drawbridge, gradually growing wider as it opened.

The huge bridge thudded down by the time they were thirty meters away. The riders could see that the portcullis was still lowered, barring access to the castle yard. The lead riders urged their horses to the beginning of the drawbridge and halted.

A mail-clad man-at-arms stepped through a small gate at the side of the portcullis and crossed the bridge toward them. He was armed with a halberd and wore a long sword at his waist. His mail armor gleamed dully in the light of the beacons set either side of the drawbridge.

The leader of the group looked up at the massive dark walls towering above him. He had no doubt that he was covered by several bowmen. This being Araluen, they would be armed with longbows, not crossbows, and they would all be expert shots.

The man-at-arms stopped a few meters short of the group.

"Do you have the password?" he asked quietly.

The lead rider shifted slightly in his saddle. *"Pax inter reges,"* he said in the ancient tongue: "peace between kings."

The foot soldier nodded and turned back to the castle, raising his right arm in a signal to the men at the portcullis. Slowly, the massive frame began to rise into the air, the movement accompanied by a distant clanking inside the gatehouse. When it was well clear of the bridge, the foot soldier waved the group forward.

"Go ahead," he said.

The hooves of their horses clattered on the hardwood boards

of the drawbridge as they trotted across in two files. When they reached the cobbled castle yard, the sound changed. There were armed foot soldiers on either side, watching them as they made their entry. One, who wore the insignia of a sergeant, gestured toward a door in the keep, the strongly built stone tower in the center of the castle yard. As he did so, a door opened at ground level and yellow torchlight spilled out onto the stone paving.

The new arrivals rode up to the open door and dismounted. Waiting servants took their horses and led them away to feed them and rub them down. The leader of the group pressed one fist into the small of his back. He wasn't used to riding long distances anymore and they had been traveling for four hours.

The man who had opened the door descended the three steps to the level of the courtyard and bowed slightly from the waist. He was gray-haired and distinguished in appearance, dressed in expensive-looking clothes.

"Welcome to Castle Araluen. I'm Lord Anthony, the King's chamberlain," he said. His tone was neutral, neither welcoming nor aggressive. The visitor nodded acknowledgment, but said nothing. Anthony stepped to one side and gestured for the new arrivals to mount the stairs. "Please come this way."

The leader of the group mounted the stairs, and Anthony fell into step slightly behind and beside him. The rest of the group followed.

As they came into the well-lit great hall of the keep, Anthony studied the man leading the group. He was small, a good five centimeters shorter than Anthony, and slightly built. His well-cut jerkin, in forest-green leather, couldn't conceal his unathletic build. His shoulders were narrow and he had the beginnings of a paunch. He held himself badly, slumping and allowing his shoulders to stoop. He wore an ornate-looking sword on his left hip, with a jewel-encrusted dagger to balance it on the right.

In spite of the weapons, this was no warrior, Anthony thought. But then, he had been told as much when he had been briefed about this visit.

He cast a quick glance over the rest of the group. All but one were taller than the leader, and they were muscular and athletic-looking. They *were* warriors, he thought. The one exception was the same height and build as the leader and there was a strong family resemblance. Anthony realized that the leader had hesitated, not sure which way to go, and he quickly gestured toward the wide staircase leading to the upper levels of the keep.

"King Duncan's rooms are on the second floor," he said, and the shorter man led the way once more.

"The King apologizes for not greeting you down here, sir," Anthony said. "His knee still troubles him and the stairs can be difficult."

The visitor sniffed condescendingly. "He's still crippled, is he?"

Lord Anthony raised an eyebrow at the insulting word and the superior tone. Stiff knee or not, Duncan was still very much a warrior. He could chew you up and spit you out, Anthony thought.

"He's able to ride again, and he walks with his dogs every day," he replied, keeping the irritation out of his voice.

"But not down stairs, obviously," the other man said.

This time, Anthony allowed his irritation to show. He stopped, facing the visitor. "No. But if that bothers you, sir, we can always cancel this meeting." He met the other man's haughty gaze and held it. You pompous prat, he thought, you're coming here to ask a favor, so you can climb down off your high horse.

They locked gazes for a few seconds, then the visitor gave way with a dismissive shrug—a typically Gallic movement, Anthony thought.

"No matter," the visitor said. "We can walk upstairs."

He resumed climbing the stairs. Anthony, feeling a small glow of satisfaction at the way the man had backed down, followed close behind. As they reached the top of the wide stone stairway, he gestured to the left.

"This way, please, sir."

A set of massive wooden doors faced them. They were guarded by two men-at-arms, who seemed to be built on the same scale as the doors. At the sight of the armed men approaching, they came to a ready position, barring the way with the long halberds they held in front of them.

"I'm afraid your men will have to wait, sir," Anthony said.

The smaller man nodded. It was only to be expected, after all.

"One of your companions can accompany you," the chamberlain added.

The visitor pointed to one of the men following him, the one who resembled him.

"My brother, Louis, will come with me," he said. He gestured to the others. "The rest of you will wait here."

"No need for that, sir," Anthony told him. "We have refreshments for them in an adjacent room." He raised his voice and called, "Thomas!"

Another door opened farther down the corridor and a

uniformed servant emerged, bowing slightly and inviting the visitors into the brightly lit room behind him.

The leader nodded and the eight warriors trooped off to the food and drink waiting for them. Anthony led the way toward the huge wooden doors. The sentries stepped aside, coming to attention as they did. Anthony knocked on the doors and a voice was heard from within.

"Come."

Anthony opened the double doors and led the two visitors into the King's office.

Duncan was seated behind the large table that served as his desk.

"My lord," said Anthony, "may I present King Philippe of Gallica, and his brother, Prince Louis."

Duncan, the King of Araluen, rose from his seat and moved round the table to greet his visitors.

"Welcome to Araluen," Duncan said, holding out his hand.

Philippe took it and they shook hands. "Thank you for receiving us," Philippe said.

Duncan shrugged the thanks aside. "We should always be willing to help our friends." He nodded a greeting to the second man. "Prince Louis," he said.

The King's brother bowed gracefully. "Your Majesty," Louis said, then straightened.

Duncan studied the two men. They looked travel-stained and weary.

"It's late and you've traveled a long way," he said. "You must be tired and hungry."

Philippe made a small moue of agreement. "It has been a hard day," he agreed.

"Your chambers are prepared for you. I'll have food and drink sent up, and hot water for a bath if you wish. Get a good night's sleep and we'll talk in the morning."

For the first time, Philippe smiled. "That would be most welcome. And we do have a great deal to discuss."

Duncan inclined his head. "I'm sure we do," he said.

2

THE OLD FARM CART WAS BATTERED AND IN DIRE NEED OF A coat of paint. The wooden axle for the right-hand wheel was dry. The grease had long since worn away and it squeaked in a regular rhythm—an annoying sound that could set a listener's teeth on edge. It didn't seem to bother the old farmer driving the cart. He was hunched over on the driving bench, urging on the mule between the shafts with a series of clicks of the tongue.

The mule needed urging. He was stubborn and cantankerous, like most of his kind, and the cart was heavy and fully laden with farm produce. Sheaves of wheat and barley filled the tray, along with a dozen sacks of potatoes, strings of onions and eight or nine large pumpkins. The bodies of nine plump ducks hung over the tailgate, heads down and jiggling with the movement of the cart as the solid wheels bumped and lumbered over ruts in the track. They would sell for their meat, of course, but their feathers would also be sought after as down for pillows. That double value would be reflected in the price the farmer would demand for them at market.

Behind the cart, tethered to the rear axle, trotted two half-grown sheep—a young ram and a ewe. They were the most valuable items that the farmer was taking to market. The ram would be used for breeding and the ewe already showed that her fleece was thick and heavy. As she grew older, she would provide abundant wool, season after season.

The farmer was a small man. Hunched down as he was, he appeared shriveled with age and a life of hard work. But, judging by the quality and quantity of the goods he was taking to market, the hard work had been well worthwhile. He wore a patched old farm smock and a shapeless straw hat crammed on his head. His trousers were rough homespun wool and his boots were leather—old, but well kept. At a time when most farm people could afford nothing more than wooden clogs stuffed with straw, they were evidence of his lifetime of industry and thrift—as well as the quality of his produce.

The road climbed a small hill and the cleared farmland on either side gradually gave way to dense woodland, where the deep shadows cast by the trees concealed any sign that somebody might be watching the road.

But somebody was. In fact, four somebodies were watching the cart slowly squeaking between the trees. The land at either side of the road had been cleared for eight or nine meters, then the tree line began. The farmer glanced idly at the dark shadows either side of the road, then settled back on the bench, moving around to find a comfortable position. He gave no sign that he had seen the silent watchers among the trees.

The leader of the group was a burly, bearded man about thirty years old. He was dressed in rough clothes—a jerkin and trousers of homespun—and a bearskin cloak. The bear's mask, and its upper jaw, served as a cap for the wearer of the cloak. At first sight, it looked impressive and dangerous—a snarling face that surmounted his own bearded, dirty features. But if one looked more closely, it became apparent that the bear had not been in the best of condition when it died. One of its front fangs was broken off halfway and there were several bare patches visible where the fur had rubbed away. The sorry appearance of his cloak and cap didn't bother the wearer. He had named himself Barton Bearkiller and had gained some notoriety in the district as the leader of a robber band, preying on the common people— farmers and residents of small villages.

Barton was seated on a low branch of a tree, watching the cart squeaking by. He looked down in annoyance as one of his men reached up and tweaked his leg.

"What?" he demanded in a rough whisper. The tweaker, whose name was Donald, grinned inanely and pointed to the cart.

"Lots of goods in that cart," he said. And when the self-styled bear killer didn't reply, he continued, "Should us go out and take 'um?"

"Why would we do that?" Barton demanded.

Donald shrugged expansively and rolled his eyes. "Wheat, potatties, punk'ins, ducks and sheep," he explained, as if Barton couldn't see it all for himself. "Us could sell a' that for a pretty penny," he explained.

Barton shook his head and sneered at his follower. "Why should we go to all that work?" He jerked his head toward the huddled figure of the farmer. "We'll let him sell them all for us."

Donald followed the direction of the gesture, nodded, then frowned. "But then," he said, "us won't be able to take them, will us? If he's sold 'um, he won't have 'um anymore."

"No," Barton said deliberately. "He'll have all the money from selling them. Lovely coin that goes chink."

Slowly, understanding dawned over Donald's grubby, unshaven features. "And us'll take the chink from him," he said.

Barton nodded, exaggerating the motion. "That's right. We'll take it from him."

Donald smiled, then the smile faded as he saw another problem. "When?" he asked. "When do we take it all from him?"

"This afternoon when he's heading home from the market," Barton told him.

Donald smiled as he saw the reasoning behind Barton's plan. "He'll come back here, with all the money . . ."

"And we'll take it from him," Barton confirmed.

Donald's smile grew wider as he visualized the scene to be played out later in the day. "He won't like that, he won't," he said, and chuckled throatily.

Barton nodded, the bearskin cap dipping as he did so. "Not one bit he won't," he said. "But do we care?"

Donald danced a step or two of a jig. "Not one bit we don't."

He looked after the cart as it disappeared round a bend in the road, so that the trees hid it from view. Faintly, the noise of the squeaking wheel carried back to them for another minute or two, then it faded away.

Barton glanced at the sun. "Might as well take it easy for a while," he said. "It'll be several hours before he comes back."

He scrambled down from the branch and found a patch of long, soft grass on the far side of the tree. He lay down and stretched out, pulling the bearskin mask over his eyes to shade them. The other two members of the band—One-Eyed Jem and

Walter Scar—followed suit, lying on the soft ground and relaxing. Donald watched them for a few seconds, wondering if he should do the same. But Barton's voice stopped him.

"You keep watch," he said gruffly. "Might be another farmer will come along."

Donald nodded, a little disappointed. The grass grew thickly here and it looked cool and comfortable.

"Aye," he said, "I'll keep watch."

It was midafternoon before the squeaking wheel heralded the return of the farm cart. The squeak was more rapid now, as the empty cart was moving faster than it had previously. The mule twitched its tail contentedly as it trotted along. It preferred the lightly laden cart to the heavier version of the morning, and now it was heading back to the comfort of its barn and a full feed bag. The farmer was still perched on the seat at the front of the cart. The tray of the cart itself was empty, save for three canvas sacks.

The cart disappeared from view as it went into a small dip in the road, and Barton gestured hurriedly to Jem and Walter.

"Across the road," he ordered them. "Donald and I will wait here. Stay undercover until we've got him stopped."

His two henchmen didn't point out that they had done this sort of thing a dozen times in the past few weeks and didn't need instructions. There was no point doing that with Barton. He had an uncertain temper at the best of times. Crouching low, although the cart was still hidden from sight, they scurried across the narrow track and concealed themselves among the trees. They were both armed—Jem with a homemade spear and Walter with a heavy spiked cudgel.

Barton retrieved his own cudgel from behind the tree where

he had been sleeping and gestured to Donald to move back to the trees.

"Get out of sight," he ordered. "Wait till I call you out."

Donald nodded several times and ran in a crouch to the tree line. The sun was lower in the sky now and it cast deeper shadows among the trees. Barton watched, then nodded in grim satisfaction. Unless you were consciously looking for the ragged bandit, you wouldn't see him.

The squeaking was louder now and he peered carefully around the tree trunk. The cart was emerging from the dip in the road and was only thirty meters away. The farmer seemed ignorant to the presence of the robber band. Barton smiled maliciously.

"So much the worse for him," he muttered.

He was a little surprised that such a rich prize was traveling alone on this road. He and his men had been preying on farmers going to and from market for the past three weeks. Most of the farmers now took precautions, either traveling in groups or hiring armed guards to escort them. In such cases, Barton and his men allowed the famers to pass unhindered. Barton might style himself as a fearless bear killer, but he wasn't about to risk his own neck in a confrontation with armed men. Not while there were still fools like this one who traveled alone.

Although, he thought, lone travelers were becoming fewer in number. He and his men would have to switch to a new location soon. He'd been planning to do so for several days. But now this rich prize would make the delay worthwhile.

The cart was ten meters away when Barton stepped out from behind the tree and moved to the edge of the road. He swung the cudgel several times, the big club making a menacing *WHOOSH* as it beat through the air.

"Stop there!" he roared, holding up his free hand in an unmistakable gesture.

The farmer hauled back on the reins and the mule stopped, swishing its tail and stomping one forefoot. It had been daydreaming about that feed bag, and now it seemed there was going to be a delay before it was strapped on. That was enough to rouse the mule's ill temper.

Still, most things were.

"My goodness. What do we have here?" the farmer said calmly.

His choice of words and accent were not the sort of rough country speech that one might expect from a simple farmer. And that should have rung a warning bell in Barton's mind. But he was too pleased with himself for caution. The sight of those well-filled sacks in the tray of the cart, doubtless bulging with coins, was more than enough to make him careless.

"I'm Barton the Bearkiller!" he roared, pointing to the bear's face above his own. This was usually enough to instill terror into his victims. This time, however, the result was not quite what he expected.

The farmer leaned forward on his seat and peered at the bear's mask with interest. "Are you telling me you killed that bear?" he asked mildly.

Barton hesitated for a second or two, puzzled by the lack of fear shown by his victim. Then he recovered, raising his weapon and shaking it above his head.

"That's right! I killed it with one blow of this cudgel!" he snarled.

The farmer peered more closely, then scratched his ear before he spoke again. "Are you sure?"

Barton was considerably startled. This was not the way this conversation was supposed to go. "*What?*" he finally asked in disbelief.

The farmer gestured toward the bear's face. "Are you sure it wasn't already dead when you found it?" he asked. "I mean, look at it. It's hardly in prime condition, is it? If it wasn't already dead, it surely must have been at death's door. You simply put it out of its misery and sent it to a better place."

"It was . . . it . . . I . . ." Barton stammered, trying to get the words out in reply. In truth, the bear had been dead when he found it. It had lived a full life and passed away from old age. But nobody before had ever questioned his claim. Frustration and rage finally overcame him, and he found his voice once more.

"Of course I killed it!" he said. "It attacked me and I killed it. That's why I'm known as Barton the Bearkiller."

The farmer remained unimpressed. "Hmmm," he said thoughtfully. "Are you sure you're not known as Barton, the dead bear's bottom? After all, the bear's head is on top and you're on the bottom. That would make more sense to me."

This was too much for the confused robber. Nobody had ever defied him before. Nobody had ever mocked him before. It was too much for him to take. He stepped toward the cart, raising his club threateningly.

"Get down from there!" he ordered. "Toss down those sacks and get down, or I'll knock your brains out!"

The farmer studied him quizzically, his head tilted to one side. "No. I don't think so," he said.

Barton let out a roar of pure rage, taking another step toward the cart, ready to swat this insolent farmer from his seat. But before he could do so, the farmer raised his hand in the air and made a circling gesture.

A second or so later, Barton felt a savage jerk as the bear's-mask cap was torn away from his head, ending up pinned to the tree behind him by a quivering arrow.

3

"So, King Philippe, tell us how can we help you?"

It was the morning after the Gallican party's midnight arrival at Castle Araluen, and Philippe and his brother were in Duncan's office. Also present were Anthony, the chamberlain, and a tall, broad-shouldered warrior who had been introduced as Sir Horace, Duncan's son-in-law and the commander of the Araluen army. They were seated around Duncan's large table. A sixth man, dressed in a curious green-and-gray-mottled cloak, sat to one side as if trying to remain unobtrusive. Philippe had to turn his head to see him. He had been introduced as Gilan, the Commandant of the Araluen Rangers. As far as Philippe was concerned, this man was the key reason for their presence here, and he kept turning to watch the still figure.

"It's my son, Giles," Philippe said, coming straight to the point. "He's being held hostage by one of my barons."

Duncan inclined his head thoughtfully. This was serious news and it didn't bode well for Gallica, a country with a notoriously unstable political history, prone to revolt and quarreling among its ruling class. Philippe had ruled over this turbulent situation for the past nine years, having seized the throne in an uprising of his own.

On the other hand, it was not entirely bad news for Araluen. When Gallica was torn by internal strife, it posed little threat to other countries. Many years past, the large and potentially powerful nation had been an aggressive and unpredictable state, threatening the peace of its neighbors and seeking to conquer new territories. But the current internal instability meant the Gallicans were too consumed by their own problems to look outside their own borders.

"How did this happen?" Duncan asked. "And who is the baron in question?"

"His name is Lassigny, Baron Joubert de Lassigny. His castle is the Chateau des Falaises. It's a powerful fortress," Philippe told them.

Duncan threw a quick sidelong glance at Anthony. The chamberlain nodded discreetly. He had heard of Joubert de Lassigny. It was part of his job to gather intelligence about ambitious nobles in Araluen and overseas who might pose a potential threat to the current peace.

"And you say this man kidnapped your son?" Duncan continued.

"Nothing so blatant," Philippe said. "It was more that he took advantage of a situation as it arose. My son was hunting in Lassigny's province when a violent storm blew up. He and his party sought shelter in the Chateau des Falaises. Unfortunately, Giles is young and didn't appreciate that Lassigny has ambitions for greater power. By placing himself into his hands, he has given him enormous leverage to advance his own position and power."

Anthony leaned forward. "Has Lassigny made any direct threat against your son?"

Philippe shook his head, with a bitter smile. "He's too clever for that. If he made a direct threat, he knows I would be able to seek support from the other barons and force him to release Giles. As it is, he says that Giles has decided to remain at Chateau des Falaises indefinitely—of his own will. The other barons are prepared to accept that at face value and stay out of the argument. None of them are particularly loyal to the crown," he said scornfully. "It's a strong fortress and my own forces aren't sufficient to besiege it and take it. I would need four times as many men as I have for that. And if I were to attack Lassigny, I might well create a revolt among some of the others. I know several of them are looking for any excuse to rise up against me."

"Has Lassigny made any direct demands from you?" Horace put the question. "Has he set a price for the release of your son?"

Again, the King of Gallica shook his head. "Nothing direct. For several years now he has been agitating for the control of the province adjacent to his own. The baron who had control of that province died some years ago and Lassigny has had his eye on it ever since."

He paused and his brother took up the narrative. "The dead baron had no heir and Lassigny has laid a claim to the land," Louis said. "It's a rich province and it will give him even greater power than he has now."

"But surely, the King can appoint whomever he chooses as baron of that province?" Horace asked. He knew that would be the case in Araluen. But not, apparently, in Gallica.

"I wish it were so," Philippe told him. "But Lassigny has a

claim to the position, albeit a thin one. A hundred years ago the two provinces formed one barony. They were divided by one of my predecessors—probably because they created a powerful base that might threaten his position. There are members of the council of barons who support Lassigny's claim. Doubtless they expect some form of reward should his claim be recognized."

"And purely by coincidence, he has raised this claim again, just at the time that your son has fallen into his hands?" Duncan said.

Philippe turned to look at him. "Exactly. The message is unstated but perfectly clear for all that. Give him the title to the neighboring province and Giles will be allowed to return home."

"I can see your problem," Duncan said thoughtfully. "But I'm not sure what help we can give you. We can hardly send troops to Gallica to reinforce your authority over Lassigny. That would be too big a provocation for the other barons. You've said that many of them tacitly support him."

"That's right."

"Then our sending troops to help you could spark a revolt among them and even a war between our two countries. I'm not prepared to risk that for something that's essentially an internal Gallican problem." He frowned, then continued. "I don't want to sound unsympathetic to your needs, but I know how our barons would react if I asked for Gallican troops to help support me." He glanced around the room at his counselors, who nodded their agreement.

"I'm not asking for troops. I'm not asking you to fight my battle for me. This is not a situation that can be resolved by force. It needs guile and subterfuge. Possibly one man."

"One man?" Horace interposed. "Who might that be?"

Philippe spread his hands in a slightly perplexed gesture. "I have no particular man in mind," he said. "That would be for you to decide and to recommend."

"I don't follow," Duncan said. "You feel one man might be able to solve your problem, but you don't know who he is. You're speaking in riddles, Philippe." There was an edge of anger in his voice. Gallicans seemed to find a perverse enjoyment in being abstruse.

Philippe recognized it and made a conciliatory gesture. "I don't mean to be obscure," he said. "It's more a type of man that I think could solve this problem." He twisted in his chair to look directly at Gilan. "One of your Rangers, perhaps."

Gilan was unsurprised. His face remained impassive. "What do you know about our Rangers?" he asked.

Philippe shrugged. "They have a certain reputation," he said. "A reputation for getting things done without necessarily resorting to brute force. It's said they can achieve the impossible."

"It's also said that we're wizards who practice the dark arts to achieve our ends," Gilan said. "But neither statement is true. The simple fact is, my men are carefully selected, highly intelligent and well trained. They can fight when necessary but they use their brains first to try to avoid fighting."

"And that's the sort of man this situation needs," Philippe said. "Falaise is a powerful castle. It could withstand a siege for years—even if I had the men and the support necessary to mount such a siege. But one man, using guile and subterfuge and intelligence, might be able to penetrate the castle and bring Giles out."

Duncan cleared his throat to interrupt. He wasn't sure he

liked the way this conversation was going. The Rangers were a very special resource. They had been founded to keep the peace in Araluen and to serve the Araluen King's needs. They were not intended to be hired out to other countries.

"One point I would like to make," he said. "The Rangers are tasked with serving the King. They're known as King's Rangers, after all."

Louis smiled unctuously. "And my brother is a king."

Duncan's brows drew together. Sometimes Gallicans could be altogether too glib, he thought. "He's not their king," he said brusquely.

Philippe responded with a typically Gallic shrug of the shoulders. "That's true, of course. But there is a brotherhood among kings, surely? And after all, a threat to one royal family is a threat to all. If it goes unchecked in Gallica, it could encourage others here as well."

There was a certain amount of truth in what he was saying, but Duncan wasn't totally convinced. Events in Gallica had no real bearing on the situation in Araluen. Yet Duncan was realistic enough to know that, while his kingdom was at peace and relatively stable, there were always undercurrents of resentment and intrigue in any realm.

"Perhaps," he allowed grudgingly. He let his gaze travel around the room, looking for some reaction from Anthony and the others. Their expressions told him they were not convinced one way or the other. "I'll need to confer with my advisers," he told the Gallican King. "I'll give you my decision tonight."

Philippe bowed gracefully, despite his seated position.

"That's all I can ask," he said smoothly.

•　•　•　•　•

After Philippe and his brother had returned to their quarters, Duncan faced his three counselors.

"Well, what do you think?" he asked. They exchanged glances. None of them seemed willing to speak first. He prompted his son-in-law. "Horace?"

The tall warrior shifted uncomfortably in his chair. "I'm not sure it's any of our business," he said eventually. "Much as I dislike the idea of anyone holding a hostage and giving out demands for his return, it seems to me it's a Gallican matter—one they should resolve themselves. Morally, I disapprove of Lassigny's actions. But practically, I'm not sure we should get involved. And it's not as if we owe Philippe any favors."

"Quite so," Duncan agreed. "And Philippe has never been a particularly friendly neighbor, has he? This situation could be largely his own doing."

"What makes you say that, my lord?" Gilan asked.

The King shrugged and gestured to his chamberlain. "You tell them, Anthony."

Lord Anthony cleared his throat and gathered his thoughts before speaking. While the Ranger Corps was responsible for keeping the King informed of potential threats or trouble within Araluen itself, Anthony maintained a network of secret agents on the continental landmass—in Gallica, Teutlandt and Iberion particularly. They reported to him on a regular basis, keeping him up to date with events and political affairs that might impact Araluen.

"He's a weak king," Anthony said eventually. "He's never been one to assert his authority over his barons. He rules by keeping them at each other's throats and he is known to accept bribes for royal favors. Consequently, Gallica has been an unstable kingdom for years, riddled with factions and corruption. This current situation is probably largely due to his own weakness and indecisiveness. Lassigny has seen an opportunity and has seized it."

"What do we know about Lassigny?" Horace asked.

"He could be a problem," Anthony told him. "He's aggressive and ambitious and quite obviously not too concerned about how he achieves his ends. He's got a strong garrison at Falaise, and a large militia to draw on. And, as King Philippe told us, he's got the support of some of the other barons."

"Just how ambitious do you think he is?" Duncan asked.

Anthony paused thoughtfully as he considered the question. "I would guess he wants more than control of the two provinces. From what I've heard of him, I'd say that's a means to an end."

"What end?" Duncan asked, although he felt he knew the answer already.

"In my opinion, he wants to take the throne. He has the power and support of the other barons—doubtless bought with promises of reward if he's successful. He's taking a big risk holding the King's son hostage. He has to be looking for more than just control of another province."

"What about Philippe's claim that an attack on one royal family is an attack on all?" Horace asked.

Anthony spread his hands, shaking his head. "He may well see it that way," he replied. "He tends to believe that he is King by some divine right. You, sir," he said, nodding toward Duncan, "hold your position and rank due to your own merits. The people are loyal to you because they respect you."

Duncan allowed himself the faintest smile. "Most of them, perhaps," he said. "But I tend to agree. Rebellion in Gallica won't necessarily lead to the same thing happening here." He turned to Gilan. "What do you think of sending a Ranger to help?"

The Commandant screwed up his face in an expression of distaste. "I don't like it," he said. "The Corps was founded to operate mainly inside Araluen—and for your benefit, sir," he said. "I'm not too comfortable with outsiders getting to know more and more about us. We've tried to maintain a low profile over the years and I don't like to see that slip away."

Duncan nodded. "I tend to agree. I don't like the idea of sending a Ranger to help Philippe. It's a little too close to treating the Corps as mercenaries for hire."

"We've used Rangers in the past to help the Skandians—and the Arridans," Anthony pointed out.

"They're friends and allies," Duncan replied immediately. "We have treaties with them and they give back as much as they get. Philippe, on the other hand, has generally treated us with disdain. Until now, when he needs our help."

"There is something else to consider," Anthony said. "It's probably in our interest to make sure Philippe retains his throne." He paused and Duncan made a gesture for him to continue with the thought. "Philippe is a weak king and Gallica is divided and fragmented. Lassigny, on the other hand, would be a strong king. He'd unite the barons and he'd create stability within Gallica."

"Surely that's to the good?" Horace asked.

But Anthony shook his head. "He's ambitious and unscrupulous," he said. "If he gained power, he might look to expand his borders. He might have to, in fact, if he were to repay the other barons who supported him in usurping the throne."

"You're saying he could be a threat to Araluen?" Duncan asked.

Anthony nodded slowly. "Certainly more of a threat than Philippe poses."

An uncomfortable silence fell over the room. At length, Duncan broke it.

"Then it might be in our interests to do as Philippe is asking."

4

BARTON TURNED IN SHOCK TO STARE AT HIS BEARSKIN CAP, now pinned to the trunk of the tree he'd been concealed behind. He looked back at the farmer, who returned his gaze, totally unconcerned and not in the least fearful. This sort of behavior in an intended victim was totally new to Barton, and his brain, never the brightest, struggled to make sense of it all.

"Oh, what a shame," the farmer said sympathetically. "Your nice cap has a new hole in it."

Still trying to make sense of what had happened, Barton looked back down the road, in the direction from which the farmer—and the arrow—had come. Sure enough, there was someone there—a cloaked and hooded person sitting astride a small shaggy horse. The newcomer was about forty meters away and was holding a bow ready, an arrow nocked on the string. He wondered why he hadn't noticed this second person before.

"Jem! Walt!" he yelled. "Lend a hand here!"

His two companions burst from the cover of the bush that had been concealing them and started back across the road, brandishing their weapons.

"Oh, I wouldn't—" the farmer began.

But before he could finish the sentence, Jem was down, rolling in agony on the ground and clutching at the arrow that had transfixed his left calf. Walter Scar looked down at his fallen comrade and stopped in mid-stride, not sure what he should do. The question was settled in the next moment as a rock hissed through the air at high speed and slammed into his head. Luckily, he was wearing a thick felt cap, otherwise his skull might have been shattered. Even so, the impact was sufficient to send him reeling. Then his knees buckled and he crashed to the road, unconscious.

Donald, on the opposite side of the road, showed more sense. Seeing his two comrades fall in quick succession, he took to his heels and ran.

For the first time, Barton's sense of disbelief was replaced by a sudden stab of fear. This was looking decidedly dangerous. Even as he had the thought, the farmer, showing more agility than one might expect of an old man, vaulted down from the cart and moved toward him.

"Let's have that club," he said, pointing at the heavy cudgel.

Now anger replaced the fear and Barton stepped toward the smaller man, taking the club back for a wide, swinging strike.

"I'll let you have it all right!" he said, and launched a killing blow.

Which never landed. The farmer moved with deceptive speed and closed the distance between them, moving inside the arc of the whistling cudgel. With his left arm, he seized Barton's right wrist and jerked it forward, deflecting the heavy club. At the same time, and in one coordinated movement, he stepped in closer, crouched and rammed his behind into the bandit's midsection. The momentum of Barton's attempted blow carried the bandit forward and off balance as the farmer's right hand joined his left on Barton's wrist. He pulled the unbalanced attacker farther forward, then lifted with his bent knees so that Barton's feet left the ground and he felt himself sailing over the farmer's shoulder.

Barton landed with a heavy thud, flat on his back. The breath in his lungs was driven from him with a loud *WHOOF*. His head hit the turf and for a moment he was stunned, bright lights dancing before his eyes. When he recovered, he found himself looking along the blade of a very sharp saxe knife, which pricked the soft skin of his throat.

"It hasn't been a good day for you so far, has it?" the farmer said, smiling.

Barton went to shake his head to clear it, remembered the saxe and decided not to. He stared at the face leaning down above him. The man was bearded and his hair and beard were shot with gray. But he was nowhere near as old as he had appeared to be from a distance. Nor was he hunched over any-more. He was a smallish man, considerably shorter than Barton's hulking frame. But his shoulders were broad and he appeared well muscled.

Barton heard the hoofbeats of an approaching horse, then heard the creak of leather as the rider swung down from the saddle.

"Are you all right, Will?"

It was a girl's voice, Barton registered with some surprise. He realized that it must have been she who had shot Jem and then, somehow, knocked Walt senseless. She came into his field of vision now, leaning over him beside the bearded man to study their captive.

"This is Barton Bearkiller," the farmer said. "Although Barton Blowhard might be a more appropriate name. Barton Bearkiller the Blowhard, meet my apprentice, Maddie Regale."

"You're a girl . . ." Barton said, even more confused than before.

The girl looked at her older companion, and said mockingly, "He's quick on the uptake, isn't he?"

The bearded man nodded in agreement. "Not much gets past him."

Barton frowned, trying to make sense of it all. The day had started so well, he thought. And now it had all fallen to pieces and he didn't really understand why or how it had happened.

"Who are you?" he said finally.

The farmer inclined his head in greeting. "I'm Will Treaty," he said. "We're King's Rangers, and you're under arrest."

Barton's spirits dropped to a new low as he realized that he'd run afoul of a pair of Rangers.

Suddenly, it all made sense. Rangers were definitely not people to tangle with. It was said, and Barton didn't disbelieve it, that they had magical powers. They could change their shape as they wished, appear or disappear at will and shoot with uncanny accuracy.

He groaned, then said, in a groveling tone, "Let me go, Ranger Treaty. Please. I'm just a poor honest man trying to make his way in the world."

Will Treaty let out a short bark of laughter. He straightened up, moving the saxe knife away from Barton's throat. Barton made a move to rise, but a warning glance from the Ranger stopped him.

"I'll accept poor," he said, "but you're anything but honest.

You and your friends have been robbing farmers on this road for the past month." He paused as the girl touched his arm. "What is it?"

"Speaking of his friends, wasn't there a fourth one?"

Will looked around. Donald had acted with more intelligence than his comrades. He was a good hundred and fifty meters away and disappearing from view over a rise in the ground.

"There he goes," Will said. "I'm sure our friend here can tell us where we'll find him. In the meantime, we'll secure this lot." He looked down at Barton once more. "You: over on your belly, hands behind your back."

His hand had dropped to the hilt of his saxe once more and Barton wasted no time in complying. The girl dropped to one knee beside him and Barton felt two leather loops slip over his thumbs. Then they were pulled tight and he was securely trussed.

"Don't go anywhere," she told him, although, lying on his stomach with his hands fastened behind him, he would be unable to regain his feet in a hurry. The Rangers strode to the other two bandits. Jem was sitting up, clutching his leg where the arrow had passed through the muscle of his calf, protruding on the other side. The wound was bleeding, but the presence of the arrow stemmed most of the flow. Jem was moaning in agony, rocking back and forth.

"If you think it hurts now, wait till we take that arrow out," Will told him unsympathetically. The robber band hadn't just taken money from defenseless farmers over the past month. They'd also been responsible for half a dozen severe beatings, leaving their victims bruised and bleeding. Most of their victims had been elderly men. All of them had been outnumbered four to one, and Will had no sympathy for the thugs who had carried out the beatings.

He knelt behind Jem and roughly dragged his hands behind his back, securing them with another pair of thumb cuffs. Maddie did the same for Walt, who was still dazed and groggy and offered no resistance.

"You used your sling on him?" Will asked.

Maddie nodded. "I assumed you wanted him alive, and I didn't have a clear shot at his legs."

Will sniffed disdainfully. "Admit it, you were just showing off." He stooped to peer more closely at Walt, raising the felt cap to study the bruise on the side of his head. "You threw a rock, did you?"

Normally, Maddie used specially cast lead shot from her sling, but she also carried a supply of smooth river rocks.

"I thought a lead shot might split his skull," she said. "A rock was safer."

Will grinned. "I doubt he'd agree with you."

Walt gazed owlishly at them, following the sound of their voices. His eyes were still unfocused and bleary.

Will slipped his hands under the bandit's arms and hoisted him upright. "Come on. Let's have you on your feet."

Walt stood, swaying uncertainly. Will waited until he was sure the dazed man wasn't about to fall to the ground again, then heaved Jem to his feet as well. He studied Jem, looking critically at the arrow that had gone through his calf. It protruded some thirty centimeters from the inside of the muscle, which would make it almost impossible for Jem to walk—the shaft would strike against his other leg with every step.

"That'll have to come out," he said.

Jem whimpered in anticipation of the pain. "Can't you just leave me here while you fetch a healer?" he pleaded. "I swear I won't go anywhere."

"I'm sure you won't," Will said cheerfully. "But we need to get that arrow out and clean and bandage the wound."

"Do you have to break it?" Maddie asked. "That's a good shaft."

Will shook his head at her lack of sympathy. "Spare a thought for our poor friend here," he said. "It'll be less painful if we break it off. Otherwise I'd have to pull the whole thing through."

With the barbed head on the arrow, there was no way they could remove it by pulling it back the way it had come. The easiest and quickest way was to break the shaft of the arrow close to the exit wound, then pull it back. Maddie gave Jem a disgruntled look.

"Who cares about less painful?" she said. "That's a good shaft."

Will made a tut-tutting noise and shook his head as he looked at Jem. "Young people can be so cruel," he said. Then he bent and quickly snapped off the shaft, pulling it back through the wound in the same motion. Jem blanched with the sudden pain and his leg nearly gave way. Will steadied him, then whipped a bandage around the wound, which had begun to ooze blood when the arrow was removed. Will tightened the bandage and tied it off, then stood, watching Jem carefully. The bandit hobbled a pace or two. It was obviously painful for him to put weight on the leg. Will turned him around and removed the thumb cuffs.

"Don't think we'll need these." He beckoned Barton to come

closer. "You can help him walk," he told the bandit leader. Then, looking again at Jem, he said, "Put your arm around the bear-killer's shoulders."

Jem did as he was told, shuffling closer and placing his left arm around Barton's heavyset shoulders. Will studied them for a few seconds, then nodded approval.

"That'll do nicely," he said. "We've got a nice long walk ahead of us."

"Where are you taking us?" Barton asked fearfully. He knew that, as an apprehended bandit, his next few years would not be pleasant.

"Willow Bend Village," Will told him. This was the village where he had sold the farm's goods. "They've got a constable there and a nice warm jail. You'll love it."

Barton's sour expression indicated that this was unlikely.

Will continued. "On the way, you can tell us where to find that friend of yours who ran off."

A crafty expression came over Barton's face. "If I do, will you ask the magistrate to give me a reduced sentence?" he wheedled.

Will regarded him without any expression for several seconds. "No," he said at length. "But if you don't, I'll ask Maddie here to shoot you in the leg as well."

Of course, there was no way he would ever carry out such a threat. But Barton wasn't to know it. It was the sort of thing that the burly robber would do himself and he assumed other people were just as vindictive as he was.

"There's a game trail off the road about two kilometers away. It leads to our cabin," Barton told him. "That's where you'll find him."

5

THEY FOUND DONALD IN THE HUT, AS BARTON HAD PRE-
dicted. Showing a distinct lack of imagination, he was hiding
under a bed. Unfortunately, the bed was several inches shorter
than he was and his feet protruded at one end.

"Bandits just aren't what they used to be," Will said with
mock regret as they thumbcuffed Donald and added him to
their little cavalcade.

"They used to be smarter then?" Maddie asked.

He shrugged. "It seemed that way. They were certainly
braver."

They continued on to Willow Bend, riding comfortably
while the former bandits shuffled awkwardly ahead of them.
Barton and Jem moved clumsily, trying to keep in step, and
the other two, with their hands secured behind them, were
constantly losing their balance on the uneven surface of the
road.

"Couldn't we ride in the cart?" Jem pleaded after they had
gone a kilometer past the spot where they had caught up with
Donald.

Will laughed without humor. "You could," he said, and Jem's

face brightened. "But you're not going to," Will added, and the outlaw's face fell once more.

They rode up the single main street of Willow Bend, watched by the curious villagers, and stopped outside the constable's watch house, which also housed the town jail. The constable, a burly man in his mid-fifties, hurried out to greet them. Rangers were important visitors and Will had donned his Ranger cloak, tossing the patched old farm smock into the tray of the cart.

"Rangers," the constable said respectfully. "Please step down."

It was good manners to wait to dismount until you were invited. Maddie and Will swung down easily now.

"I'm Will Treaty. This is Ranger Maddie Regale," Will said. He saw the constable's eyes widen slightly at his name. Will Treaty was a larger-than-life figure in this part of the country. In most parts of the country, in fact. Will jerked his thumb at the four forlorn figures who had preceded them.

"These are the men who've been preying on farm folk going to market," he said. "You can keep them in your jail until the magistrate makes his monthly rounds. Then they can serve their sentence at Castle Redmont." He handed across a rolled scroll. "This is my deposition. You can give it to the magistrate. Until he hears their case, you can use them for any unpleasant tasks you might have in the village."

The constable took the scroll and tucked it into his belt. He rubbed his hands together expectantly. There were always plenty of dirty, unpleasant laboring tasks to be carried out in the village. Privies had to be dug, cesspools to be drained and cleaned. Barton and his gang wouldn't be left sitting idle while they waited for their trial.

"How did you come upon them?" he asked. For obvious reasons, Will's plan of posing as a farmer going to the market had not been widely known.

"I took Malcolm Tillerman's place," Will told him. "And took his products to market. These sad specimens tried to rob me on the way back. Malcolm's money is in the cart there. You can pass it on to him with my thanks. I hope I got a good price for his goods."

The constable grinned. "Not as good as he would have," he said. Malcolm was known in the district as a man who drove a hard bargain. He turned back to the watch house behind him.

"Barney! Joseph!" he called. "Out here, please!"

Two heavyset men emerged from the watch house—members of the watch were usually on the large side. They were dressed in the simple uniform of the town watch—a leather jerkin over wool trousers and knee-high boots, with a heavy leather belt carrying their keys and their truncheons, the twin symbols of their office.

"Get these four inside," the constable told them, and they shepherded the bandits into the building.

"If you have a local healer, you might get him to look at that leg wound on the blond one," Will said. "I've bandaged it but it'll need cleaning to stop it getting infected."

"We've an apothecary in the village," the constable told him. "I'll send for him."

Will nodded. "Do that. And for now, we'll bid you good day and be on our way."

The watch house had a small yard at the rear. They unharnessed the mule from the cart and left both in the yard, carrying the leather money sacks into the constable's quarters for safekeeping. Then, making their farewells, they mounted Bumper and Tug and rode off, heading for the highway that led to Castle Redmont.

"Why do you call me Maddie Regale?" Maddie asked after they had been riding for some time. Will turned in the saddle to look at her.

"I have to call you something," he said. "Just 'Maddie' doesn't seem to be enough somehow."

They rode on for several hundred meters before she spoke again.

"You could call me Maddie Altman," she suggested. "That's Dad's name, after all. So it's really my name too."

"I could," Will replied. There was a note of doubt in his voice. "But Horace's name is relatively well-known and recognized. He's quite a famous figure, after all. People might put two and two together and figure out that you're his daughter."

"So?" Maddie asked.

"So then they would realize that if you're his daughter, you're also Cassandra's daughter, and the second in line to the throne. And you know that we prefer to keep that fact secret."

It had been agreed, several years before, that if Maddie were to serve as a Ranger's apprentice, and eventually as a Ranger, her relationship to the royal family must be concealed. Rangers needed to maintain a high level of anonymity. In addition, the knowledge that she was second in line to the throne might endanger her life. She could be targeted by enemies seeking to put pressure on the King. It would certainly draw attention to her and make it difficult for her to maintain the secrecy that was so much a part of a Ranger's life.

"So, why Regale?" she asked. She pronounced it the way

Will had, in the Gallic fashion, so that it sounded like *Regahl*, rather than *Regail*.

"Initially, I thought of calling you Maddie Royal," Will said. "Being as you're a princess and such. But I realized that would be almost as bad as calling you Altman. People would soon twig that you actually *were* royal. Then they'd realize you're a princess and we'd be back where we started."

"So where did Regale come from?"

"It's similar to Royal. It means much the same thing, but it's not as obvious. Particularly when we pronounce it in the Gallic fashion. Most people won't make the link." He paused. "Don't you like being Regale?" he said eventually.

She shook her head. "Maddie Regale," she said derisively. "It sounds like 'madrigal' if you say it quickly."

"A fine dance, the madrigal," Will told her, grinning.

She sniffed. "A fine dance, maybe. But a dumb name. I don't like it."

"I think it suits you," Will said, teasing her. "It's melodic and happy, just like you."

"Well, I wish you'd think of another name for me," she said.

He shrugged. "Wish away," he said. "You should be grateful I thought of that one. I'm not good at names. It takes me ages to think of a name when I get a new dog."

"Thanks for comparing me to Sable," Maddie said. Sable was Will's current border collie, a descendant of Shadow, his first dog.

"Think nothing of it. I'm very fond of Sable," he told her.

"Maybe I should just revert to plain old Maddie," she said, "and skip having a second name." But before she finished, Will was shaking his head, all traces of humor gone from his expression.

"You need a second name," he said seriously. "Everyone does. If you don't have a second name you feel somehow detached and rootless. You feel incomplete. I should know," he added. "I spent half my life without a second name—just known as 'Will, the orphan boy.'"

She was somewhat surprised by the intensity of his feelings. "Was it really that bad?" she asked.

He shrugged, a little embarrassed that he had exposed that aspect of his life. "I guess I was happy enough," he said. "But all the others in the ward—Horace, Alyss, Jenny and George—they all had family names. They might have lost their parents but they knew who they had been. They knew where they came from. I didn't and I guess I felt . . . I don't know . . . left out somehow."

She regarded him with interest. She was surprised to hear that he had ever felt so insecure. Will was such a capable person, sure of himself and full of confidence. It was difficult to think of him feeling inferior.

"I guess I'll stay as Maddie Madrigal then," she said.

He smiled. "You could do worse."

When the shadows lengthened, they were still three or four hours away from Redmont and their cabin among the trees. They were in no rush, so they made camp in a sheltered glade a little way from the highway.

Maddie enjoyed camping out with Will. He was an excellent camp cook and he always served up a delicious dinner. Somehow, the fact that they were eating it in the open air, with the scent of woodsmoke from their fire wafting around them, made it taste even better.

As did the strong, sweet coffee they drank afterward.

It was a fine night so they didn't bother with their tents. They spread out their bedrolls and wrapped themselves in their cloaks to sleep. Maddie lay on her back, gazing up at the stars as they wheeled slowly overhead, and sighed contentedly.

"I love this life," she said quietly. "I don't think I could ever go back to living in the palace and being a princess."

"You may need to take over as queen one day," Will told her.

She shook her head. "Someone else can do that. I'm a Ranger. I love being a Ranger."

"That's what makes you a good one," Will said, and she turned in surprise to look at him. He rarely uttered such words of praise. She waited for him to say more but his deep, even breathing told her he was already asleep.

Or was pretending to be.

6

WILL AND MADDIE RODE SLOWLY UP THE HIGH STREET OF the little village below Castle Redmont, nodding to the villagers who called greetings to them as they passed by. Will was a popular figure in the village. He had grown up in Redmont, first in the ward that Baron Arald maintained for orphaned children, then as an apprentice to Halt, one of the most famous of the Rangers.

In more recent years, Will's fame had gone on to equal, or even surpass, that of his mentor, and the local people were proud that two such renowned figures lived in their fief. It set Redmont above the neighboring fiefs and the folk who lived there enjoyed sharing the reflected glory of the two illustrious Rangers.

And now Maddie, who had been in the fief for the past four years, was adding her own achievements to those of the other two. Less than a year ago, she had foiled a plot to seize the throne of Araluen. And before that, she had assisted Will in unmasking and destroying a gang of kidnappers who had been carrying out their vile work on the east coast of the kingdom.

All in all, there were plenty of reasons why the villagers

might feel proud of their Rangers and glad to greet them as they passed by.

They rode past Jenny's restaurant. Jenny herself was sitting in the sun outside her establishment, drinking coffee and keeping an eye on her staff as they prepared the tables for the evening's trading. She raised her cup to them as they passed, accompanying the gesture with a broad smile. She and Will had grown up together in the ward, and Jenny had helped him settle Maddie in when she had first arrived, a spoiled and self-centered princess who was badly in need of discipline.

Will waved to his old friend, and glanced quizzically from her to the young girl riding beside him. How things had changed, he thought. These days, he would trust Maddie with his life—in fact, he had just done so when they had confronted Barton Bearkiller and his gang. Maddie sensed he was watching her and tilted her head in a question.

"What?" she asked.

But Will didn't answer directly. She'd had enough praise lately, he thought, and he was never one to overdo that sort of thing. "I thought we might eat at Jenny's tonight," he said instead.

Maddie nodded enthusiastically. "Sounds good to me," she said. "Should I ride over and ask her to keep a table for us?"

Will shook his head. "She'll always fit me in," he said. "That's one of the advantages of being an old wardmate."

At the top of the hill, they left the village and turned right into the narrow trail between the trees that led to their cabin. As they came closer, both horses began twitching their ears and sniffing the air.

"They're glad to be home," Maddie observed.

But Will disagreed. "There's someone at the cabin," he said. "They can scent whoever it is."

They emerged from the trees into the clearing around the cabin and Maddie saw that he was right. There was a small, shaggy horse standing by the tethering rail outside the cabin and a gray-and-green-cloaked figure was sitting on the verandah, legs stretched out, enjoying the sunshine. Their horses whinnied a greeting to the tethered horse and it responded.

"It's Halt," Maddie said, recognizing his horse initially. Their visitor's face wasn't so easy to make out, as the shadow from the verandah roof fell over him, reaching down to shoulder level.

"What's he doing here?" Will said to himself. They rode up to the cabin and Halt rose to greet them as they came near.

"Good morning," he said cheerfully, although he was only just correct. Midday was only a few minutes away. He shook hands with Will as the younger man dismounted, then enveloped Maddie in a bear hug. Halt was very fond of his former apprentice's apprentice. He had been instrumental in having Maddie selected for training as a Ranger—the first female Ranger in the history of the Corps. Seeing how well she had turned out, he felt his choice had been more than justified.

"What brings you here?" Will asked when Halt had disengaged himself from the hug. Halt jerked his thumb at a black-and-white form sprawled on the end of the verandah in the sun—lying on her back with her rear legs splayed out and her forepaws folded back on themselves.

"I thought you'd be home today, so I brought Sable down from the castle," he said. While Maddie and Will had been hunting the market gang, as they had been known, Halt and

Lady Pauline had taken care of Will's dog. At the mention of her name, Sable's tail thumped on the boards of the verandah several times. Otherwise, she made no movement at all.

Will raised one eyebrow. "I could be overwhelmed by such a welcome," he said. "Obviously she hasn't missed us. I assume you've been spoiling her as usual?"

Halt grinned. "Not me. Pauline."

His wife was fond of dogs in general and Sable in particular. Sable, sensing this, as dogs will, made a huge fuss of Lady Pauline whenever she saw her. As a result, Pauline was constantly giving her treats and patting her, rubbing her ears and her belly. When Sable stayed with Halt and Pauline, she became accustomed to this sort of treatment far too quickly. It usually took several days for Will to retrain her in what he considered to be proper dog behavior.

"The stove's lit and the coffee's on," Halt told him, and Will nodded his appreciation.

Maddie stepped forward and took Tug's bridle in one hand, Bumper's in the other. "I'll get the horses settled," she said.

Will unfastened his travel pack and bedroll from behind Tug's saddle and slung them over his shoulder. "Thanks," he said. "We'll pour you a coffee while you're doing that." He and Halt went inside while Maddie led the two horses to the stable at the rear of the cabin.

They were nursing mugs of coffee, with another full mug waiting for Maddie, when she rejoined them. She added a heaped spoonful of honey to the steaming liquid and stirred it.

Will gave her a pained look. "I already did that."

She shrugged. "You never put enough in," she said, and tasted her drink. "Perfect."

Will shook his head. "Maybe that's because I have to pay for the honey," he muttered. Then he turned to Halt. "So what's behind this visit? Other than the need to bring Sable back."

While they had been waiting for Maddie, they hadn't discussed the reason Halt had been waiting for them. Instead, they had talked about inconsequential matters, with Will describing their encounter with the self-styled bear killer and his thugs.

"A carrier pigeon arrived from Gilan yesterday evening," Halt said. "The King has summoned us to Castle Araluen."

"Is it urgent?" Maddie asked.

The two older Rangers exchanged a glance. "A summons from the King is *always* urgent," Will told her. "Should we get going straightaway?" he asked Halt.

Halt made a demurring gesture. "There's no need to rush," he said. "After all, nobody will know when you actually arrived back, or when you received the message. We can get going in the morning. Get a good night's sleep tonight and we'll leave after sunup."

Will nodded. "That sounds fair enough. Did Gilan give you any idea what this is all about?"

"Just said, come at once. I imagine it's important."

"What makes you think so?" Maddie asked.

Halt shrugged. "The tone of the message for starters. And pigeon messages can go astray all too easily," he said. "If it's a delicate matter, it's never a good idea to put in too much detail— just in case the message falls into unfriendly hands."

"Is that likely?" Maddie asked, the doubt in her voice obvious.

"Unscrupulous people in the past have been known to train

falcons to capture or kill message pigeons," Halt told her. "Confidential information can be quite valuable if the wrong person gets hold of it."

"Maybe it's a mistake to use pigeons for messages," Will said. "They're altogether too peaceful. They can't defend themselves."

"Some years back, we tried training ravens to carry messages. It'd take a brave falcon to attack a raven," Halt said. "But it didn't work out."

"Why not?" Maddie asked, and the white-haired Ranger hid a grin.

"Ravens talk too much," he said. "They can't keep a secret no matter how hard they try."

Maddie rolled her eyes, as only a teenage girl can do. "There are times when you're very amusing, Halt," she said. "This isn't one of them."

Halt finished his coffee and stood up. "Young people have no sense of humor," he said, with some dignity. He pulled up the cowl on his cloak and turned to the door.

"I'll see you at sunup," he said. "Pauline will come down later to collect Sable."

They made their farewells and he mounted Abelard, wheeling the Ranger horse toward the narrow path through the trees. Will and Maddie watched as he rode away, finally disappearing round the first bend.

Will rubbed his beard thoughtfully. "That's unusual," he said, more to himself than to Maddie.

She cocked her head curiously toward him. "How do you mean?"

"Well," he said, turning to go back into the little cabin, "Halt's semiretired these days and he's never gone on a mission with us. I wonder why Duncan has summoned all three of us to the castle."

Maddie considered the point and found she had no answer.

"I expect we'll find out when we get there," she said.

"I expect so."

7

"BUT WHY MADDIE?" SAID CASSANDRA. "WHY SHOULD SHE be involved in this?"

Horace sighed. "Cassandra, we've discussed this before—"

His wife interrupted before he could go any further, ignoring him and speaking to her father. "I can understand why you'd send Will. After all, he's the best Ranger you have. But why should Maddie go as well?"

"She's a Ranger," her father said patiently. He knew what was on her mind and he knew they were in for an argument.

"She's your granddaughter," Cassandra replied. "And she's second in line to the throne. Yet you're willing to place her in danger."

"The world is a dangerous place," Duncan told her. "Even for princesses. Maddie has chosen to join the Rangers and live their life. I can't make exceptions for her."

"But it will be dangerous!" Cassandra protested.

"Just as it was dangerous for you to ransom Erak from the Tualaghi tribesmen. Just as it was dangerous for you to travel to Nihon-Ja to find Horace."

"That was different!" Cassandra protested. "I was—"

"You were the heir to the throne. You accepted that there was a responsibility that went along with the privilege. That's the way we have to live our lives, Cassandra."

"I just don't see why it's necessary for her to go. Let Will do it. He can handle it on his own."

"He'll be a lot better off if Maddie's with him," Gilan said quietly. He had been expecting Cassandra to object to the idea of Maddie accompanying Will on the secret mission to Gallica. He knew how Cassandra felt about her daughter's role as an apprentice Ranger. She had opposed it from the start and had never fully accepted it.

Cassandra turned to face him. "How do you figure that?" she challenged.

"A stranger traveling alone is more likely to excite suspicion than a father and daughter traveling together. That's how they'll be seen. A man traveling with his daughter will be seen as relatively harmless. After all, what father would willingly expose his daughter to danger?"

"So you admit she will be in danger?" Cassandra said.

Gilan nodded. "Of course I admit it. She's a Ranger, after all, and that's part and parcel of a Ranger's life."

Cassandra opened her mouth to object but Horace forestalled her.

"We agreed to this when she decided to join the Corps," he said. "If she's a Ranger, she has to take her share of dangerous situations. We can't pick and choose what she does. We can't insist that she only goes on safe missions."

"Not that there are too many of them," Gilan observed.

But Cassandra wasn't willing to give in just yet. "*You* agreed to this. I never wanted her to be a Ranger in the first place."

"And yet she is one," her father said firmly. "And as a Ranger, she has to undertake her share of hazardous duties. Otherwise she might as well quit the Corps."

"That'd be fine by me," Cassandra said bitterly.

"So you'd rather have her sit meekly around the castle, practicing her needlework and learning court etiquette?" her father said. "That's pretty poor training for a future queen. It was something you never accepted. You knew you had to be out in the real world, learning how to lead men and defend your country in times of war."

In her heart, Cassandra knew they were right. As a young woman, she had led an exciting, and often dangerous, life. She had traveled the world, fought in battles and faced the kingdom's enemies countless times. The idea of remaining safely at home in Castle Araluen had been anathema to her and she knew she couldn't impose such a restriction on her daughter. If Maddie was to be queen one day, she had to experience the real world, with all its hazards. That way, she would be equipped to rule the country wisely and bravely. Cassandra knew all this. But that didn't mean she had to like it. She scowled at the three men sitting opposite her.

"I hate it when you all gang up on me," she said.

Her father smiled fondly at her. "Now you know how I used to feel," he told her. "It's not easy to send your only daughter off into the world. But it's something we all have to do. And Maddie's experiences as a Ranger will make her a better queen when the time comes."

He looked away from her as there was a discreet knock at the door to his office. "What is it?" he called.

The door opened to admit one of his servants. "My lord,

there are three Rangers here to see you," he said.

Duncan made a beckoning gesture. "Thank you, Miles. Please tell them to come in."

The servant opened the door wider and stood to one side to admit the three gray-and-green-cloaked figures. Halt, Will and Maddie strode into the room, Maddie staying slightly behind her superiors. They stopped before Duncan's big desk while the servant withdrew, closing the door behind him.

Halt, as the most senior of the group, spoke. "You sent for us, my lord?"

Duncan rose from his seat to greet them, wincing slightly as he placed weight on his injured leg. "Halt! How good it is to see you! And you, Will, of course."

He reserved a special smile of welcome for his granddaughter. He felt a sudden surge of pride seeing her in her Ranger uniform. Even though she was still an apprentice, she had already proven her skill and courage several times over.

"Maddie," he said, "I trust you've been behaving yourself?"

She smiled widely in return. "Not too much, Grandfather," she said.

Then Horace and Gilan stepped forward to greet the newcomers and the room was full of warmth and welcome. Cassandra held back for a few seconds, then impulsively rushed forward and enveloped Maddie in a hug, too full of emotion to speak, her eyes bright with tears.

Maddie, a little overwhelmed by the effusive greeting, was somewhat taken aback. "Mum!" she exclaimed. "Settle down!" She met her father's eyes over Cassandra's shoulder and raised her eyebrows in a question. He made a gesture with his hands, which she took to mean, *Your mother's a little emotional. Go with it.* She nodded and allowed her mother a few seconds to compose herself.

Cassandra finally brought her emotions under control and released Maddie to Horace's embrace. Will stepped forward then and hugged Cassandra. He thought he understood the reason for her display of emotion. Obviously, he and Maddie were being sent on a mission. Equally obviously, Cassandra was upset by the fact. There was nothing new in that, he thought. His old friend was extremely protective when it came to her daughter.

"I'll look after her," he said softly. For a moment or two, she buried her face in his shoulder. Then she recovered and stepped back, smiling into his eyes.

The greetings went on for several more minutes, then Duncan called the group to order. They pulled chairs around the table and waited expectantly for him to tell them why they were here. He wasted no time getting to the heart of the matter.

"Will, I want you and Maddie to go to Gallica," he said.

Maddie and Will exchanged a quick glance. One thing about life as a Ranger, Maddie thought, you never knew what was coming next.

Will scratched his beard. "Gallica?" he said. "What's going on there that concerns us?"

Will leaned back, nodding, as Duncan finished explaining the reason he had summoned them to Araluen.

"Makes sense," he said. "A father and daughter traveling together don't attract as much attention. People don't seem to be as suspicious as they might be if I were on my own."

"That's what I thought," Gilan said. "After all, it worked

before when you were hunting those child robbers on the east coast."

"But why do we care if there's trouble in Gallica?" Maddie asked. "After all, it's not as if Philippe has ever done us any favors." She realized that she might have sounded somewhat heartless and hurried to amend her statement. "I mean, I'm sorry that his son has been kidnapped, but it hardly involves us, does it?"

"Perhaps not," Horace told her. "But it's probably better for us if Philippe remains on the throne. This Lassigny type could be a problem for us if he managed to replace Philippe. And there's not much doubt that's his eventual intention. The more power he gains, the greater a potential threat he is to us."

Maddie nodded as she saw the reasoning behind her father's words.

Halt was frowning slightly. "My lord," he said to Duncan, "I take it you don't want me to go with Will and Maddie. Why did you want me here?"

Duncan hesitated a second, then replied, "I always value your input, Halt. We have to work out how these two will be disguised. After all, they'll have to have some plausible reason for wandering around the Gallican countryside."

Halt nodded slowly. He suspected there was something Duncan wasn't telling him. Whatever it might be, he was sure he'd find out in due course, so he was willing to wait until the King was ready to say more.

8

THE MEETING BROKE UP SHORTLY AFTERWARD. THE THREE
new arrivals were given time to freshen up and eat after their
long journey. Then Gilan, Halt, Will, Horace and Cassandra
assembled in Gilan's office to make plans for Will and Maddie's journey to Gallica. Maddie wasn't required for that meeting so she went in search of Ingrid, her former maid and
companion, who was now a senior member of Cassandra's
staff. Duncan had other matters to attend to—a king was
always busy—and he trusted his senior officers to come up
with a workable plan. He didn't need to be concerned with the
details. The ability to delegate was one of the hallmarks of a
good leader and it had been a feature of Duncan's reign. He
chose reliable people as his subordinates and left them to get
on with it.

"Why buy a dog and wag your own tail?" he had been known
to say.

"Shouldn't that be, why buy a dog and bark yourself?"
Cassandra had once asked him when she was a young girl.

He had shrugged. "Bark, wag your tail, dogs do both. Why
do either if you've got one?"

"So are we getting a dog?" she had asked eagerly, but he shook his head.

"No. I'll have to do my own tail wagging for a while," he said. "Besides, if you lie down with dogs, you get up with fleas."

That night, Cassandra had gone to bed a confused little girl.

The five friends sat in Gilan's tower office, a big pot of coffee on the table between them. Once cups had been poured and generous quantities of honey spooned in, they sat back and discussed the best method for Will and Maddie to travel unobtrusively in Gallica.

"You'll hardly blend in," Horace observed. "You're foreigners. People will notice you."

"I speak Gallican," Will said.

Halt raised an eyebrow at him. He was fluent in the language himself and had taught Will, so he knew his former apprentice's shortcomings. "With an appalling Araluen accent," he pointed out. "Say *good morning* and they'll pick you for a foreigner straightaway—before you even get to *morning*."

Will shrugged. He knew Halt was right. He'd never managed to get his tongue around the Gallican accent.

"Well, we can't simply ride around Gallica for no reason," he said. "We'll be bound to attract attention that way."

"Best way to avoid attention is to divert it—attract it to something else," Gilan observed. There was silence for some ten seconds while they all thought about this.

"You need some sort of reason for traveling," Cassandra said finally. "Something that distracts people from the fact that you're not locals."

"You could pretend to be tinkers," Horace suggested. They

all turned pained gazes upon him. Seeing their expressions, he spread his hands in a question. "What?"

"Why does someone always suggest that?" Gilan said. "Tinkers have a reputation as petty thieves, and that means people watch them closely. They don't blend in."

Horace frowned. "But in romance stories and sagas, heroes often disguise themselves as tinkers," he protested.

"They often fight dragons and fly on magic horses too," Will told him, and Horace subsided, realizing that what his friend said was true.

"I'm sure not all tinkers are dishonest," Cassandra put in. "It's probably just a few bad ones that have given the others a bad reputation."

"So we could have a sign that says, 'We're honest tinkers'?" Will asked. "That should do the trick."

Cassandra scowled at him and he grinned.

"Whether tinkers are dishonest or not," Halt said, "they have that reputation, and people tend to be suspicious of them."

"Besides," Will continued, "what if someone actually believed us and trusted us and asked me to mend a pot with a hole in it? I'd be totally out of my depth."

"That's true," Halt said. "You're no handyman, are you?" He rubbed his beard thoughtfully. "When you went to Macindaw years ago, you posed as a jongleur. Maybe that would work again."

Will considered the idea and nodded slowly. He actually had quite a talent for playing the mandola, and he had a pleasant singing voice.

"That might work," he said. "I think I can remember the tricks of the trade that Berrigan taught me." Berrigan was a former Ranger who had been forced to retire from the Corps when he lost a leg. He had found a new identity and purpose for himself as a jongleur—a traveling musician—and had carried out several intelligence operations for the Corps in the past.

"Do you still play your lute?" Halt asked.

Will turned an exasperated expression on him.

"It's a mand—" he began, then seeing that Halt was trying, unsuccessfully, to smother a grin, he simply agreed. "Yes, I do. As a matter of fact, I've got it with me," he said. For years, Halt had been trying to get a rise out of him by pretending he didn't know the difference between a lute and a mandola. Usually, he succeeded.

But now Will frowned as a thought struck him. "But what about Maddie?" he asked.

Gilan shrugged his shoulders. "Couldn't she accompany you? I mean, sing along with you?"

"Can she sing?" Halt asked. He didn't notice that both Cassandra and Horace looked away, avoiding eye contact with him.

Will hesitated. He liked his young apprentice and hated to say anything derogatory about her. "Like a bird," he said finally.

Halt spread his hands in a satisfied gesture. "Well, there you are."

But Will continued. "The bird I had in mind was a crow," he said uncomfortably.

Horace and Cassandra both nodded.

Gilan was unconvinced. "Oh, come on. She can't be that bad," he said, but Maddie's parents turned to him.

"She is that bad," Cassandra finally said.

Gilan eyed her suspiciously, suspecting that she might be using this as a pretext for excluding Maddie from the mission.

Seeing that he was unconvinced, Will decided the best way would be to let Gilan see for himself.

"If you send for Maddie, and have someone fetch my mandola, I'll show you," he said.

Gilan dispatched his assistant, Nichol, a second-year apprentice, to fetch the instrument and Maddie. Nichol arrived back with the instrument five minutes later. Maddie was a few minutes behind him.

Will was tuning the eight strings of the mandola when Maddie arrived, curiosity written all over her face. She assumed that the group had come up with an idea as to how she and her mentor would travel through Gallica. She looked at the mandola in Will's hands with obvious interest.

"There's a suggestion that we might travel as jongleurs," he said, "with me playing and both of us singing."

Maddie nodded enthusiastically. "Sounds good to me."

Will looked down at the instrument to avoid her enthusiastic gaze. Like so many tone-deaf people, Maddie had no idea that her singing was totally off-key.

"Remember 'The Whistling Miller'?" he said, and she nodded. He struck a chord. "Come in on the chorus."

He played a clever little introduction, then began singing.

"The whistling miller of Wittingdon Green
had the loudest whistle you've ever seen . . ."

He got no further. Halt held his hands up in protest. "Whoa! Whoa! Back up the hay cart there!" Halt said.

Will looked at him, puzzled. "Problem?"

Halt nodded explicitly. "Yes. Problem. How can you see a whistle? I take it it's not an actual instrument, it's the noise this miller person makes?"

"That's right," Will agreed.

"Then he should have had the loudest whistle you'd ever heard."

"It doesn't rhyme that way."

"Well, it doesn't make sense your way," Halt said, with some heat. "It's ridiculous."

"It's a song, Halt. It's poetic license."

"People always say that when they're being dumb. This is a dumb song."

"I could always do 'Graybeard Halt' . . ." Will suggested. For a long moment, they locked gazes. Halt hated that song. He finally made a gesture of defeat.

"All right. Go ahead with this 'Visible Whistler,'" he said.

Will continued from the spot where he'd stopped.

"He'd whistle all night and he'd whistle all day
and if anyone asked him, he would say . . ."

Halt held up a hand once more and Will stopped, a little annoyed. No singer likes to be constantly interrupted and he suspected Halt was doing it on purpose.

"What now?" he said tersely.

"If anyone asked him what?" Halt asked.

Will scowled at him. "We're about to get to that," he told his old mentor. "If you'd stop interrupting, you'd know what they asked."

"Well, get on with it," Halt said unapologetically, and Will, taking a deep breath, continued.

"I'll teach you to whistle, it's easy, you know,
just purse your lips in a kiss and blow."

He nodded to Maddie to join in on the chorus. She did so with considerable energy.

"Whistle high and whistle low,
it's easy to whistle once you know.
Whistle high and whistle low,
just purse your lips and blow and blow."

Will hit a final chord and the song came to an end. Maddie looked at the audience expectantly.

"Well, what do you think?" she said.

Nobody spoke for a moment, then Gilan said softly, "Good grief."

9

Will gestured to the door leading to the anteroom outside Gilan's office.

"Maddie, perhaps you could step outside for a minute while we talk?" he said. She shrugged and let herself out. Once she had gone, the others exchanged a look. Halt, whose own ear for music wasn't the strongest, frowned thoughtfully.

"I take it that wasn't exactly good?" he said.

Cassandra raised her eyebrows. She was a mother, and mothers never want to say anything negative about their children.

"Maybe she's got a little bit better than she used to be," she said tentatively.

Horace gave a short bark of derision. "Do you *think*?"

Cassandra reluctantly shook her head.

"So she's no good?" Halt said.

"It's not as if she doesn't try," Cassandra said. "She's very enthusiastic."

"For which read *loud*," Horace put in, and Cassandra gave him an angry glance.

"Put it this way, Halt," Gilan said. "Maddie couldn't carry a tune in a bucket."

"She has what they call a cloth ear," Will added. "We some-times sing together after dinner in the evening. And I'll grant you she is enthusiastic. And loud. And totally off. She doesn't sing on the note. She doesn't even sing very near it."

"All right!" Cassandra snapped. "We've established that she's not the best of singers. Can we leave it at that, please?"

"Sorry," Will said, making a pretense of holding his hands up in self-defense.

"Well, if she can't travel as a singer, what can she do?" Halt asked, sensing that this conversation was getting into dangerous waters. Again, there was a long silence in the room.

"Maybe Malloy could help," Gilan finally suggested.

"Malloy? Dad's jester?" Cassandra asked.

"He's a little more than that," Gilan told them. "Malloy's in charge of all entertainment at the castle. He hires enter-tainers for the King. And he's quite talented himself. He's a jester, of course. But he also dances, and sings quite well. And he juggles too. Maybe he'll have an idea about what she might do."

Will shrugged. "It's worth a try."

Gilan rang the small bell on his desk that summoned Nichol. The young apprentice opened the door and stepped in. Behind him, Maddie was looking expectantly at them.

"Just a few more minutes, Maddie," said Gilan. Then, addressing Nichol, he said, "Nichol, can you fetch Malloy here, please." He reconsidered that statement. Nichol was sixteen, and sixteen-year-olds aren't renowned for their tact. "Give him my compliments and ask him if he could spare us a few minutes of his time, please," he amended.

Nichol *was* sixteen and was imbued with all the ennui that a teenager can muster. He was an adept at eye rolling and sighing. He did both now.

Fetch Maddie. Fetch the Ranger's mandola. Fetch Malloy, the twin gestures seemed to say.

"Yes, sir," he replied heavily, and withdrew once more.

"He's a ray of sunshine, isn't he?" Will said.

Gilan nodded. "It's no fun for him being stuck here as an administrative assistant," he said. "I'll have to get him some field experience soon."

"Send him to me." Will glowered. "I'll give him field experience."

Gilan grinned. A few weeks with Will, and Nichol mightn't feel so put upon here at Araluen, he thought.

"I might just do that," he said. "He's a good kid at heart but this job can get pretty boring."

"Hah!" Will snorted.

Cassandra smiled at him. "When did you become a grumpy old man?" she asked.

Will jerked a thumb in Halt's direction. "About five minutes after I met him," he replied. "He taught me everything I know."

"Fortunately," said Halt, smiling, "I didn't teach him everything *I* know."

Several minutes later, Nichol returned, tapping at the door and then entering.

"Malloy the jester is here, sir," he told Gilan. Perhaps he had sensed Will's annoyance because he was brisk and businesslike now and his eyes stayed solidly in one plane.

Gilan smiled at him. "Thanks, Nichol. Show him in, please. And send Maddie in as well."

The jester was tall and lean, with an athletic build, slim hips and broad shoulders. He had prominent cheekbones and an aquiline nose. His hair was short cropped and he was clean shaven. He wore a subdued version of the traditional jester's outfit—a red-and-green-quartered jerkin and yellow hose, but without the extra tassels and bells and long, pointed shoes. His short-cropped hair was beneath a felt cap, rather than the traditional headgear adorned with bells and baubles.

He was well muscled and moved gracefully. Studying him, Will felt Malloy was a physical match for any warrior he had ever seen—and he was right. Malloy, when necessary, could wield a sword with frightening speed and precision.

Gilan made the introductions. Malloy, of course, knew Cassandra and Horace. And he recognized Maddie, although he maintained the popular protocol that she was merely an apprentice Ranger and not the second in line to the throne. Since Dimon's unsuccessful attempt at a coup, most of the senior palace staff knew about Maddie's dual identity. But it was tacitly agreed that they would not acknowledge it or discuss it. When she was dressed as a Ranger she was known as Maddie. When she appeared in court attire, she became Princess Madelyn.

"We need your advice, Malloy," Gilan said. "Will here is going on a mission disguised as a jongleur. He plays the mandola and sings."

Malloy nodded in Will's direction. "I've heard you're quite capable, sir," he said.

Will smiled. "I get by."

"Maddie will be going with him," Gilan continued. "But we need to find her some sort of role as well."

"I can sing with Will, can't I?" Maddie interrupted, looking around the assembled faces. Nobody answered for a few seconds.

Then Halt, with a tact he rarely exhibited, answered her. "You've got a nice voice, Maddie. But it's not really . . . up to professional standards." He was very fond of Maddie and didn't want to see her embarrassed.

She looked a little crestfallen, but nodded her acceptance. "If you say. But I'm willing to practice if you think that'd help."

"Let's see what Malloy suggests," Halt told her. "He's the expert."

Malloy nodded briskly. In his years at the castle, he had heard Maddie sing from time to time. He stood in front of her now, sizing her up.

"Hmmm. You look fit enough," he said. "How about tumbling? Are you any good at that? That's something I could teach you relatively quickly." He looked to Gilan. "I take it there's some urgency about this?" he asked. There usually was when Rangers were involved, he knew.

Gilan replied. "Yes. We need to get her ready in a few weeks."

Will held up a hand before Malloy could go any further. "Tumbling and acrobatics might be a problem," he said. "Maddie's certainly fit and has excellent balance and agility, but she was hit by a javelin some years ago, and her hip is a little stiff."

"Does it cause you pain?" Malloy asked.

She shrugged. "Not generally. But when I get tired or exert myself a lot, it does stiffen up." She spread her hands apologetically. "Sorry."

"Not your fault," Malloy said. "I'll have Sanne look at that."

"Sanne? Who's that?" Maddie asked.

"She's one of my people. She's a triple threat—juggler, tumbler and knife thrower. I thought I'd get her to coach you.

Maybe she can teach you to juggle—although with this time frame we wouldn't get past the basics. We'd need something else if people are going to believe you're a professional entertainer."

"Maddie can throw a knife," said Gilan, and Malloy's interest was piqued.

"Really? How well?"

Maddie looked at Gilan questioningly. He indicated a portrait of one of Duncan's ancestors hanging on the wall behind his desk.

"Show him," he said.

Maddie's hand went to the double scabbard on her left side. She drew back her arm in one smooth movement, then jerked it forward. Her throwing knife caught the light as it spun across the room, thudding to a halt exactly halfway between the eyes of the elderly knight in the portrait.

"That well," said Malloy. "I think we could work with that."

"Great-Uncle Hesperus is looking a little the worse for wear," said Cassandra.

Gilan grinned. "Never liked that painting anyway."

10

THE FOLLOWING MORNING, ON MALLOY'S INSTRUCTIONS, Maddie was waiting in the armory hall on the keep's second floor. She looked around as she waited. She hadn't been in this long, empty room since her mother's final practice duel with Dimon before the Red Fox Rebellion. The room was a vast space, well lit by tall windows that lined the southern wall. At one end, racks held practice arms and armor—wooden swords, axes and halberds, padded jerkins and leather helmets equipped with metal mesh face protectors. There was a rack of steel swords for more realistic training.

She noted the rounded points and blunted edges on the swords. Not too realistic, she thought.

The floor was timber, well worn by the movement of thousands of feet over the years, as warriors practiced their skills with the various weapons in the racks. The floorboards were scarred and gashed where overenthusiastic strokes had missed their mark and damaged them. The gashes had been sanded and filled, but were still visible.

"Good morning. I'm Sanne. Malloy asked me to work with you."

Maddie turned at the voice. Sanne was a young woman in her mid-twenties. She was petite but well muscled, and fit-looking. She pronounced her name as *Sahna*. She had pleasant, regular features, and her shoulder-length light brown hair curved down in a heavy wave on the right side of her face.

She was dressed in a thigh-length jerkin, in a diamond pattern featuring the traditional jongleur's colors—red, green and yellow. Below the jerkin she wore yellow hose and ankle-high red leather boots. Maddie noted that her shoes were not fashioned in the usual entertainer's style, with long, curved tips and bells. Then she recalled that Malloy had said Sanne was a tumbler. She guessed that long, pointy-toed shoes would be an encumbrance for tumbling.

Before Maddie could reply, Sanne continued. "You're Princess Madelyn, right?"

Maddie grinned and shook her head. "Call me Maddie," she said.

She stepped forward and offered her hand. Sanne shook it briefly. Maddie noted the strength and firmness of Sanne's grip as the jongleur studied her with some curiosity. Maddie was dressed in an outfit similar to Sanne's—a thigh-length jerkin over tights. But the colors were more subdued, dull green and brown as opposed to the bright diamond pattern on Sanne's clothes.

"You don't look like a princess," the entertainer said.

Maddie shrugged. "I'm spending my time these days as an apprentice Ranger," she explained, then added, "But that's to be kept confidential."

Sanne frowned. "Oh yes," she said. "You were the one who spoiled Dimon's little game eighteen months ago, weren't you?"

Her curiosity was now tinged with a certain level of respect. Maddie sighed. After she had played such a prominent role in the downfall of the Red Fox Clan, she had known it would be difficult to keep her identity a complete secret—certainly not among the staff at Castle Araluen.

"There were a lot of people who spoiled his game," she said. "My mother was one, in particular. But as I said, we keep my role as a Ranger confidential."

Sanne nodded, understanding the reasoning behind the instruction. It could be dangerous if too many people knew about Maddie's double identity. Rangers, after all, preferred to maintain a low profile, and having people bowing and scraping to Maddie would be a continual nuisance—and one that could identify her as a member of the royal family and imperil her life.

"I'll bear it in mind," she said. Then, with the matter of Maddie's identity dealt with, she said, "Now, what can I do to help you? Malloy said I was to train you as a jongleur."

"I'm going on a mission with my mentor, Will Treaty," Maddie began. She noticed Sanne's eyes widen slightly at the mention of Will's name. Her teacher was a famous figure in Araluen—almost mythical, in fact, as Halt had been before him—although few people could actually claim to have seen either one of them. As a result, there were wild rumors about the two Rangers: People said they were tall as giants, broad-shouldered and heavily muscled. The less educated folk of the country also said they could appear and disappear as they chose, and they were skilled in the art of magic.

The truth was, while both men were heavily muscled in the arms and shoulders from long practice with their powerful war bows, they were, like most Rangers, somewhat shorter than the norm. Their reputation for appearing and disappearing at will was due to their training and field craft, and the use of their cloaks, which were mottled green and gray and helped them merge into the forest background. All Rangers knew that the real key to remaining unseen was to remain still, even when you were sure that an enemy had spotted you. Nine times out of ten, he hadn't.

Maddie was always amused by the reactions of people who met Will for the first time. There was an air of disbelief and even disappointment.

Can this be the mighty Will Treaty? their expressions seemed to say. *Surely not!*

"We're traveling undercover," she continued, "disguised as entertainers. Will is posing as a minstrel. He plays the mandola quite well and sings."

"What about you?" Sanne asked.

Maddie hesitated. "I don't play the mandola," she said. She didn't mention the singing. She was beginning to suspect that her singing wasn't all that it might be. She was relieved when Sanne didn't press the point. The young woman looked her up and down appraisingly, then walked in a small circle around her.

"You look fit enough," she said, almost to herself. "Can you tumble?"

"I'm not sure. I—"

Sanne cut her off with a brief wave of her hand. "Try this," she ordered, setting the leather satchel she wore over her right shoulder on the floor.

Without any further preparation, she took three quick paces and, on the third, sprang high in the air and spun in a forward somersault, landing on both feet with barely any sound of impact and in perfect balance.

Maddie noted that the soles of her red boots were soft leather, which accounted in part for the noiseless landing. She took a deep breath, composed herself, then sprang forward, throwing herself high in the air and tucking her head under as she rolled into a somersault.

She completed the movement well enough, although she was much closer to the floor than Sanne had been and her fingers brushed the floorboards.

But, as she landed, her weak hip gave way slightly and she stumbled, taking three small paces to recover. Sanne frowned. Maddie cursed under her breath. She had hoped her hip might stand up to the strain. She tapped it now.

"I've got a stiff hip," she explained. "I was hit by a javelin several years ago and it never healed properly."

Sanne chewed her lip thoughtfully. "Hmmmm. So I see. It'll definitely be a problem for tumbling. Given time, we could probably cure it. But it'd be painful. Are you up for that?"

"I'm not worried about pain," Maddie said. "But time is the problem. We only have a few weeks. Maybe after that I could work on freeing up the hip."

"Well, a few weeks won't do it," Sanne told her. "We'd better look for something else. Can you juggle at all?"

"Two balls," Maddie said. "No more than that."

Sanne said nothing. Stooping to the satchel she had set on the floor, she took out two soft juggling balls and tossed them to Maddie, nodding in approval as the young Ranger deftly caught both of them.

"So far so good," she said. "Now let's see how good you are."

Maddie set herself, a ball in either hand, then began. She tossed the ball in her left hand in the air, tossed the ball in her right hand laterally to her left, then caught the first ball in her right hand. She continued, sending the two balls around in a loop.

After half a dozen of these sequences, Sanne held up a hand for her to stop.

"All right. That's enough."

Maddie caught the last ball and waited for Sanne's verdict. She thought she'd done reasonably well. Two balls only, perhaps, but not at all bad.

"So what was that?" Sanne asked.

Maddie looked surprised. "I was juggling," she said.

But Sanne shook her head. "No. You were just throwing one up and passing the other across to your empty hand. That's what most people think is juggling. *This* is juggling."

And, without any apparent effort, Sanne set the two balls flying in opposing loops in the air, tossing the left-hand ball so that it flew in a circle over to her right hand, then the right-hand ball so it intersected the path of its partner, landing in her left hand. And as soon as she caught each ball, she launched it again to maintain the pattern in a one-two-three-four rhythm, with each ball flying high in the air and crossing over her body as it did so.

After a few rounds, she stopped and cocked her head at Maddie.

"Let's see if we can get you doing it like that," she said.

11

⟨⟨⟨⟨⟨⟨⟨⟨⟨⟨⟨⟨⟨⟨⟨⟨⟨⟨⟩

"ALL RIGHT," SANNE SAID, "THERE ARE A FEW THINGS TO remember." She reached out and put her hands on Maddie's shoulders, squaring them off. She moved Maddie so that she was directly in front of her.

"Stay nice and balanced, with your legs slightly bent and both feet evenly on the ground. Now take a ball in each hand."

Maddie did as she was instructed, watching Sanne expectantly.

"Relax," Sanne told her. "You're tensing up. Now bring your elbows in close to your body, with your forearms out at ninety degrees." She waited until Maddie was positioned properly. "Now toss the ball in your right hand up and across your body, and catch it in the left hand."

Maddie obeyed. The ball smacked into her left palm. She glanced at Sanne, who nodded approval.

"Good. Now toss it back to the right hand."

Maddie tossed the ball up again, but this time had to reach out to catch it, as it descended some thirty centimeters in front of her. Sanne held up a hand for her to stop.

"See that?" she said. "You had to reach out for the ball to catch it. That means you threw it too far out in front. The balls have to stay in the same plane, just going up and down so they land in your hand without you having to snatch at them. Try it again."

Maddie did, frowning in concentration, making sure the ball flew up vertically when she released it. It plopped easily into her catching hand this time.

"Better. Do it again."

Toss, fly, plop. Once more the ball landed smoothly in her hand. She tossed it again, back the other way.

"Good," said Sanne. "Keep that up. One. Two. Three. Four. One. Two. Three. Four. Toss. Catch. Toss. Catch."

She stopped counting the rhythm but Maddie continued to toss and catch the ball, counting to herself under her breath.

"You can count out loud if you like," Sanne told her.

The seventh time Maddie launched the ball in the air, she tossed it too far to the front again and snatched at it, missing it and knocking it to the floor. She swore quietly.

Sanne retrieved the ball and tossed it back to her. She grinned sympathetically. "That's the biggest problem to overcome," she said. "But you've just about got it."

Maddie began the sequence again, muttering between clenched teeth. "I can see why you don't use balls that will bounce." The balls were made of leather and filled with what felt like grain of some kind.

"Yes, you'd be scrambling all over the room retrieving them if they did," Sanne said. She watched Maddie throw the ball a few more times, then held up a hand for her to stop. "Fine. Your throwing is pretty consistent, although it's a little high. Try to toss it just above head height."

She handed Maddie a second ball. "All right, let's try two.

Toss the ball in your right hand and, when it reaches head height, toss the ball in your left hand to pass inside it. And toss both the same height in the air."

Maddie settled herself, preparing for this new challenge.

"Don't tense up," Sanne told her. "The secret to juggling isn't the catching. It's the tossing. If you toss them correctly, staying in the same plane, they should land naturally in your catching hand. Ready?"

"Ready," said Maddie tersely, her eyes focused on the space in front of her.

"And remember, if you toss it correctly, you don't have to look at it. Just let it float out there in front of you. Now, one, two, three, go."

Toss, toss, catch, catch.

"Excellent! Do it again."

One. Two. Three. Four.

Maddie grinned triumphantly as the second ball plopped back into her right hand, finishing the sequence.

Sanne nodded approvingly. "Good. Now toss the left-hand ball first."

For a moment, Maddie hesitated, adjusting her thinking to the reversal of the action. Then she complied.

One. Two. Three. Four.

The final ball fell into her left hand, and she nearly dropped it.

"Do it that way again," Sanne told her. This time, she completed the sequence without nearly spilling the ball. She tried again, then again. The third time, the final ball flew too far in front of her. She snatched it out of the air but her rhythm was spoiled and she stopped. She bit her lip in annoyance.

"Stay calm," Sanne instructed. "You're doing well."

"Except I think I've got it right and then I throw too far out to the front," Maddie replied.

"Try practicing standing close to a wall," Sanne told her. "That might help."

Maddie thought about the instruction and nodded. "You're right. That might do it. What's next?"

Sanne smiled at her. "Next, I'm going to take it easy for a couple of days while you practice until you've got it right. Then we'll add a third ball into the mix."

"Couldn't we do that now?" Maddie asked. "I think I've almost got the two balls worked out."

"*Almost* isn't good enough," Sanne replied. "You need to be completely comfortable with the two balls, so you can do it automatically, before we move on."

"But—" Maddie began. She was impatient to improve.

Sanne held up a hand to stop her. "Gilan told me you Rangers have a saying about practice," she said. "What is it?"

"Most people practice till they get it right. A Ranger practices until he doesn't get it wrong."

"Or *she*, in this case," Sanne told her. "Jugglers have the same rule. Keep practicing and I'll see you in two days."

"Oh, all right," Maddie said. She began another sequence but, inevitably, on the third passage, she snatched at one of the balls and dropped it. She swore quietly.

Sanne grinned. "See what I mean?" she said. She headed for the stairway, leaving Maddie tossing and catching, tossing and catching, her tongue protruding from her teeth.

"Are you planning on poking your tongue out at the audience?" Will asked her the next day as she practiced her toss-toss-catch-

catch routine in the sitting room of their suite of rooms.

"What?" she asked distractedly.

He shrugged. "It's just, some people might take offense. And it's never a good idea to offend those who are paying you."

Maddie nodded and withdrew her tongue inside her lips. But after a couple of tosses and catches, it slipped out again, unnoticed. Unnoticed by her, that is. Will noticed immediately.

"You're doing it again," he said cheerfully.

She swore under her breath. Her tongue went back in and instantly she missed the next catch, so that the ball hit the floor and rolled under the settee.

"Blast it," she said bitterly, stooping to retrieve the ball. She began the pattern again. This time she managed eight or nine sequences before one ball flew erratically and she dropped it again. This one rolled under an armchair and, once more, she went down on one knee to retrieve it. Will watched with some interest.

"If you practiced in front of the table or the bed, you wouldn't have to crawl around the floor to retrieve them," he pointed out.

"Shut up," Maddie said tersely, her eyes flicking back and forth to follow the flight of the balls. This time, she completed over a dozen sequences before she snatched at a ball and dropped it, sending it rolling across the floor. Sighing, she retrieved it and moved to the dining table to practice. This time, she completed fifteen patterns before dropping a ball. But this time, the ball landed on the table, rolled once and came to a halt. She retrieved it easily.

"Told you so," Will said. She drew in breath to make a pithy reply, then realized he had been right and said nothing.

Toss, toss, catch, catch, she continued. Will watched for a

while, then realized there was no further need for comment. Her tongue was withdrawn and she kept the balls rotating evenly, without dropping any.

He went back to reading a report about pirate activities on Araluen's northwest coast.

12

SANNE REVIEWED MADDIE'S PROGRESS THE FOLLOWING morning and nodded approvingly.

"Good work," she said. "Let's add the third ball and we're under way."

She handed Maddie another ball, placing it in Maddie's right hand, so that she held two balls there and one in her left.

"Okay, here's the sequence: Toss with your right hand. Toss with your left hand. Catch with your left hand. Toss with your right hand. Catch with your left hand."

Maddie frowned. "Say that again," she requested, and Sanne repeated the sequence.

"Like this," she said, and demonstrated. With the extra ball in play, the sequence now became toss-catch-toss-catch-toss-catch. Maddie tried it and instantly felt as if she was back to square one. The smooth rhythm she had built up with two balls deserted her and balls flew erratically, causing her to snatch at them and drop them.

"I'll never get this," she said bitterly.

Sanne smiled at her. "Of course you will. It just needs practice. Start again."

Maddie did so and, after a few muffed sequences, the pattern clicked and she had the balls rotating smoothly. She smiled in triumph and promptly dropped one.

Sanne stooped and retrieved it for her, handing it back to her. "See? I told you," she said.

Maddie scowled. "Yes, but I dropped one that last time."

Her instructor shrugged. "Maybe. But you *didn't* drop one the previous four times. That's progress."

"If you say."

"I do. All you have to do now is practice that three-ball sequence for a couple of days and you'll have it. But for now, let's try something different."

"Gladly," Maddie said. She put the balls away in her jerkin pocket and followed Sanne to the end of the practice hall. For the first time, she noticed that there was a head-high object there, covered with a thick linen cloth. Sanne pulled the cloth away and revealed a large round board, shaped in a circle and with twelve numbered segments marked on it. It looked like a giant version of the target boards Maddie had seen the castle garrison throwing small darts at when they were relaxing.

From her ever-present satchel, Sanne produced a canvas tool wrap. Unrolling it on a side table, she revealed five identical knives. Simple in design, each one consisted of a wooden handle riveted to a straight steel blade that tapered to a double-edged point. There were no crosspieces and no fancy decoration on the hilts. She passed one to Maddie, who tested its weight and balance. In spite of the simple, almost primitive design, she found the knife was perfectly balanced and weighted.

Transferring the knife to her left hand, she reached for another and tested it. It felt identical to the first. She raised her eyebrows.

"These are good," she said, passing them back and forth from right hand to left, testing them further.

Sanne smiled. "Thank you," she said. "I made them myself."

"They're almost identical," Maddie said, studying the two simple blades, holding them alongside each other to measure each against its companion.

"Not almost," Sanne corrected her. "They *are* identical. Weight and balance for each one is exactly the same as the other." She indicated the round target, nearly six meters away. "Try one," she said.

Maddie paused, testing the heft and balance of the knife for a second, then threw with a deceptively casual action. The knife caught the early morning sun streaming through the tall windows as it spun across the room, then thunked solidly into the target a few centimeters to the left of the junction point of the twelve numbered segments. The knife had spun past the central point on its final spin and the hilt was angled at about twenty degrees higher than the blade. Sanne looked at her, a small moue of surprise on her features.

"Pretty good," she said. "Try another one." But before Maddie could comply, she held out a hand to stop her. "Aim for a different part of the board," she said. "If you hit that first knife, and there's every chance you might, you could split some of the wood off the hilt. Then I'll have to rebalance it."

Maddie nodded and spun the second knife into the widest part of the number one segment, at the top of the target. Another solid *thunk* and the knife was quivering in the wood. Without commenting, Sanne handed her a third knife. This one Maddie placed in the number nine segment.

"Can you throw underarm?" Sanne asked, handing her a fourth knife.

Without replying, Maddie spun the knife underarm into the number three segment, opposite her previous throw.

"And round arm?" Sanne said, passing across the final knife. Maddie hurled it in a sideways throw, placing it a centimeter from the first knife in the center of the board.

Sanne frowned. "I told you not to throw near the other knife," she said.

Maddie shrugged and grinned. "I've got the feel for them now," she said. "I knew I wouldn't hit it."

Sanne went to reply, then looked at the neat placement of the five knives in the target and realized Maddie wasn't boasting, but speaking the truth. Well, perhaps she was boasting just a little, but she obviously knew what she was doing when it came to throwing knives.

"So you say," Sanne said eventually, then moved forward to retrieve the knives from the board.

"Well," she continued, "I can see that I don't need to teach you how to throw a knife. But I can teach you a little show business to go along with it."

"Show business?" Maddie asked. For the past three and a half years, knife throwing had been a serious business for her, with no room for fancy throwing and showing off.

Sanne nodded. "Throwing a knife well is good," she said. "But the audience has to see some element of risk in it if they're going to be entertained."

"Risk is entertaining?" Maddie asked.

The performer smiled indulgently. "Of course it is. People love to be frightened," she said.

She moved up to the target and wheeled a new apparatus from behind it. It was a pulley wheel and crank handle, with a leather belt running from the pulley. She looped the belt over a matching pulley at the back of the target board, flicked off a retaining strap and pulled the cranking apparatus until the leather belt was taut. She gave a few experimental tugs on the crank handle and the target board turned slowly in time with the crank. The two pulleys were different sizes, so that the wheel turned at twice the speed as the pulley Sanne was cranking.

"Hit number five," she said suddenly, catching Maddie by surprise.

Hurriedly, the Ranger peered at the turning target wheel and located the number five segment. She took a few seconds to assess the speed at which the wheel was turning and threw, aiming off to allow for the fact that the numbered segment would have moved in the time it took for the knife to reach the target.

Thunk!

The knife thudded into the nominated segment on the outer edge of the wheel. It wasn't quite central but Sanne nodded approval.

"Excellent," she said. "Now hit number eleven."

She continued turning the crank, keeping the target board rotating at a constant speed. Familiar with the movement now, Maddie threw without the same delay. This time, the knife hit the outer edge of the eleven segment, exactly in the center.

"Good work," Sanne called, a little short of breath from the effort of keeping the heavy board turning. "And number three."

Maddie was ready with another knife. Her eyes narrowed as

she sought the number three, assessed the trajectory she would need and threw.

Thunk!

Once again, it was a perfect throw.

"This time, halfway into the center—number seven."

The target was narrower now, as the segments tapered down the closer they were to the center of the board. Maddie took a second to assess the new conditions, then hurled another knife, spinning and catching the sunlight, to thud into the board at the nominated point. Sanne stood up from the crank and let the board slow down and eventually come to a stop.

She grinned at Maddie. "You're better at this than juggling."

Maddie shrugged. "I've thrown a lot of knives over the past three years," she said. "We have to practice with knives that aren't balanced like these, so we can throw any type of knife."

Sanne indicated the two knives at Maddie's belt. "But your own knives are balanced for throwing," she said.

The apprentice Ranger nodded. "They are. Although not as well as these." She pointed to the knives Sanne had brought to the session. "These are excellent."

Sanne nodded in recognition of the compliment. "They have to be," she said.

"There's one thing," Maddie said. "You said you were going to add an element of risk. There's no risk in simply hitting a rotating target."

The juggler smiled. "There is when there's a person strapped to it," she said.

13

At Sanne's invitation, Maddie stepped forward to study the target board once more. Looking closely, she could see there were two handholds at the nine and three positions, and gaps in the board at the five and seven positions.

"You place one of the audience on the board," explained Sanne. "They hold on to the handgrips, and you pass leather straps through the gaps here to fasten their feet to the board. Then you have someone turn the crank and you have a live target spinning slowly on the board. The object, of course, is to miss them—but to do it with the smallest possible margin."

"Of course," said Maddie, eyeing the handles and strap holes. "I guess the trick is to aim to hit them when they're at a certain point, knowing the rotation of the board will take them away from the spot you're aiming at."

"As long as the person on the crank keeps turning at a constant rate—so I'd advise you to use your master for that task, not a volunteer from the audience."

"Yes. I don't think I'd be wise to rely on someone who's been drinking for several hours," Maddie replied.

"And don't make the target anyone too important, just in case."

"I can see that might be unwise," Maddie said thoughtfully. "So what's next?"

"Practice," Sanne told her. "Practice your juggling so you can get those three balls flying without dropping them. And practice throwing with the wheel turning. Get one of the castle servants to crank it for you. Or ask Will if he's got the time. It'll be good to get him used to the apparatus."

"You won't be with me?" Maddie asked.

Sanne shook her head. "You don't need me anymore. I've shown you all you need to know. Now you need a week or so to get the movements right. Particularly the juggling. I'll check back in a week to see how you've progressed. My guess is you'll be ready to go. Your juggling won't be anything spectacular, but it'll be adequate. And your knife throwing will compensate for that."

"I'm not going to have to juggle those knives, am I?" Maddie asked anxiously. She envisioned those gleaming knives spinning in the air in front of her. It was not a comforting image.

Sanne smiled. "I don't think you'll have time to perfect that. We'll keep the juggling to the balls."

She patted the young Ranger on the shoulder encouragingly. "Don't worry. You'll be fine. You've got a lot of natural talent and you're already a perfectly competent knife thrower. We just have to add a bit of show business to that."

"And avoid actually hitting anyone with one of the knives," Maddie said.

Sanne nodded. "That would be ideal, yes," she said. Then, gathering her leather satchel and slinging it over her shoulder, she prepared to leave.

"I'll check you out in a week," she said. "In the meantime, if there's anything that's bothering you, feel free to send for me and ask me."

"There's a lot that's bothering me," Maddie said, remembering how the juggling balls tended to spill from her hands as if they had a life of their own. "But I'm not sure if just asking will fix it."

Sanne grinned, knowing what she meant. "I know the juggling seems well-nigh impossible at the moment," she said. "But you'll be surprised how quickly you improve."

"I certainly hope so," Maddie replied.

The week passed quickly, with Maddie applying herself to the two disciplines of juggling and knife throwing. Her life as a Ranger had left her well accustomed to practicing and perfecting new physical skills. She alternated between the two, ensuring that she spent sufficient time on each to ensure improvement, without becoming stale.

Will watched her approvingly, seeing her ability improving as each day went by. In the evenings, she put the knives and juggling balls away and gave herself a complete break from the work, so that the following morning she could approach it totally refreshed.

After two days, she had a life-size dummy made and strapped to the board, and co-opted two sturdy servants to crank the handle and make it rotate. She counted time for them, ensuring that they didn't go too fast or too slow, but turned the wheel, and the dummy, at a constant speed as the knives thudded into the target board. The servants watched with some degree of awe. They were impressed by her knife-throwing skills. But when she asked if either of them wanted to take a turn strapped to the wheel, they hastily declined.

She grinned and didn't press the matter.

Her juggling was improving rapidly. She was sending the three balls swooping through the air with great aplomb and only ever dropped one on rare occasions—usually when she was interrupted or distracted. She became so confident, in fact, that she decided she'd try juggling three of the throwing knives, reasoning that it would make a dramatic beginning to her knife-throwing act.

But knives were a lot more daunting than balls. She spent ten minutes accustoming herself to the feeling of tossing a knife in the air so that it rotated once, landing hilt-first in her catching hand. All the time, she was conscious of the sharp point as it spun slowly in the air. Eventually, she became proficient with one knife and moved on to two, as she had with the juggling balls. But the minute the two sharp points were spinning in the air, she panicked and skipped away with a startled yelp, letting them thud point-down into the floor of the practice room.

"I'll leave the juggling to the balls," she muttered, as she pried the knives loose, studying the two new gashes in the floorboards that she'd have to smooth over.

Will, meanwhile, had his own work cut out. He needed to learn a new repertoire of songs—particularly those that were popular on the continent. Fortunately, there was a lot of traffic back and forth between Araluen and Gallica so far as entertainers were concerned, and a protégé of Malloy's had only recently returned from a tour of Gallica and Iberion and was able to show Will some of the newer and more popular tunes.

In addition, he was supervising work on their transport—a

small, gaily painted and decorated cart that would carry their equipment as they traveled, and provide shelter for those times when they might need to camp on the road. It was a short, high-sided cart, capable of being pulled by one horse—either Tug or Bumper. The cart had a high canvas top, held erect by three bent steel hoops set into the sides. Once Maddie's throwing board and crank handle were loaded, there would be room for her to sleep inside the cart, under cover. Not a lot of room, mind you, but room nonetheless.

"What about you?" Maddie asked.

Will shrugged. "I can sleep on the ground, under the cart," he said. "I've had worse beds."

Maddie had been about to offer to alternate with him but then decided that if he felt that way, he could stay under the cart. He saw the momentary hesitation and turned away, smiling. She was learning fast, he thought.

Sanne returned, as she had promised, on the seventh day and assessed Maddie's progress. She nodded in satisfaction as the young girl sent the balls spinning in a smooth cascade.

"You've come a long way," she said, then gestured to the target board in the corner. "Have you tried this with a live subject yet?"

"Not so far," Maddie admitted. "I've been using that dummy." She indicated the burlap sack with rough arms and legs attached, all stuffed with straw.

Sanne examined it, noting the lack of tears or holes in the burlap. "Nothing like practicing with the real thing," she said. "It adds that necessary frisson of danger."

Maddie grinned. "Are you volunteering?"

Sanne backed away hurriedly. "Not me," she said. "I don't get paid enough for that." Her gaze lit on Will, who was standing by, watching with interest. He saw her appraising him and held up his hands in protest.

"Not me either!" he said. "I'm a valuable officer in His Majesty's forces!"

"And yet, you were the one who taught her how to throw a knife?" Sanne challenged.

"Well, yes. But not at me," he pointed out.

"Come on, Will," Maddie wheedled. "Don't you trust me?"

"Neither one of us wants to hear the answer to that," he said. But he began to move toward the target board, albeit reluctantly. Grinning broadly, Sanne adjusted the board so that it was upright. Will stepped up onto the foot stirrups and took a firm hold of the handgrips. The two women quickly strapped him in, with straps on both hands and feet, so that he was secure.

Sanne held up a hand as Maddie reached for the first knife. "Not yet," she said. "I want you to see something."

She wound the crank until Will was head down, then stopped.

"See how he's dropped a little on the board?" she said. "There's always some slack in the straps and you have to allow for that."

"She can see," Will said, upside down and somewhat red in the face as a consequence. "Now can we keep moving?"

Sanne laughed softly and began cranking again. "Set the rhythm," she told Maddie, and the young Ranger began to count time. After a slight hesitation, she threw the first knife, sending it thudding into the board a few centimeters from Will's left armpit.

"Good!" said Sanne. "Did you mean it to be that close?"

"Pretty much," Maddie replied.

Will, his voice alternately straining and relaxing as he rotated, asked a question. "How close was she?"

Sanne looked at him in mild surprise. "You didn't see?"

"Can't see with my eyes closed," Will replied.

14

THEY LEFT CASTLE ARALUEN FOUR DAYS LATER. THE LITTLE cart, festooned at all four corners with red, yellow and green flags that fluttered gaily in the wind, rolled smoothly along with Tug between the shafts. Bumper trotted obediently beside his older companion, the two of them tossing their heads and shaking their manes in companionable conversation as they went.

Although neither horse had been bred as a cart horse, both had the necessary nuggety strength and endurance to pull the cart easily. It was light in weight and not heavily laden. The knife-throwing target was the bulkiest piece of equipment they carried, and usually either Maddie or Will walked beside the cart to lighten the load still further.

"Sorry about this," Will had told his horse as he guided Tug between the shafts. He sensed there was a certain indignity involved in pulling a cart. But Tug was a Ranger horse and he understood the necessity for going undercover. They could have used a cart horse, of course, with the two saddle horses tethered behind the cart. But it might have roused suspicions for a pair of jongleurs to own three horses.

At least I don't have to wear that ridiculous red-and-yellow getup, Tug had replied, and Will sighed ruefully.

As a Ranger, he was used to wearing subdued colors and not drawing attention to himself. Jongleurs did the opposite. Their gaudy clothing was designed to catch the eye, invite attention and provoke interest. Jongleurs wanted to be seen. Such high visibility meant that they were often asked to perform without having to ask permission or to spend excessive time attracting a crowd.

They took the cart down to the small quay a few kilometers from Castle Araluen, where cart, horses and Rangers were loaded aboard a tubby little merchant ship called *Jaunty Lady*, which had been chartered by the King for the journey to Gallica. The craft made its way downstream to the sea, propelled by oars and current with a speed belying its lines. At the river mouth, the crew set the sails on the ship's twin masts and she forged out into the open sea, rolling and pitching with the short, steep waves.

"How about a tune for the lads while they work?" the skipper requested of Will. He was a short, tubby man, built rather like his ship, and with his long hair greased with tar and held back in a pigtail by a piece of twine. A shabby felt hat crowned his head, all style and shape beaten out of it by years of being drenched in seawater coming over the bow in solid waves.

Will nodded agreeably. It was some years since he had performed in public and he could use all the practice he could manage. It was one thing, he knew, to sing by the fire after dinner among friends. Singing for total strangers, who were ready to notice the slightest fault or hesitation, was a different matter altogether.

The ship's crew of four were mainly occupied with the business of bailing the ship dry, removing the considerable volumes of seawater that sloshed in over the bow and ran down into the bilges. There was a hand pump mounted by the foremast and they took it in turns cranking the handle up and down, keeping a clear stream of water spurting back over the side. A song with a good, solid rhythm would help them along, he reasoned.

As usual when asked to perform unexpectedly, he found his mind empty when he came to selecting a suitable song. Berrigan, who had tutored him many years before, had told him this was one of the fundamental differences between an amateur performer and a professional. A professional never hesitated. He always had a string of suitable tunes ready to perform.

"I'm out of touch," he muttered as he searched his repertoire. Finally, he settled on a sea shanty that had a strong, basic rhythm the men could work to. He set to, strumming the mandola in the stirring introduction, then followed with the first verse and chorus. He was interested to note how the men working the pump immediately conformed to the rhythm of the song. After the first run-through, they joined in on the chorus, where a sailor bemoaned the fact that his love's father had rejected him as a suitor for his daughter and sent him to sea and a life of hardship.

It was a common theme in sea shanties, he thought, and in spite of the inherent melancholy in the words, the sailors joined in cheerfully, bellowing out the words with a will, their actions on the pump adding a somewhat violent emphasis to the words.

Of course, as with most shanties it had been written by a landsman poet, who made the usual mistake of confusing a sheet with a sail, instead of the rope that controlled the sail. And he described the cheery dash of salty brine in the face with all the enthusiasm and romance of one who has never endured it. Still, the sailors didn't seem to mind. It helped ease their labors as they worked the pump.

Will followed up the shanty with a non-nautical tale of a lad who worked for a wagoner and, once again, was rejected by his lady love's parents. Seemed that it didn't just happen to sailors, he mused.

But again, the song had a driving chorus that lent itself to the task the sailors were carrying out.

He finished that song and was searching his mind for another when the skipper called the hands to tend the sail and altered course south. The wind and sea were now on their beam, and the *Jaunty Lady* was no longer butting her way into a head sea. As a result, the water smashed over the bow in vastly reduced amounts and there was no further need for pumping.

"Good songs, those," the skipper told Will, and handed him a large silver coin. Will nodded his thanks and put it away into his purse.

Maddie had watched the interplay between Will and the crew with interest. Initially disturbed by the surging actions of the *Jaunty Lady*, she had begun to feel somewhat better as she had something other than her stomach to concentrate on.

Will noticed how the color had returned to her cheeks. "Got your sea legs?" he asked. He was one of those fortunate people who had never been affected by the rolling or pitching of a ship under his feet.

She nodded. "It was touch and go for a few minutes there," she said. "But I'm all right now."

She had never been on board a ship at sea before and, to be

truthful, her discomfort had been initially due to uncertainty and fear. It took her some time to realize that the *Lady* was riding the waves like a gull, and when she rolled one way, she inevitably would roll back. Once that realization came, she could relax. And once she relaxed, the tension in her stomach subsided.

Will nodded. "Always be careful if you're on a ship with Halt," he said. "Never lend him your hat if he asks for it."

She frowned, trying to figure that one out. He explained by miming the action of throwing up into a hat and she looked at him wide-eyed.

"Halt gets seasick?" she asked.

He grinned cheerfully. "Every time."

She shook her head in disbelief. The idea that the indomitable Halt, so self-assured, so confident, could ever suffer from something as mundane as mal de mer was a revelation.

The crossing took the better part of two days. *Jaunty Lady*, despite her name, was a slow sailer and the prevailing winds were adverse to their course. But in the midafternoon of the second day, they slipped through the harbor entrance of Ontifer, a small port on the Gallican coast, and secured alongside a stone pier. Since the pier was only a meter and a half higher than the deck of the ship, there was no need to rig a hoist to lift the horses and cart ashore. A wide section of the bulwark was removed and a sturdy gangplank was shoved in place. Tug and Bumper were led up the wooden ramp, stepping gingerly as it flexed under their weight and moved up and down with the action of the small waves inside the harbor. Then the sailors, with the help of three stevedores from the shore, tailed onto the cart and ran it easily up the gangplank and onto the quay.

Will thanked them and paid them for their work, then hitched Bumper into the traces on the cart.

"Your turn, boy," he said quietly, and Bumper flicked his ears at him. Like Tug, he accepted the indignity as part of the job. Will mounted the cart and settled into the driving seat. The whip remained in its socket. It was for show only and would never be needed. With horses like these, all that was needed was a click of the tongue.

At that sound, Bumper leaned forward against the neck yoke and strode off down the narrow street that led from the quay and into the village proper.

"We'll head for Philippe's castle first," Will said. "I want to make sure the situation hasn't changed and that his son is still being held at Falaise."

There was no need to tether Tug to the cart. Like all Ranger horses, he was trained to remain with his master. Tug trotted alongside his friend. Maddie rode on the seat beside Will, peering around her curiously at the sight of a foreign village.

The village returned the favor, with its inhabitants stopping in their mundane tasks to stare at the gaily colored, be-flagged cart and its brightly dressed inhabitants. Nothing much happened in Ontifer and the sight of the two jongleurs riding past drew considerable attention. Most of those watching were hoping that the newcomers might stay the night and perform. That would add a spice of novelty to the uneventful day-to-day life of the little fishing port.

But Will had other ideas. "We'll make as much distance as we can today. We want to meet with Philippe as soon as possible," he said.

Of course, that didn't mean they wouldn't stop en route to

perform. If they simply rode straight to the palace, they might arouse suspicion. But on this, their first day ashore, Will wanted to make up as much distance as he could.

"So where will we stop tonight?" Maddie asked. Will had studied the map of the surrounding area the night before on board ship.

"There's a small town called Aules about fifteen kilometers inland. We should make that by sundown. We'll camp on the common there and see about performing in one of the taverns."

"Why not stay at an inn?" Maddie asked.

But Will shook his head. "We're jongleurs. We don't have the money to stay at inns and taverns. We'll perform there, but we'll camp on the green or the common. That's what people would expect."

Maddie nodded. She hadn't thought of that. After the hard plank bunk she had slept in on *Jaunty Lady*, the thought of a soft bed in an inn had been very tempting. She sighed. Undercover work meant making sacrifices, she thought.

15

They continued traveling northeast, heading for Philippe's castle at La Lumiere. En route, they stopped each evening in larger villages, where they could expect to find an audience.

"Time you got used to performing," Will told Maddie at their first stop, and she agreed, wetting her lips nervously. At the thought of performing, she found, they had suddenly gone dry.

They pulled into the main square of the village, where a combined inn and tavern called Les Trois Canards, or "the three ducks," took up most of one side of the square. There was an open area outside the tavern, where tables and chairs were set up so that patrons could enjoy the fresh air while they ate and drank. A large canvas awning was folded back. In times of less pleasant weather, Maddie assumed, it could be rolled out to provide shelter for the customers.

In the center of the square, a low stone wall marked off a level area of raked sand and fine gravel, where a dozen men were playing a game similar to bowls—except the balls they were using were made of highly polished metal and they tossed them underarm at a target jack, rather than rolling them along the ground, as the Araluen version of the game was played. They paused in their game to watch the arrival of the jongleurs' cart.

Several of the tables outside the tavern were occupied and the customers looked up curiously as the wagon pulled to a halt and Will and Maddie clambered down. A serving maid who was pouring wine for one group finished her task and hurried inside. A few minutes later, a stoutly built man with a long apron tied round his waist emerged from the interior and eyed them with professional interest.

"That'll be the innkeeper," Will said in a low aside to Maddie, and she nodded. Even though the square was technically public property, the fact that the tavern had tables and chairs set up there gave the innkeeper a proprietorial interest. Good performers could mean a boost to his daily takings, as they would attract customers to the tavern and encourage them to eat and drink while they were entertained.

On the other hand, poor performers could have the opposite effect. An out-of-tune singer or a clumsy tumbler could drive customers away, to eat and drink in the privacy of their own homes. For that reason, the publican took a keen interest in itinerant performers who arrived. He strode across to the cart now, casting a practiced eye over its two brightly clad occupants.

"Bonjour," he said. His tone was neither welcoming or unfriendly. He spoke Gallican but Will replied in the common tongue. Even in a remote village like this, it would be widely spoken, he knew.

"Good morning, good sir," he said cheerfully. "My name is Accord and this is my daughter, Madelyn."

Like Halt before him, Will sometimes assumed a Gallican nom de guerre based on his real name: thus, Treaty became

Accord. He bowed now to the tavern keeper, a deep, exaggerated movement, wherein his right arm snatched the feathered hat from his head and described a wide curve, the hand turning over two or three times during the action. His right leg stretched out in front of him and his head was lowered almost to the level of his knee. He straightened gracefully, replacing the green cap with its yellow feather on his head.

The tavern keeper, whose name was Maurice, studied him closely, then flicked his gaze to the young girl standing nearby.

"Entertainers, are you?" he said, now speaking the common tongue.

"Indeed we are, sir," Will said effusively. "I am a humble singer of songs: love songs, work songs, songs of brave deeds and chivalry." He stepped closer and turned his head slightly to view the man with his right eye while he continued in a lowered voice, which somehow managed to carry to those seated nearby. "Or if it's your pleasure, good sir, I can sing you songs of witches and wizards and wickedness. Of evil deeds in the night that will bring terror to your heart."

Ghost stories set to music were a popular genre in Araluen and Gallica, and Will had a large stock of them. They were best sung on cold and rainy winter nights, while the audience huddled around the fire in the darkness and the wind whistled around the walls outside.

Maurice, however, was unimpressed. He'd seen plenty of jongleurs in his time. He glanced at Maddie. "What about the girl?" he asked.

Maddie and Will exchanged a quick glance and he gave her an imperceptible nod. She took a deep breath, then launched into a spiel that Sanne had taught her. "It's not enough to turn up and say, 'Hi. I'm Maddie. I juggle a bit and throw knives.' You've got to sell the act," Sanne had said. Now Maddie set out to do that, as she had been taught.

"Why, good sir, I juggle!" she said brightly. The three juggling balls appeared, seemingly from nowhere, in her hands and she began to loop them in a rapid cascade. Maurice was relatively unimpressed. Then she continued.

"But anyone can juggle, of course. I'll wager you can yourself!" And with those words, she tossed the three balls in quick succession to the surprised man.

He tried to catch them but was caught off guard, and the balls spilled across the fine gravel of the sitting area. Moving quickly, Maddie retrieved them and stowed them out of sight under her jerkin in a swift, practiced movement.

"Or perhaps not?" Maddie continued, and several of the drinkers at the tables laughed at Maurice's sudden discomfiture. He went to say something but Maddie's bright smile robbed the comment of any offense.

Maddie laughed and skipped away from him, her eyes alight and her smile wide.

"But my real talent lies elsewhere," she declared, and, before he could ask what it might be, she produced one of the gleaming knives and tossed it, spinning, in the air, catching it and tossing it again. She might not be able to juggle three knives, but she could easily toss and catch one. The sudden appearance of the gleaming, razor-sharp blade caused a few intakes of breath around the tables. Maurice's eyes narrowed as he saw it.

"Yes, my lord, I am skilled with the blades of danger, the knives of dire peril. Razor-sharp . . ."

As she said these words, she caught the knife by the hilt and slashed at an apple that Will had tossed in front of her. The fruit fell to the ground in two pieces, ample proof that the knife wasn't blunted for safety. She tossed it, spinning, once more.

"... ready to cut, slice or slash!"

She balanced the knife, hilt down, on her forehead and moved in a circle, keeping it upright. Then she nodded it off and caught it again, sending it spinning once more, so that it was never still.

"Or to flash through the air at my target!" she said.

As she had been moving and talking, Will had quickly unloaded the target board from the back of the cart and set it up. Now she turned and, without seeming to pause to aim, sent the knife spinning through the air to thud into the very center of the target.

A few murmurs of appreciation came from the patrons at the tables. Several of them raised their tankards of wine in salute. She grinned at them as she skipped across to the target and reclaimed her knife.

She brandished it under Maurice's nose and he took an involuntary half pace backward. There was more laughter from the tables.

"But now, my lord, step this way, if you please ..."

She took hold of his elbow and moved him to stand in front of the target board. As he took his position, a little reluctantly, Will handed him two inflated balloons, made from pig's bladders, and attached to the ends of two light canes.

"... and hold my balloons for me."

Sensing what was coming, Maurice started to protest as she walked quickly away from him. He had the good sense, however, to remain still, not exactly sure what was coming, but knowing that any movement on his part might be a mistake.

He was right. Maddie suddenly spun on her heel and released the knife, followed by a second, previously unnoticed, in her left hand. The two whirling blades spun across the intervening space and popped the two balloons in rapid succession, then thudded into the board.

The balloons were filled with brightly colored, tiny pieces of paper, which now filled the air as they were released. Maurice didn't have time to flinch as a sustained burst of applause came from the tables. And Maurice noticed that the dozen men playing boules had left their game and sauntered across to sit at the tables. They gestured to his waitress and ordered jugs of wine. Seeing his customers suddenly double in number, he was prepared to forgive the girl for using him as a foil.

"Very well," he said. "Continue." He brushed several small pieces of the colored paper from where they had settled and hastily moved away from the girl before she could use him as a target again. She smiled and nodded her thanks to him, then addressed the audience around her, who were eager to see what she might do next.

She moved some fifteen paces from the target board. She now had all five knives held by their tips in her left hand, splayed out in a fan shape. In her right, she produced a large silver coin.

"Gentles all," she called to the expectant crowd, "here is a silver crown. And it's yours if you can bamboozle or confoozle me. See the target? There are numbers painted on it. Call a number at random and I'll hit that segment with my knives. If I miss, the silver crown goes to the man who has called the number."

"And if you hit it?" called one of the drinkers good-naturedly.

Maddie skipped lightly across the open space to stand in front of him, her eyes twinkling with mischief.

"Then, sir, I know you will be generous when the time comes to reward my performance," she replied. The men around the speaker grinned agreement as she let her gaze wander across them.

"Quatre!" cried a customer at another table, hoping to catch her on the hop. But she held up a hand.

"Please, sir, in the common tongue if you will. If I have to pause to translate, I'll probably miss."

"Then hit four!" the man cried. Maddie spun on her heel, plucked a knife from her left hand and sent it flashing underhand at the target. It thunked into the three segment, missing the nominated target by ten centimeters. Some in the crowd groaned their disappointment. Maddie contrived to look a little disappointed, and spun the silver coin toward the man who had called out. He caught it happily.

Always make a mistake early on, she heard Sanne's voice say in her mind. *You don't want to appear too good too soon.*

Seeing the caller rewarded, others eagerly took up the challenge.

"Six!" called another and this time Maddie threw overarm. The knife hit the number six segment, but only just. It was close enough to the dividing line to encourage more calls.

"One!"

Thunk! The knife quivered in the exact center of the nominated segment.

"Nine!"

Thunk! Again, dead center.

"Twelve!"

Thunk!

More voices called out numbers, but Maddie held up her empty left hand, indicating that she needed to retrieve her knives. She did so, then skipped lightly back to her throwing position and signaled for more calls.

This time she threw faster than before, and varied her throws: right handed, left handed, over arm, side arm. For her final throw, she turned her back on the target, her right arm poised with the knife in hand. She held up her hand for silence. When she had it, she called the last target herself.

"Center!"

And in one movement, she spun on her heel and released the knife, sending it thudding into the small circle at the center of the board, where the twelve segments joined. The audience roared their appreciation and she swept down into an exaggerated bow, right leg forward, and both hands and arms spread out to the side.

Realizing the show was over, the audience cheered her and sent a shower of coins her way. As she scampered about collecting them, Will stepped forward, his mandola slung, and launched into a popular country song.

The tavern customers, already in good spirits after Maddie's display, joined in immediately. Maddie slipped past Will to deposit the considerable pile of coins—many of them silver—in a lockbox at the rear of the cart. He winked at her as she passed him.

"Well done," he said.

16

THEY PERFORMED ANOTHER NIGHT IN THE VILLAGE, AT Maurice's urging.

"Tomorrow is six-day," he told them, "and seven-day is a day of rest for the farms around here. That means the farmworkers will be coming to town to relax, to eat and to drink. And once word gets out that there are entertainers here, they'll come in big numbers. You could expect a much larger audience if you stay another night."

"And you'll have many more customers," Will said.

Maurice shrugged, a typical Gallic movement. "I make no secret of that fact," he said. "But the more customers at Les Trois Canards, the more coin there will be for me and you. We both win."

Eventually, Will agreed to stay another night. The tipping point came when Maurice offered them bed and board in the tavern.

"My beds are renowned for their soft mattresses," he said. "Far better than sleeping on the ground, or in your cart. And Hortense, my chef, is renowned in the district for her ragout. There will be no charge, of course."

"That's very gracious of you," Will said. He knew the tubby landlord would stand to make a killing with the extra trade he would enjoy once word of the jongleurs went round the district.

They moved the cart into the cobbled yard behind the tavern and settled Tug and Bumper into the small stable there, leaving them with full bins of hay and troughs of fresh, cool water.

Maddie sat on the edge of Will's bed that evening as they prepared for their performance.

"I thought we were in a hurry to get to La Lumiere," she said.

Will nodded. One of his mandola strings had broken and he was fitting a new one as he talked. The tip of his tongue protruded slightly between his lips as he wound the string on and tensioned it.

"I am," he said. "But if anyone is watching us, they might wonder why we would turn down the opportunity to make good money."

"Is anyone watching us?" Maddie asked.

Will shrugged. "I don't know. But it's always best to assume that someone is," he told her. "We'll make up the time in the early part of next week. The taverns and inns won't be as busy on the first few days. It'll be less suspicious if we keep moving on."

His voice was strained as he said the last few words. He was bringing the new string up to full tension and that always was a nervous moment, waiting to see if it would take the strain or, as occasionally happened, snap.

He sounded the string several times. It reached the correct note, then it slipped a little, as new strings always did. He wound it tighter, holding the instrument well away from his face, just in case. Finally, the new string settled and held its note. He sighed,

unaware that he had been holding his breath during the restring-
ing operation.

Maddie, watching him, grinned. "Dangerous things, those
mandolas," she said.

He nodded gravely. "Could take your eye out if you aren't
careful," he said. He strummed a few chords gently, making sure
that the string was now set and holding its tune. Then he stood
and headed for the door.

"Come on. Time to perform."

As Maurice had predicted, the inn was packed and the outdoor
tables were filled. He had hired an extra waitress for the night
and two girls hurried between the tables, refilling wine and ale
tankards, joking with the customers and bringing steaming
platters of local sausage and potatoes and onions to set down
beside the hungry farmworkers.

Hortense's ragout was also a popular choice, with a constant
supply of bowls being delivered to the tables, along with fresh,
crusty loaves of long bread.

The inn was buzzing with a dozen different conversations.
Laughter rang out from the crowded tables and patrons called
greetings to one another. Will and Maddie had already set up
the target wheel outside the inn, where it was illuminated by
four flaring torches. The inn itself was too cramped for the
knife-throwing act, with a low ceiling and crowded tables.

"We don't want you killing any patrons," Will had said. "Bad
for business, you know."

He waited until the majority of the crowd had finished their
meals. "Never perform while they're eating," he told Maddie. "It
splits their focus." Then he strode into the main room of the

tavern, his mandola slung around his neck, and struck a loud chord. The patrons looked up and a low cheer went around the room as he launched into the comic tale of Wollygelly the cross-eyed sorcerer. He smiled to himself as he sang. The last time he had performed this song in public had been in the northern fief of Macindaw, when he was trying to smoke out a sorcerer known as Malkallam.

The audience quickly picked up on the chorus and joined in, laughing at the ridiculous antics of the witch and sorcerer. There was a round of eager applause at the end of the song, and coins showered around him. Maddie moved quickly around the room, retrieving them and keeping them safe.

Will sang for another thirty minutes or so, alternating loud, boisterous sing-along ditties with more melancholy ballads and sad tales of unrequited love. Love never seemed to be requited in those songs, he mused. When he concluded, there was a storm of applause. Maddie brushed by him, intent on collecting the coins.

"They must be starved for entertainment," she said slyly. He grinned at her and held up his hands for the crowd to settle down. Then he invited them outside to watch Madelyn and the Blades of Deadly Peril. Maddie rolled her eyes, but there was a concerted movement toward the door.

Once again, she performed to enthusiastic applause. After a brief display of juggling, she produced her knives. The audience leaned forward with extra interest. There was something strangely fascinating about the sight of a fresh-faced, attractive young woman handling those razor-sharp blades with such skill and dexterity.

The serving maids moved back and forth among the patrons,

passing out jugs of ale and wine as fast as they could fetch them. In the tavern itself, busily refilling the jugs and handing them to the girls, Maurice smiled happily to himself. It was a very profitable night, even considering the fact that the entertainers had been provided with meals and comfortable beds. The fact was, he hadn't had to turn away any paying customers for the rooms Maddie and Will used, and the two bowls of ragout cost him very little.

"All in all," he said, "it's a good result."

Will and Maddie set out early the following morning, on the seventh day of the week. Maurice saw them off, having provided a good breakfast of fresh sweet rolls and butter, with a pot of fragrant coffee to wash them down. He yawned as the little cart trundled off down the main street of the village, heading for the high road.

"I never knew performing could be such fun," Maddie said as Tug ambled along, pulling the cart at a gentle pace, Bumper keeping step beside him.

Will grinned at her. "You're starting to like the sound of applause," he said.

She nodded. "Yes. It's kind of . . . invigorating, isn't it? You enjoy it, don't you?"

"I do," he said seriously. "It's such a reversal of our usual behavior, staying concealed and out of sight. But yes, it can be quite addictive to hear people clapping your efforts to entertain them."

"And paying for them," she said. She was silent for a few seconds. "Still didn't convince anyone to ride on the wheel. That'd really add some excitement to the act."

She had cajoled the audience the night before, trying to persuade someone to volunteer to be strapped to the rotating target wheel—but with no success.

"Maybe you shouldn't miss with that first throw," he suggested.

She thought about it, then shook her head. "Sanne says it's good showmanship to make a mistake early. It adds an edge of danger to the performance."

"Perhaps she's right. But showing you can make a mistake isn't conducive to having volunteers act as a target."

"I make the mistake on purpose," she pointed out.

He pursed his lips. "You know that and I know that. The whole point of it is the audience doesn't know it. They just see that you can make a mistake. So they're not too enthused about the idea of becoming a target."

"Maybe you could do it," she suggested hopefully.

Will kept his eyes on the road ahead. "Maybe you could have your head examined," he said.

They trundled on, changing horses every three hours and eating up the kilometers at a steady rate. They camped by the road that night and the following two nights. Early in the week, there was little sense in seeking an inn or a tavern to perform in—the audiences would be smaller as people settled into their working week. The key time would come later, when farmworkers and villagers would be looking to the end of the week and a chance to relax.

On the fifth and sixth days, they sought out villages and performed once more. It seemed that this part of the country saw few jongleurs, as the audiences were appreciative and generous and the pile of coins in their lockbox grew more substantial.

But still Maddie couldn't convince a volunteer to ride the wheel. And still Will abjectly refused to do it.

"Don't you trust me?" she said in a wheedling voice.

"No," he said flatly.

"But you taught me. You've seen me throwing knives for years."

"That's why I don't trust you," he said.

On they went, moving farther and farther inland, coming closer and closer to La Lumiere. Word of their presence spread ahead of them, by some mysterious method. They began to find that they were expected in the villages they visited, and greeted enthusiastically.

"That bodes well," Will told her as they turned in after another successful night. "If our reputation precedes us, it's going to be easier to get permission to perform at Philippe's castle."

"And that's what we want," Maddie said.

"And that's what we want."

17

WILL EASED BACK GENTLY ON THE REINS AND BROUGHT THE little cart to a halt.

"That's quite a castle," he said quietly.

"More a palace, I'd say," Maddie replied.

Chateau La Lumiere was an incredible sight. They were both used to the splendor and majesty of Castle Araluen, but the Gallic King's home was something else again. Araluen was spectacular, with its soaring towers and flags fluttering from different vantage points. But while it was beautiful, it was also obviously a functional stronghold. La Lumiere was not quite as large as Castle Araluen, but it possessed an elegance in all its lines. It was faced in white marble, so that the midafternoon sun glittered off its walls and spires. And a dozen flying buttresses formed elegant archways around the central structure that concealed their underlying strength and power in a show of seemingly delicate beauty.

Where Araluen's crenellations were square and unadorned, those on the wall of this castle were ornate and decorative, providing a graceful, lacy trim to the castle itself.

The castle stood on top of a steep hill, with the access road snaking back and forth in a series of switchbacks to meet it. Small buildings were clustered together on the hill, seeming to cling to the steep slope. They housed the villagers who served and supplied the needs of the castle. All of them were white-washed to match the gleaming marble facing of the castle walls. Presumably that was done by order, Will thought. No gray or dowdy houses would be tolerated in sight of the stunning white castle that crowned the hill.

Will surveyed the steep road leading up to La Lumiere. He passed the reins to Maddie and began to clamber down from the cart.

"You drive. I'll walk. That'll take some of the load off Tug."

She nodded and flicked the reins lightly, clicking her tongue at the same time. Tug leaned forward into the yoke, and as he did, she released the brake and let the cart roll forward. Bumper, keeping pace with Tug, snorted encouragement.

Up they went, winding back and forth with each switchback. The higher they went, the more densely packed were the buildings of the village. And they began to see individual houses and businesses: a tannery, set as always on the outskirts of the village. Nobody wanted a tannery and its incumbent smells too close to the center. Likewise a smithy, although in this case, it was for safety reasons that the smithy and its forges and fires were kept to the outskirts of the settlement. Then houses and shops fringed the road, becoming more numerous as they moved on.

As always happened, as they moved through the village, people emerged from their houses and places of business to eye the unmistakable jongleur's cart.

Eventually, a hundred meters from the summit, they broke

clear of the lines of buildings on either side of the road and emerged onto a paved section that led to the castle's main gates. The slope was easier here as they came closer to the summit of the hill, and Will swung himself up onto the cart again. Maddie made to hand him the reins but he shook his head.

"You keep driving," he said. "I want to look around."

His eyes darted around the castle walls, taking in the well-sited bastions and redoubts. He studied the gatehouse. It was highly decorative and quite elegant. But beneath that elegance he could see that it was well built. It commanded the last stretch of the access road, with two fighting towers, one either side of the gate, and a heavy drawbridge. At the inner end of the bridge, he could see the lower section of a portcullis. Doubtless, the grille work would be highly decorative and stylish, but no less of an impediment than a straightforward iron grille would be.

"Wouldn't care to attack this," he said out of the side of his mouth.

Maddie, who had been more impressed by the beauty and grace of the building, glanced sidelong at him. "Why so?" she asked.

He pursed his lips before answering. "Oh, it's very beautiful and very graceful," he said. "Quite Gallic, in fact. But it's also highly functional. All that decoration doesn't make the walls any lower or the gate any weaker. It's a narrow road access to the gates, and set on a steep hill as it is, it'd be difficult to site siege machines anywhere close."

"I suppose so," Maddie said thoughtfully, looking at the castle with new eyes.

The massive gates stood open, allowing access to a vaulted entryway some five meters deep, with the portcullis situated at the rear. There were four pike men standing guard outside the gates, dressed in mail and wearing the peculiar hat-shaped helmets that Gallic foot soldiers favored. Their white surcoats bore the golden lily device that was King Philippe's coat of arms.

"Gates are open," Maddie said.

"If we'd looked at all threatening, they would have had plenty of time to close them," Will told her.

Two of the pike men stood forward, moving to the center of the roadway to block their progress. One of them raised his two-meter-long pike so that it was diagonally across his chest. The other held up his right hand in a signal for them to stop. Their two comrades remained on either side of the gateway, their pikes grounded and held vertically.

Will twitched the reins and Tug came to a halt a few meters from the guard with his hand raised. As the cart stopped rolling, the foot soldier lowered his hand.

"Identify yourself," he demanded, although their identity was plain to see.

"I'm Will Accord and this is my daughter, Maddie," Will told him. "We're traveling entertainers," he added unnecessarily—their gaudy cart and brightly colored clothing identified them as such.

The guard grunted, unimpressed. "Where from?" he asked curtly.

Will half turned in his seat and swept his arm in a wide arc, indicating the direction from which they had arrived.

"From Araluen originally, good sir," he said. "But we've been traveling in your beautiful country this past week or so."

"Not my country. The King's," the guard said.

He seemed a surly brute, Will thought. But he smiled

regardless. "No less beautiful for that, sir," he said.

The guard tested that statement for a few seconds, studying it to see if there were any insult inherent in it. Eventually, he decided that there wasn't. He half turned his head and called to one of the guards behind him.

"Fetch the gate marshal," he said. "He'll need to see these two before we admit them."

"Friendly place," Maddie muttered.

Will, keeping the smile fixed on his face, replied in the same low-level tone. "Shut up."

The guard was returning now, followed by a gray-haired, gray-bearded man in a black-and-silver uniform. The sleeves of his black jerkin were slashed in places to reveal the silver cloth beneath. In spite of the gray hair, he moved easily and swiftly. A sword hung at his belt, denoting his rank as an officer. The hilt was bound in black leather and a heavy silver pommel was mounted at its end. The scabbard repeated the colors of black and silver—black polished wood and leather with silver trim. A long dagger, its hilt and scabbard similarly trimmed, hung from the right side of his belt.

"I take it this is the gate marshal," Will said. He eyed the man keenly. He would be the officer given the responsibility of deciding who might or might not be admitted to the castle. Judging by the quality of his clothes and weapons, it was a senior appointment. Will eased down from the seat of the cart as the man approached and swept off his hat, stooping in the deep and graceful bow he had perfected over the previous week.

The gate marshal looked at him. His eyes were dark and alert, taking in every detail of the cart, and its two occupants.

"Jongleurs, eh?" he asked. His tone was brisk and no-nonsense.

Will nodded. "Yes, my lord. Traveling through this fair country and looking for admittance."

"I'm no lord," the man replied gruffly. "Address me as Sir Guillaume. Or, if you can't get your tongue around that, just as sir."

"Yes, sir," Will said agreeably. "My name is Will Accord of Redmont and this is my daughter, Maddie."

Sir Guillaume was pacing briskly around the cart. He patted Bumper briefly on the muzzle, then peered inside the cart at the equipment contained there.

"From Araluen," he said. It was a statement, not a question.

"Indeed, sir. We arrived in your country a week ago."

"So we heard," Guillaume said, and Will and Maddie exchanged a quick glance at those words. Quick as it was, it did not escape the marshal's notice. "Oh yes. We have excellent information services. And we keep track of newcomers to our country." He stopped his pacing and stood before Will, feet apart and hands on hips. "We've heard good things about you," he said.

Will inclined his head in appreciation of the compliment.

The marshal continued. "You have permission to enter the castle. Take your cart and horses to the stables. You'll be assigned a room."

"Thank you, Sir Guillaume," Will said.

The marshal nodded briskly. "Tonight you can perform in the general dining hall for members of the staff and garrison," he said. "We'll take a look at you then and see if you're good enough to perform for His Majesty and his court."

"And when might that be, sir?" Will asked.

"Tomorrow night. The King dines his court on six-day evening. It'll be in the royal banquet hall." He paused, then added meaningfully, "If you're good enough."

"And as for payment, Sir Guillaume?" Will let the question hang.

The marshal nodded. It was a natural-enough question. "Tonight you can collect from the audience as you normally might. For tomorrow, a fee will be agreed in advance." He took a breath and was about to add more but Will forestalled him.

"If we're good enough," he said.

A trace of a smile touched the marshal's lips, then was gone. "If you're good enough," he agreed.

18

GILAN AND HORACE WERE PACING THE BATTLEMENTS OF Castle Araluen, deep in conversation. Horace was planning to exercise his cavalry with the castle's archers, in a combined operation.

"I was thinking about when we were being pursued by the Red Foxes, at that river crossing," Horace said.

"The archers and cavalry worked pretty well together, as I recall," Gilan said.

Horace nodded. "Granted. But we had a select bunch of both with us at the time—the best archers and the best troopers. And we were improvising, making it up as we went along. I'd like to formalize the whole thing so that all our archers and all our troopers are able to train for an operation like that."

While Gilan was nominally the Commandant of the Ranger Corps, he also oversaw the training of the castle's force of archers. That was only sensible, as he was one of the best shots in the kingdom, along with Halt and Will.

He nodded now as he considered what Horace had said. "That makes good sense," he said.

Horace, encouraged by his reaction, expanded on his idea. "And I'd like to do it in reverse," he said.

Gilan smiled. "You want them to ride backward?"

Horace gave him a weary look. "No. I'd like to practice with our troopers attacking across a river, and the archers shooting over their heads in support."

"That would require a bit of practice," Gilan admitted. "It'd be a little riskier than holding off a pursuing force."

They passed through one of the corner towers and emerged on the far side, out onto the battlements once more. A sentry on duty, surprised to see the two senior officers, stiffened to attention.

"Relax," said Horace, and the man reverted to an at-ease position. The two friends had started to resume their walk and conversation when Gilan stopped and indicated a tall figure leaning on the battlements halfway along the wall.

"Who's that?" he said, although he was reasonably sure he knew.

The sentry, who wasn't familiar with the idea of a rhetorical question, answered immediately. "It's the King, sir," he said. "He's been there these past forty minutes or so."

"Odd," said Horace, lengthening his stride to approach Duncan, who was staring out over the grassy parkland below, looking to the east. Gilan had to hurry to catch up with the tall knight's long strides.

Duncan heard them coming and turned, a smile creasing his face as he recognized two of his most trusted, and capable, officers. "Good morning, Gilan. Morning, Horace," he said.

The two returned his greetings. Gilan studied the King shrewdly. Behind the smile of greeting, he could see the lines of worry on the King's face. Something was bothering him.

"Is there a problem, sir?" he asked. Gilan was never one to beat around the bush, which was one of the many reasons Duncan valued him as an adviser.

The King gestured vaguely to the east. "I was thinking, Will and Maddie should be well on their way by now," he said. "They're due to reach Chateau La Lumiere any day."

"And you're worried about them?" Gilan said.

Duncan nodded slowly. "And I'm worried about them."

"Any particular reason, sir?" Horace asked.

Duncan hesitated before answering. "Nothing specific. Just an uncomfortable feeling. I don't like sending two of my Rangers out to take care of someone else's problem."

"I can't say I'm keen about it myself, sir," Gilan agreed. "It does make them seem a little like mercenaries."

"I agree." Duncan nodded. "Although I think Anthony's point about keeping Philippe on the throne is a good one."

"Better the devil we know," Horace said.

Once again, Duncan nodded. "Exactly."

"But you don't entirely trust Philippe," Gilan put in. It was a statement, not a question.

"That's right. He's never been a particularly trustworthy person. And if things go wrong for Will and Maddie, he's liable to leave them twisting in the wind."

"Do you have something in mind, sir?" Horace asked.

Duncan paused before committing himself to an answer. "I'd feel better to know they had a little backup standing by in case they need it," he said. "Just a couple of good people—and I don't think I want Philippe to know about them."

"Anyone in particular, sir?" Horace asked.

Duncan met his gaze for a long moment and Horace sensed that he might well be one of the "good people" to whom Duncan referred. But instead of saying so, Duncan turned to Gilan.

"Is Halt due to visit us anytime soon?" he asked.

Gilan allowed the ghost of a smile to cross his face. "I'm sure that could be arranged, sir," he said.

Duncan looked away to the east again, as if he could see his two Rangers, far away in Gallica.

"Good," he said at length. Then he repeated it. "Good."

19

WILL AND MADDIE PERFORMED THAT NIGHT FOR THE LOWER ranks of the castle's population—the garrison and staff members—in a large dining hall on the ground floor of the keep.

They were well received. Life in a castle, after all, tended to be boring and uneventful, so any diversion or form of entertainment was usually welcomed. That said, Will and Maddie provided excellent entertainment. Will's singing and playing were well above average and he had a good repertoire of songs.

And Maddie's knife throwing was an exciting act as well, with the added spice of implicit danger from the razor-sharp throwing knives she handled with such apparent nonchalance and unerring accuracy. With Will's suggestion in mind, she left out the deliberate mistake at the beginning of her act. But she was still unable to cajole any member of her audience to allow themselves to be strapped to the rotating target wheel. The suggestion, when she made it, was greeted by good-natured ribaldry and absolute refusal.

They had an established order to the program now. Will would open proceedings with a twenty-minute set of songs. Then he would introduce Maddie. In the vast dining hall there was plenty of room for her to perform. When she was done, he would resume, inviting the audience to sing along with him, while Maddie circled the room with a large sack, offering it to the audience so they could put their coins into it.

She was gratified by the growing weight of the sack as she moved through the long tables, and the preponderance of silver and gold coins that went into it—there were few of the less valuable coppers, she noticed.

She also noticed the marshal standing at the back of the hall, watching Will perform. Sir Guillaume caught her eye and gave her an approving nod. He beckoned her over to him. She bowed politely as she reached him and he gave her a quick smile.

"Very good work," he said. "Tell your father you'll be performing for the King and his nobles tomorrow night. I'll speak to him about a fee in the morning."

She bowed again, a quick nod of her head. "Thank you, Sir Guillaume," she said. "I'll let him know."

He nodded several times. There was a nervous energy about him that infused all his movements. "Good. Good. Your quarters are satisfactory, I trust?"

They had been assigned a small suite of rooms on the third floor of the keep—where the senior servants and staff members were accommodated.

"Very comfortable, sir. Much better than our cart."

The smile flashed quickly again and was gone. "I'm sure," he said. "Well, I shall talk to your father tomorrow."

He turned away and left, threading his way through the crowded tables to the door. Maddie turned around and saw Will had been watching them. She headed back to the front of the room, collecting more payment as she went. As she passed by him, she said in a low voice, "We're performing for the King tomorrow."

He nodded acknowledgment and began another song while she went back to the small table reserved for them at the side of the dining hall. It was a nonsense song with a repeating chorus about a bucket with a hole in it, the audience joining in with gusto. She knew that it was the antepenultimate song of his set. She sat at their table and poured herself a cup of coffee from the jug there. She yawned discreetly—it wouldn't do for the audience to think she was bored by Will's singing and in truth she wasn't. She was simply tired. The nervous energy that filled her when she was performing had left her, and she felt flat and exhausted as the adrenaline drained away from her system. Ten more minutes, she thought, and she could head for her warm and comfortable bed on the third floor.

The following day around noon, they were summoned to Sir Guillaume's room on the ground floor of the massive gatehouse structure.

"His Majesty will be pleased to see you perform this evening, for him and his knights and nobles," he told Will, who nodded.

"And the fee?"

Guillaume leaned back in his high-backed wooden chair. Will and Maddie were standing in front of his desk.

"Some might consider the honor of performing before royalty to be sufficient reward," he said.

Will sensed that his protest wasn't genuine. Rather, it was part of a haggling process. "Some might," he replied, his tone leaving no doubt that he was not one of the aforementioned "some."

Guillaume nodded briefly. He hadn't expected Will to agree to the idea. "Then a fee of forty eagles will be paid," he said.

Will pursed his lips. An eagle was the Gallic unit of currency, a gold coin worth about one and a quarter Araluen royals. It was a reasonable offer, he thought. But on the low side and definitely not overgenerous.

"We made nearly that much from the common folk last night," he said.

Guillaume shrugged. "Then you were most fortunate," he said. But, seeing Will's determined expression, he hastily amended the offer. "Very well, the fee will be fifty eagles." He paused and added meaningfully, "And that is the final offer."

Will nodded. "Agreed," he said immediately.

Guillaume made a quick note on a piece of parchment on the desk before him. "You'll be paid after the performance," he said. "I assume that you'll be moving on tomorrow?"

And don't let the door hit you in the backside on your way out, Maddie thought, concealing a grin.

"Unless His Majesty insists that we stay over and perform again," Will said.

Guillaume raised his left eyebrow and tapped the figure he had written on the parchment. "At this price, don't bank on that happening," he said, and they took their leave.

As they made their way across the cobbles to the keep tower once more, Will grinned down at his companion. "Well, now you can tell your grandchildren that you've performed for royalty," he told her.

Maddie smiled back. "And for fifty eagles," she said.

He looked at her in surprise. "Who said you were getting any of that? You're doing it for the honor."

• • •

The royal dining hall was on the second floor of the keep. It was a more lavish affair than the hall where they had performed the previous night. It was smaller, as was the audience. And it was furnished more opulently than the rough-and-ready trestle tables of the general hall. Richly woven tapestries and paintings—presumably of the King's ancestors—hung from the walls. The room was lit by dozens of candles in candelabra, with a massive chandelier holding at least fifty candles hanging over the center of the room. There were approximately forty knights and nobles, seated at eight tables in front of a raised dais, where the royal table was set. A space had been left between the tables and the dais. This was where Will and Maddie would perform.

On the dais, a table was set for the King and his senior court members: his wife and her lady companion, his brother, his chamberlain and three other high-ranking nobles. Whereas the common folk the night before had sat on uncushioned wooden benches, the King and his party, and the knights and nobles in the lower part of the hall, sat on carved chairs, with high backs, comfortable cushions and carved armrests. At the far end of the room from the royal table, a huge fireplace dominated the wall. A hearty fire was blazing in it as Will and Maddie made their way unobtrusively into the room, standing to one side.

A noisy buzz of conversation filled the air as servants made their way among the tables, carrying roast meats and fowls, and platters of steaming vegetables. They placed them on the tables and the diners helped themselves, carving and spearing pieces of meat with the long daggers that had been set on the table before them. They used wooden platters and forks as well, loading the platters with food and then eating. Nobody seemed to feel that they should stop talking while they ate, and a hubbub of voices, each raised so its owner could be heard over his neighbors, filled the room.

At the royal table, the King ate little, Maddie noticed. His gaze wandered over the throng assembled before him, studying them, assessing them. There was no sign of affection in his eyes. They were as cold and unblinking as a basilisk's. She shivered briefly at the sight of them. King Philippe was not a man you would want to antagonize, she thought.

From time to time, he would lean to one side and say a word or two to his brother, seated on his right—Louis, Maddie knew from Gilan's briefing. He was an interesting character as well. A sardonic, superior smile was fixed on his face and he would respond to the King's comments with loud guffaws of laughter. But the laughter never reached his eyes, she noticed, and they had the same cold intensity that his brother's had.

Philippe didn't speak to his wife, a haughty, tall and strikingly beautiful woman sitting on his left, whose jet black hair was worn long and marked with a white streak on the right-hand side. Maddie assumed it was a cosmetic effect and not a sign of aging. From time to time, the queen would utter an aside to her lady-in-waiting. The two would then laugh briefly. Maddie had the distinct impression that the queen's comments were barbs aimed at the diners at the lower tables. She sniffed disdainfully, thinking of the cheery, convivial banquets she had attended at her father's court in Araluen, or the more informal, boisterous affairs at Baron Arald's Redmont.

The Gallic court, by contrast, would appear to be one where snide comments and thinly veiled snobbery were the order of the day.

It had been agreed that the performance would not begin until the main meal had been eaten. Now, as servants carried away the ravaged carcasses of ducks and geese and the dismembered joints of beef and pork, the King nodded to the majordomo, a white-bearded, straight-backed man who carried a metal-shod black rod as his staff of office. He, in turn, made a signal toward the side door of the dining room and two servants hurried in, carrying the target wheel for Maddie's performance, draped in a heavy linen cover. Some of those present noticed and stopped talking, eyeing the draped apparatus with interest. Others, farther away, continued to talk and laugh, until the majordomo, resplendent in his uniform of gold and silver—Philippe's court colors—slammed his staff down on the floor three times. Three resounding reports echoed through the room, and the diners' conversations lessened, then died away as the majordomo thundered in a stentorian voice:

"My lords and ladies, knights and nobles, pray silence for the King's entertainment!"

Will looked sidelong at Maddie and grinned. "Tense up," he whispered. "We're about to go on."

20

PHILIPPE, LOOKING SOMEWHAT DISINTERESTED, WAVED A languid hand for the entertainment to begin. Will stepped forward and launched into his opening song, a stirring tale of chivalry and valor, describing the courageous battle of a knight in white armor against a trio of evil trolls. It was a popular song, he knew, and one well suited to this type of audience. When he sounded the final ringing chord, he received an enthusiastic round of applause from the lower tables. The King and his party, he noticed, as he glanced quickly in their direction, allowed themselves a few bored handclaps. He shrugged and continued with his set list of songs.

By the end of the set, he had the audience clapping enthusiastically and calling for more. Not the royal table, of course. Taking their lead from the King, they maintained an aloof, disinterested air. They clapped perfunctorily and even carried on conversations while Will was performing.

"Tough crowd," he muttered to Maddie as she moved into the open performance space beside him. She grinned at him, knowing he was referring to the royal party, not the wider audience, who were obviously enjoying themselves. Politely waving aside the audience's cries for an encore, Will introduced Maddie, referring to her this time as the Mistress of the Blades of Peril. She smiled to herself. Some nights it was the blades of death, others the blades of danger.

Will moved quickly to where the target wheel stood and stripped away the linen cover. A murmur of interest ran through the room. The assembled crowd had been wondering about the apparatus concealed under the cover.

Maddie, calling the numbers that she was aiming at, sent the five blades whirling and thudding into the board in rapid succession—every one hitting her nominated target. Then Will set the wheel spinning and she repeated the sequence. The audience were enthralled. Even the King lost his look of indifference and leaned forward slightly to watch.

As the act progressed, Maddie moved on to more difficult feats, having the wheel turn faster and faster while two servants worked the crank handle as she called the tempo for them, standing with her back to the spinning wheel and whirling as a number was nominated, hurling the knives without seeming to pause and hitting the target every time. The crowd became more and more fascinated and appreciative. The applause became louder and longer.

Finally, Maddie neared the end of her act. She faced the audience, her knives held in a loose fan in her left hand, and flung out her right arm toward the target wheel.

"My lords and ladies!" she cried. "May I have a volunteer?"

There was a stir of interest among the crowd as they wondered what was coming next.

"Is there a brave soul among you who will ride the spinning wheel of peril while I continue to throw my knives?"

A murmur ran through the audience, but nobody volunteered. Maddie gave a quick frown of frustration. Having a live volunteer strapped to the spinning wheel would form a climactic end to her act. But so far, she had been unable to cajole anyone to participate. She took a breath to try to convince someone to volunteer. But a voice from the high table forestalled her.

"What's this? Are none of my brave knights valiant enough to volunteer? Is Gallica to be shamed before our Araluen friends?"

It was Philippe. He had risen from his chair and was surveying his knights and nobles with a superior sneer on his face. His voice was high pitched and nasal. The tone of it was hectoring and dismissive.

Maddie turned to him, smiling. "It's no matter, Your Majesty—" she began, but he waved her to silence with an imperious gesture.

"Of course it matters, young lady. It's an insult to your skill that none of my brave knights will volunteer to assist you. But I know there is one here with the courage to do so . . ."

He paused dramatically as the room watched warily. Then he pointed to his brother, Louis, sitting beside him.

"Prince Louis, my brother, will volunteer to be your assistant," he declared, with a note of triumph in his voice. A murmur of surprise and relief went around the room. But Prince Louis recoiled in his chair, his face going pale.

The King turned to him, smiling disdainfully. "Isn't that so, brother?"

Louis, speechless, could only shake his head.

"Come now, Louis, on your feet. Show these cowards what real courage is."

"Your Majesty . . . Brother . . ." Louis finally found his voice, then was lost for words once more. He cringed away from the King in his seat, as if distancing himself would make the command go away.

Will, watching from the side of the hall, shook his head. Maddie caught his eye, a confused and frightened look on her face as she wondered how to handle this.

What a family, Will thought. It was obvious that Philippe was enjoying belittling his younger brother, embarrassing him in front of the entire company. There must be undercurrents between them for the King to feel the need to assert his dominance over the prince in this way. But such a course held potential danger for Will and Maddie. If he allowed this to proceed, they could well make an enemy of Prince Louis.

He strode now to the center of the room and bowed to the King.

"My lord!" he cried. "Generous though Prince Louis's offer might be, I'm afraid I cannot allow it. The thought of having royalty strapped to her target wheel might well be too much for my young daughter." He phrased his objection so that he seemed to accept that the prince would allow himself to be strapped to the wheel.

Philippe frowned at the interruption. "*You* cannot allow it?" he said. "Who are you to gainsay a king?"

Will mentally cursed himself for his unfortunate choice of words. He bowed deeply. "Your pardon, Majesty. My respect for you and your royal family is too deep to allow any of you to take such a risk. It would be a tragedy of the deepest kind if your brother were to be injured. After all, his blood and yours are the same. Any injury to him would be an injury to you."

Philippe smiled thinly. "I admit it would be tragic if Louis were to be wounded," he said. "But your daughter needs someone to assist her."

"Then let me do it," Will said quickly. "Let me take the prince's place on the wheel." He turned his gaze to the pale-faced Louis. "Would Your Highness permit me to take your place?" he asked, continuing the pretense that Louis had actually volunteered.

The King, still smiling, turned to his brother and Will knew he had handled this situation correctly. Philippe wanted two things, he sensed. He wanted to embarrass and belittle his brother. And he wanted to see someone risk their life on the wheel.

Louis nodded quickly. When he spoke, his voice was pitched a trifle higher than normal. "Yes! Yes! By all means. Go ahead," he said. He was still cowering back in his large, high-backed chair, as if trying to stay as far away from the King as was possible.

The King made a gesture of acquiescence toward Will. "Then, seeing that Louis is willing, we give our permission."

Louis sank a little further into his chair as he heard the words. Will bowed, then moved toward the wheel. Maddie hurried to his side to help strap him into position.

"Don't miss," he told her grimly as she tightened the straps around his wrists.

"Don't worry," she replied. She signaled to the two servants to crank the wheel, counting time for them. When they had the wheel rotating at the speed she wanted, she strode back to her mark. Silence hung over the room as her arm went back, then forward.

Thunk!

The audience cheered as the knife thudded home, missing Will's outstretched hand by a few centimeters. The next four knives followed in quick succession, missing by the same small margin. Signaling for the servants to stop cranking, Maddie strode forward to retrieve the knives for a further demonstration. She signaled for the servants to begin cranking again but, this time, Philippe's voice interrupted her.

"Faster this time!" he demanded, and pounded the table with the rhythm he wanted. The others at the high table joined in and the wheel began to turn faster. Maddie assessed the speed for a few seconds, then delivered another volley of knives, each one just missing Will's hands, feet and head.

Then, before the King could demand more, she faced the audience and bowed deeply. The assembled knights and nobles cheered and began to throw coins to her. As she hurried to the wheel and released Will, the cheers redoubled, praising his courage. Will and Maddie held hands and bowed to the audience, to the left, the right and the center. Then they turned and bowed to the King at the high table as well, holding the bow for some seconds.

"Well done," Philippe said, with a marked lack of enthusiasm. He tossed a chamois purse to Will. It clinked as he caught it. "Your reward," he said briefly. It seemed he was disappointed that Will had escaped unharmed.

Will bowed again, then approached closer to the dais.

"Your Majesty, if I may be so bold, I have a gift for you from Araluen. May I present it?"

Another languid wave of the hand greeted the request. Will mounted the stairs quickly and took a silver medallion from around his neck, laying it on the table before the King. Philippe glanced at it, incuriously at first. Then his eyes narrowed.

The medallion was embossed with a crown. Beneath it were three words.

Pax inter reges.

Later that night, when the castle was sleeping, Will and Maddie were summoned to the King's quarters.

21

UNTIL WILL HAD HANDED HIM THE MEDALLION, PHILIPPE had no idea that the two jongleurs were the agents sent by Duncan to help rescue his son.

He had been expecting one person—a man. And he had been expecting that person to be a Ranger, not a brightly clad troubadour. The fact that the two jongleurs had come from Araluen had struck him as a coincidence, nothing more. After all, travelers from Araluen passed through Gallica every day.

The reason for the secrecy had been explained to Will by Duncan before the two Rangers had set out on their journey.

"Castles are full of informants, gossips and out-and-out spies," he had said. "And I imagine that Chateau La Lumiere is worse than most, given the intrigue and the state of politics in that country at the moment. We don't want this fellow Lassigny to get any hint that you're working for Philippe. So you need to wait for the right moment to reveal your identities to the King."

The medallion had been the way they would do this. The inscription, *Pax inter reges,* was the same phrase Philippe had used to identify himself when he first visited Araluen to seek Duncan's help.

Now Maddie and Will were escorted through the dark corridors and stairways of the castle to the King's private chambers. It was well after midnight and the castle was dark and sleeping, so there was nobody awake to see them. Only a few lighted torches set in sconces illuminated the passageways as they followed the King's servant to the sixth floor of the keep, where Philippe's quarters were situated.

The servant paused outside the door and knocked twice. It was obviously a prearranged signal as he didn't wait for permission to proceed, but pushed the door open and stood aside to let Maddie and Will enter. After the dimness of the palace corridors, they were both dazzled by the bright light of a score of candles in the room. Philippe sat behind an ornate desk, in a gilt-encrusted chair with spindly curved legs, upholstered with satin cushions. Will smiled wryly. It was the total antithesis to Duncan's functional work-scarred pine table and plain high-backed chair.

Prince Louis sat to one side, on a banquette similar in style to his brother's chair. There were two more such chairs set opposite Philippe and he waved the Rangers to them, with a somewhat distracted expression on his face. Will bowed, a brief nod of his head. Maddie, watching him carefully, followed suit. Then they both sat.

"You," Philippe said after several seconds. "You are Duncan's people?" There was a note of puzzlement in his voice.

Will nodded. "That's correct, my lord."

The frown on the King's face deepened. "I was expecting a Ranger. A warrior. Not a pair of jongleurs," he said, looking from one to the other, then shaking his head.

Will smiled. "King Duncan felt that a pair of jongleurs

would be less likely to arouse suspicion, sir," he said. After the events in the dining hall, he had decided that he didn't like the Gallican King. Nor did he trust him. As a result, he now eschewed the use of the royal title *Your Majesty* with a more egalitarian *sir.*

Philippe didn't seem to notice. He pointed at Maddie. "But she's a girl," he said, his tone leaving no doubt that he considered girls and women to be some sort of inferior group. "This is a dangerous mission you've embarked on. Surely Duncan realizes that?"

"I'm sure he does, sir," said Will. He glanced sideways at Maddie and saw that her cheeks were flushed with color. He knew that was a sign she was suppressing her anger. "But she's highly capable," Will added.

"But . . . a *girl*!" Philippe repeated. He spread his hands in further bewilderment.

Will glanced at Louis. The prince was nodding in agreement with his brother.

"I can assure you, sir, Maddie is highly skilled and well able to look after herself—and me if it comes to that. And the fact that she is a girl makes it less likely for people to suspect our true purpose—as you have just demonstrated, sir."

The King's cheeks flushed. He wasn't accustomed to having people disagree with him—particularly people whom he considered to be his inferiors—which accounted for most people in the world. He could think of no fitting reply to the infuriatingly calm man before him, so he fell back on his dignity and royal protocol.

"You will address me as 'Your Majesty,'" he said angrily.

But Will shook his head. "No, sir. That's a form of address I reserve for my own king."

Philippe sat bolt upright, his eyes wide with surprise. Nobody spoke to him in that manner! *Nobody!*

"You're insolent, jongleur—" he began but Will interrupted him.

"I'm answerable to King Duncan, sir. I'm here because he ordered it, nobody else."

"I could have you arrested!" Philippe said, his voice rising angrily.

But again, Will shook his head. "It wouldn't be a wise thing to attempt," he said, and before Philippe could proceed further, he elaborated. "If you do, who's going to rescue your son from Baron Lassigny?"

Philippe realized Will was right, and made an immense effort to stifle his anger. He glowered at the jongleur. I'll deal with your insolence when I no longer need your help, he thought.

Will gave him a few more moments to control himself, then said in a reasonable voice, "Now, perhaps you could tell us the latest situation with your son so we can get on with the business of bringing him back to you?" Sensing that Philippe was finding it difficult to speak calmly, he gave him a lead.

"Has the situation changed in the last three weeks?" he asked. "I take it he is still held hostage at Chateau des Falaises?"

Philippe nodded, then said in a thick voice, "Yes. He's still a hostage. Nothing has changed."

"Do you have maps of the area around Falaise?" Will asked. "It would be useful for us to see them."

Regaining his equanimity more and more with each moment, Philippe nodded and jerked open a drawer in his desk, pulling out several sheets of parchment.

"I had these copied for you," he said.

Will could see that they were charts and maps. As the King passed them across, he turned them so he could see them right side up and fanned them out. Maddie rose from her chair to lean over his shoulder and study them as well. Will traced a series of roads with his forefinger, leading from La Lumiere to Falaise.

"This looks like the quickest route," he said, half to himself. He consulted the scale marked on the base of the map. "We could be there in . . . three days. Maybe four."

"Riding hard, you could do it in two," Philippe suggested, but Will shook his head, smiling to rob the action of any insult.

"We have to maintain our cover as jongleurs," he explained. "That means traveling slowly and stopping to perform along the way. Then, when we arrive, we'll be more likely to gain access— just as we did here."

Philippe nodded, seeing the logic of the statement. He was still furious with Will but he was suppressing his feelings. This insolent, confident man was his best chance to have his son back safe and sound. He couldn't afford to antagonize him. If he did, the jongleur was likely to abandon the mission altogether and return to Araluen.

"I suppose so," he said. There was another silence as he realized he had nothing to add to the conversation. He looked at his brother. "Louis, is there anything you want to say?"

The prince sat up straighter and pulled at his chin, thinking. Then he asked: "Why didn't you sing 'La lune, elle est mon amour'?"

Will looked at him with disbelief. "What?" he asked sharply.

Louis made a gesture with both hands spread out, as if

explaining to a simpleton. "'La lune, elle est mon amour,'" he said. "It's a love song. A beautiful one."

Then, inexplicably, incredibly, he began to sing.

"La lune, elle est mon amour

Elle voyage dans le ciel de mon coeur . . ."

He hummed a few more bars of the melody.

Good grief, thought Will, we're talking about rescuing his nephew and he wants to talk about his favorite love song!

"I'm afraid, sir, I don't know that one," he said.

Louis smiled at him. "You should learn it. It's very beautiful."

Will shook his head slowly and turned to Philippe. "Was there anything else, sir?" he asked.

Philippe thought for a few seconds, then shook his head. He didn't seem to see the incongruity of his brother's actions. Will rose, gathered the charts together and took a deep breath. Maddie followed suit.

"Then, sir, we'll get some sleep. We'll leave after first light tomorrow."

Philippe nodded several times, as if resuming control of the situation and the conversation.

"That would be best," he said, and gestured to the door. "I won't detain you further."

Outside, the same servant was waiting to escort them back to their rooms. Maddie looked at Will and said, in a low voice, "'La lune, elle est mon amour'?"

She spread her hands in a gesture of disbelief. "Holy cow, what a family!"

"I was thinking much the same thing," said Will.

Maddie was silent for a few moments. Then she spoke again. "I'm wondering why you didn't confirm that we're Rangers. You intimated that we were simply jongleurs," she said. Will glanced quickly at the servant leading them, making sure he was out of earshot.

"I don't altogether trust Philippe," he said. "Or his brother. The less they know about us, the better. If they think we're just spies and not Rangers, that might be better for us."

22

THEY LEFT LA LUMIERE SHORTLY AFTER DAWN THE FOLLOW-
ing day. Not surprisingly, neither Philippe nor Louis rose early
to see them on their way. As they clip-clopped gently along the
high road toward Falaise, Will felt as if a giant weight had been
lifted from his shoulders. The atmosphere at the royal palace
had been oppressive and dismal, he thought. Philippe's infuriat-
ing air of superiority, and his penchant for bullying and belittling those under him, had left an unpleasant taste in Will's
mouth.

Maddie obviously felt the same. "That's a good place to be
out of," she said.

"He's a strange person all right."

Maddie frowned thoughtfully. "Why do you think he
behaves like that?" she asked. "That business with his brother,
trying to force him to act as my target, and embarrassing him in
front of the whole room. What does he gain by doing that?"

"A sense of importance, I guess."

"But he *is* important. He's the King, after all. What does he
have to prove?" She paused, then added, "My grandfather doesn't
seem to think that sort of thing is necessary."

"Philippe would seem to be lacking in self-esteem. He's constantly doubting his ability to rule—and rightly so, if you ask me. He's looking over his shoulder all the time, trying to see if there's someone about to supplant him. And the most likely candidate would be his brother. So he puts Louis down in front of the others, shows him up as lacking in courage. Duncan doesn't have to do that. He's a strong king, and he's well respected for that strength. He has a natural authority that Philippe will never match."

"I can't imagine anyone talking to my grandfather the way you spoke to Philippe," Maddie said, grinning at the memory.

But there was no answering smile from Will. Instead, he answered seriously. "I shouldn't have done that. But he annoyed me with his superior air and insufferable tone. Once we're done with this mission, we'd be wise to leave this country as quickly as we can."

"You don't think he'll be grateful when we bring his son back safely?" Maddie asked. She had no doubt that they would be successful in their task.

But Will shook his head. "A man like that doesn't forget an insult. He'll be looking for ways to get his revenge." He paused. "Even Louis will be looking for ways to get back at us."

"Louis? What did we do to him? You saved him from having to be my target."

"*That's* what we did to him. We showed him up as a coward. He'll forget it was his brother who engineered it—after all, there's little he can do against the King. So we'll be the logical target for his spite."

Maddie shook her head wearily. "As I said, what a family."

Will nodded. "Makes you glad we don't live here," he replied.

• • •

Nightfall found them still on the road, with no sign of a village nearby. Accordingly, they turned the little cart off the road at a clearing and camped for the night. It was no hardship. They were used to sleeping out and both were excellent camp cooks. There was no sign of rain so Maddie chose to sleep in the open, rather than in the cart, preferring the fresh night air to the slightly stuffy, confined atmosphere inside.

In the morning, they had a quick breakfast of toasted bread and cheese, washed down with several cups of coffee, and continued on their way.

They had been traveling for an hour when Maddie noticed Will leaning out from the driving seat of the cart to peer behind them.

"Something wrong?" she asked.

He frowned and scratched his chin. "Don't know. I've got an itch in the back of my neck."

"Your neck is itchy so you scratch your chin? That's a novel way of treating it," she said.

But he made a dismissive gesture. "The itchy neck is a figure of speech. I get the feeling that someone's behind us."

She leaned out her side of the cart and peered back down the road. She could see for about two hundred meters before the road went round a bend. There was nobody in sight.

"I don't see anyone," she said.

Will glanced at her. "Neither do I," he told her. "But I just have a . . . *feeling* there's someone there."

"Following us?"

He shrugged. "Well, if he's behind us, he's following us. But whether he's doing so deliberately is another matter."

The day wore on. They stopped for lunch, and to spell the

horses, at midday. While Maddie made coffee, Will paced back along the road the way they had come, going about fifty meters before he stopped and turned back.

"Neck still itching?" Maddie asked him. His feeling that they were being followed was setting her own nerves on edge. Will was rarely wrong when it came to sensing danger nearby, she knew. In the years they had been together, she had learned to trust his instincts.

"Thought I saw something—or someone—for a second or two. But the trees are too thick to be certain. We'll keep going."

They reached another small village late in the afternoon and performed at the tavern there. While Maddie entertained the crowd in the small square outside the tavern, Will prowled around the outskirts of the audience, staying in the shadows and studying the people watching Maddie. He took note of one man—a swarthy, bearded man in a blue cloak who was sitting alone, nursing a tankard of ale. He was well dressed and his clothes were somewhat more refined than the coarse homespun of the villagers. He looked a little out of place among the simple county folk.

The tavern offered no accommodation so they parked the cart on the village green and camped once more. As they rolled into their blankets, Will told Maddie about the man.

"Of course, he could just be an ordinary traveler," he said.

"Or not. But if he's not, who would want to have us followed?" Maddie asked.

The older Ranger merely shrugged. "In this country, who knows? Nobody trusts anybody here—and with good reason." He paused, lying on his back and looking up at the stars.

"We'll see if he's still with us tomorrow."

23

THERE WAS NO SIGN OF THE STRANGER THE FOLLOWING morning when they departed.

Presumably, he had paid one of the villagers to give him a room for the night, but if so, he had kept out of sight in the morning. Will had actually strolled through the village before breakfast, looking for some sign of the traveler, or perhaps his saddle horse. He assumed, from the quality of the man's clothes, that his horse would be a cut above the rough-coated cart horses that would normally be found in the village. But of course, many of the houses ranged along the main street had barns or stables at their rear, and the horse, if it were there, could easily be concealed in one of them.

"Can't see him anywhere," he told Maddie as he climbed aboard the cart and settled into the driver's seat.

"Maybe he left earlier," she suggested.

He inclined his head doubtfully. "Maybe."

Maddie noted that Will had put aside his brightly colored jongleur's outfit and was dressed in dull brown and gray trousers and jerkin, but she didn't comment on the fact.

He waited until midmorning, when they had traversed a

long, straight section of the road, some three hundred meters in length, and rounded a sharp corner at the end. As they went round the corner, he leaned out, peering back down the road. There was no one in sight. He let Bumper pull the cart another twenty meters, then clucked his tongue to bring the little horse to a stop.

"Did you see something?" Maddie asked.

"Not yet." He dropped lightly to the road, then hurried to the rear of the cart. Maddie heard a dull clatter as he opened the secret compartment under the cart. After a minute or so, he returned to the front of the cart. He had his longbow strung and slung over his left shoulder, and a quiver of arrows clipped to his belt.

"Move up another twenty meters or so. Then stop and get your bow. I'll cut back through the trees to see if anyone's following. Stay quiet. If he's coming, I don't want him to hear you."

Maddie nodded and took the reins from where he'd looped them around the brake handle. She clicked her tongue at Bumper and the little horse pushed forward. When they had gone another twenty meters, she stopped, swinging the cart so that it was across the road, allowing her to see back to the corner.

Will had already disappeared into the trees.

Will slipped quietly through the thickly growing trees and foliage, cutting off the corner they had just rounded and heading back down the long, straight stretch. Fifteen meters from the corner, he stopped beside a tall, thick-trunked elm, leaning against the rough, ridged bark, his dull-colored clothing blending easily into the background. He slipped the bow off his shoulder and peered out to the road. He was close to the edge of the trees and could see back the way they had come for some distance. So far, there was no sign of anyone following them.

He sank to one knee behind the tree and listened, turning his head slowly from side to side, searching for some small noise that would tell him a rider was approaching. After several minutes, he heard the faint jingle of harness, then the soft sound of a horse's hooves on the hard-packed surface of the road.

"There you are," he muttered softly to himself.

The hoofbeats came closer, becoming more noticeable as they did so. Will waited, still as the tree behind which he sheltered. His heart rate had accelerated and he felt a tightness in his belly. He strove to keep his breathing deep and even—although there was little chance that the approaching rider would hear him breathing.

He remained still, allowing only his eyes to move as he saw a dim shape moving past the spot where he crouched in hiding. He couldn't make out much in the way of detail from his cramped and awkward viewing position, but he had an impression of something blue moving beyond the tree line. Then the rider was past him and had nearly reached the bend in the road. Will rose silently to his feet, stepping through the trees to emerge on the road, and nocking an arrow to his bowstring as he did so.

He heard a sharp exclamation of surprise as the rider rounded the corner and saw the cart a mere forty meters away, stopped across the middle of the road.

There was a sudden jingle of harness as the man tugged sharply on his reins, beginning to wheel his horse about and move back down the road.

Only to find Will blocking his line of retreat.

Will stood in the center of the road, bow raised and drawn,

the arrow pointing unwaveringly at the new arrival.

"You can stop right there," he said quietly. "And get down off the horse."

The rider hesitated, glancing back over his shoulder to where the cart barred the way. For a moment, he was tempted to try to escape in that direction. Then he realized that the cart's driver was also dismounted, and training a bow on him.

"Run either way and one of us will shoot you," Will cautioned him. "Now dismount and turn your horse loose."

Reluctantly, the rider swung down from his saddle. But he kept the reins held in his right hand. Will gestured with the arrow.

"Turn your horse loose," he repeated.

The man spread his hands in a gesture of appeal. "He'll run off," he protested. He spoke in the common tongue, as Will had been doing. But a strong Gallic accent was obvious.

"That's the general idea," Will said.

"But . . ." the man began.

Will made an imperious gesture with the bow and the half-drawn arrow. The stranger dropped the rein that he had been holding. The horse, sensing the tension between the two men, danced skittishly for a few paces. He was a highly strung animal, which suited Will's plan.

"Now slap him on the rump," he ordered. For a second, it looked as if the man would demur once more. But the cold look in Will's eyes stopped him. He slapped the horse resoundingly on the rump. It reared its head up, whinnying in surprise, then took off at a canter, back the way they had come. Will stepped to one side as it clattered past. He swiped at its rump with his bow, urging it to a faster pace. The horse, tossing its head and whinnying indignantly, continued down the road until it disappeared around the distant bend.

"That should delay you for a few hours," Will said pleasantly. "Now, who are you and why are you following us?"

"Following?" the man said, assuming a puzzled look.

Will cut him off. "Don't mistake me for a fool," he said curtly. "You were behind us all of yesterday. And you were in the tavern last night when my daughter was performing. Here you are again, still behind us. Why?"

The man shrugged. "I'm simply traveling this road, as you are," he said. "I'm not following you."

"Yet with a fine-spirited animal like that, you choose to move at the same snail's pace as our little cart, staying well back out of sight," Will pointed out. "I'll ask you again. Who are you, and what are you up to?"

The man's shoulders sank as he realized that his explanation wouldn't hold up.

"My name is Egon of Tourles," he said unhappily. "I am under orders to follow you and observe you."

"Whose orders?"

Egon paused for a few seconds, then replied. "The Royal Prince Louis," he admitted.

Slightly taken aback, Will lowered the bow, releasing the tension on the half-drawn string.

"Prince Louis?" he repeated. "The King's brother? Why does he want us followed?"

Egon shrugged uncertainly. "He wants to know that you are living up to your end of the arrangement. He is worried about the safety of his nephew."

Will took a deep breath. He glanced at Maddie, who had

moved back down the road to stand a few meters away, where she could hear the discussion. He shook his head, then addressed Egon once more.

"Did it occur to him that your presence might give us away?" he said. "That you might draw Lassigny's attention to us?"

Again, Egon shrugged. "Only if I was spotted," he said defensively.

Will finally lost his temper. "*We* spotted you!" he shouted. "You're not terribly difficult to spot! You go blundering about the countryside in your fine clothing, on your fine horse, for all to see. What makes you think Lassigny and his men would be any less observant?" Before Egon could answer, he continued. "And do you realize that if they did notice you following us, it would draw attention to us and ruin our mission?"

Egon jutted his bottom lip unhappily. "I suppose so," he agreed.

"Oh, you do? How good of you! You great blundering idiot! Go back to Prince Louis and tell him you were recognized. Tell him you could have jeopardized our mission and his nephew's life. Tell him if he sends someone else—*anyone* else—to keep an eye on us, I'll put an arrow in him. And I'll put one in you if I see you again. Then I'll abandon this mission and return to Araluen. And he can explain it all to King Philippe."

Egon said nothing. He stood, hanging his head in embarrassment and fear.

Will raised the bow once more. "Toss down your sword," he ordered. Egon's hand went instinctively to the sword at his waist. It was a fine weapon, the hilt decorated with gold wire and a large ruby pommel.

"My sword?"

Will motioned with the arrow. "Get rid of it. And the dagger." Egon was carrying a matching dagger in a sheath on the opposite side of his belt. Reluctantly, under the threat of the arrow nocked on Will's bow, he drew both weapons and let them fall to the road.

"Now get going," Will ordered.

The man gestured uncertainly at his weapons, lying at his feet. "But—"

"Go!" Will shouted. "Go back to Chateau La Lumiere and tell your prince that you are an incapable idiot."

Head down, Egon began trudging back down the road, walking awkwardly in his high riding boots. Will watched him go, then stooped and picked up the sword and the dagger. He glanced at them once, then tossed them far into the forest beside the road.

He glanced up, caught Maddie's amused gaze and shook his head.

"What a family!" he said in disgust.

24

THEY SAW NO FURTHER SIGN OF EGON. THE FOLLOWING DAY,
Will saddled Tug and rode back along their tracks to make sure
he was no longer following.

Satisfied that their would-be shadow had left, he returned to
the cart and they continued on their way.

The high road, the most direct route to Falaise, cut across a
wide, looping river at two points. In doing so, it traveled virtually
due north. To the west, a range of low mountains, steep and
rocky, provided a barrier to travel. A narrow mountain track ran
across the range, but it would necessitate a long detour to reach
Falaise that way. The main road was more direct and more easily
traveled, in spite of the fact that it necessitated crossing the river,
La Rivière Cygnes, in two places—once by way of a ford and the
second time via a bridge. Will indicated the ford on the map
Philippe had provided.

"We should reach the ford in a few hours.," he said. "Pity
there's no bridge there. I guess we'll get our feet wet."

Maddie leaned forward from under the canopy that covered
the driving seat of the cart and surveyed the sky. There were

dark clouds on the eastern horizon and a strong wind was pushing them westward.

"We may get more than our feet wet," she said. "There's rain in those clouds."

Will glanced up at them. "We should be all right," he said. "A little rain won't hurt us."

As it turned out, the clouds contained more than a little rain.

They pulled off the road late in the afternoon, with the ford still nowhere in sight. Will had hoped to cross before dark, but the scale of the map wasn't accurate and the distance to the river was apparently much greater than it indicated.

"Why am I not surprised by that?" he asked.

For a few minutes, he debated pushing on. But he didn't want to risk crossing an unknown ford in the dark. They set up their camp. It was Maddie's turn to cook and she quickly built a fire, setting four plump pigeons on green sticks to roast over the flames, moving them closer as the fire died down to red-hot coals. Fat sizzled and spat from the grilling birds and a delicious scent filled the air. She set a pot to boil with quartered potatoes in salted water, and tore up some greens they'd been supplied by the castle kitchen before they left. These, with an oil and lemon juice dressing, would make a fresh-tasting salad.

Will watched her work and smiled. "I've taught you well," he said. It was a matter of some pride among the Rangers that they could all cook nourishing, tasty meals over a campfire, and Will and Halt were two of the best camp cooks in the Corps. Knowing this, Maddie was quietly pleased at Will's words of praise.

The trees around their small campsite were swaying more and more as the wind freshened, seeming to be almost alive as they moved from side to side in a stately unison. They grew close together and the branches and trunks groaned as they rubbed against each other with the movement. Maddie looked up at the sky, where roiling clouds were quickly blanking out the stars.

"That rain's not too far off," she said.

Will studied the sky as well. The wind was strengthening with each moment and he could smell the rain in it. He rose from his comfortable spot in front of the fire. "I'll get the rain blankets on Tug and Bumper," he said.

The rain blankets were waterproof tarpaulins, lined with woolen material, that went over the little horses' backs and kept them warm and dry in bad weather. Of course, they could manage quite well with their natural coats, but there was no sense in making them suffer discomfort if it could be avoided.

With their heightened senses, the horses could smell the coming rain as well, and they submitted readily to having the blankets put in place. Even Bumper, who was inclined to turn such an exercise into a game, only dodged and skipped away two or three times before standing, head lowered, while Will slipped the cover over his head and strapped it under his belly.

They ate quickly. While Will was boiling a pan of water to clean the platters, the first big raindrops began to hammer down. Then a spear of lightning split the sky and a massive reverberation of thunder boomed out.

A second later, the rain hit them, driven by a sudden, ferocious wind and sheeting down on the campsite.

"We'll leave these for the morning," Will said, dumping their platters and spoons in the boiling water and leaving the pan over the fire. It would be extinguished within a few minutes, he knew. Maddie quickly packed up the cooking utensils, seized the coffeepot, half full of fresh coffee, and their mugs and clambered into the back of the cart, where the rain was drumming down on the canvas roof. Will led the two horses round to the lee side of the cart, where it would shield them from the worst of the wind and rain. They nosed up against it, grumbling and nickering. Then Will clambered into the cart as well.

Normally, when they camped, he rolled his bedding out on the grass under the cart. Tonight, the ground there was already centimeters deep in rain.

There was another vicious crack and lightning flared, lighting the sky around them. Will made himself comfortable in the cart. It was cramped, but not unbearably so. Maddie passed him a mug of coffee and he sipped at it gratefully. In the few minutes it had taken him to organize the horses, he had been quite drenched and the hot drink was most welcome.

It was the mother of all storms. The cart shuddered with the constant booming of thunder and fierce wind and rain that slammed into it—the wind driving the rain almost horizontally in solid sheets of water. The lightning was vicious and intense. Each jagged fork lit up the interior of the cart, so that the canvas roof showed bright white, with the dark outline of the frame seared across it. The image was left burned onto their vision for several seconds after the light had faded.

Maddie felt Bumper shoving his muzzle against the canvas close by her. She wriggled her hand under the point where the canvas hood met the timber side of the cart and stroked his velvety nose with her fingertips.

"Nothing to worry about, boy. Just a little thunder and lightning," she crooned softly.

"He's frightened of storms?" Will asked.

She shook her head. "Not frightened. He doesn't like the

sudden noises and flashing of lights. He's okay if he knows I'm close by."

The end of her sleeve was soaked with the icy rain and she withdrew her hand, tucking it under her blanket and pulling the warm, soft wool up to her chin. She quite enjoyed sleeping while it rained—even when it was a savage storm like this one. She felt warm and safe under her blanket and the noise and flaring lightning only added to the sensation of being dry and secure in the cart.

Then a trickle of water found its way through a seam in the canvas cover and ran down into her ear, and the spell was broken.

The storm gradually rolled over them and over the mountains to the west. The rain persisted, as did the wind, for a few hours more. Around four in the morning, it died away to a gentle patter. An hour before daybreak, something woke her. She lay in her warm blanket for a few seconds, wondering what it had been. Then she realized: The rain had stopped.

The sun rose on a bright, clear day, with not a breath of wind.

25

WILL AWOKE STIFF AND CRAMPED. THE CART WAS SMALL and, with Maddie's target wheel and their other paraphernalia packed inside, the space left for sleeping was cramped. Maddie, of course, had her usual sleeping space where she could stretch out comfortably. But Will had been confined between the target wheel and the side of the cart and had lain awkwardly. When he awoke, his back ached and his neck was stiff.

He stretched and groaned. His neck would be stiff for some hours, he knew. Still, there was nothing for it. If he hadn't slept in the cart, he would have been drenched. He untied the flap at the back of the cart and peered out. The sky was blue, with a few puffs of white cloud sliding slowly across it—a far cry from the brutal weather the night before.

"You'd think butter wouldn't melt in its mouth," he said to himself.

He swung his legs over the tailgate of the cart and dropped lightly to the ground—right into a shin-deep puddle of rainwater that lay there. He cursed quietly and picked his way to a dry piece of ground. Inside the cart, Maddie laughed, guessing what had happened.

"You said we'd be getting our feet wet," she said, reminding him of his prediction of what would happen at the ford. As her comment brought that thought to his mind, a worried frown crossed his face. He looked up and down the road, and at the cleared space to either side. Vast sheets of rainwater lay everywhere, pooled in the depressions in the roadway and the soft ground to either side. There had been so much rain the night before that it had been unable to drain away.

"We may have a problem," he said. He moved around to the side of the cart where Tug and Bumper were still standing. They had found a slightly higher patch of ground, where the rain hadn't collected. They nickered good-naturedly to him as he unstrapped the tarpaulin blankets and laid them over the shafts at the front of the cart to dry. The two horses wandered a few paces, looking for fresh grass to crop and bending their necks to drink at some of the deeper puddles.

He walked back to the rear of the cart, looking for a dry approach. But there was none and he shrugged fatalistically. His feet and leggings were soaked now anyway. He waded through the rainwater and pulled the canvas flap aside. Their saddles and tack were stacked on the left-hand side of the cart. He took his saddle, saddle blanket and bridle and backed away. Maddie watched him going and scrambled to the back of the cart, finally forsaking the warmth of her blankets.

"Going somewhere?" she asked as he moved to a dry patch of ground and whistled for Tug to join him.

"I'm going to take a look at that ford," he said as he quickly saddled Tug. "All that rain last night could mean it's not there anymore."

She frowned. That thought hadn't occurred to her. "What do we do if it's flooded?"

He nodded toward the mountains looming above them in the west. "According to the map, there's a track across the mountains. It's a long way around, but we may have to go that way."

He swung up into the saddle and wheeled Tug toward the roadway. Maddie watched as they cantered off, splashing through the pooled water on the road. Will called back to her.

"You can get breakfast ready while I'm gone."

Holding Tug to a steady canter, and without the cart to slow them down, he reached the ford in fifteen minutes. He brought Tug to a halt on the high ground of the bank, before it sloped down to the river's surface where the ford should have been.

"Damn," he said quietly to himself.

Tug's ears pricked at the sound of his voice. *Are you talking to me?*

He sighed. "Not really. Just annoyed. We should have crossed last night."

He took the map from under his jerkin and unfolded it, studying the notations at the site of the ford. They indicated that the river at this point was fifty meters wide and a meter deep—easily passable for the cart and the two horses. What he now saw was something entirely different. The ford, as such, had simply disappeared, obliterated by the surging waters that flooded the riverbed.

The crossing was now at least one hundred and fifty meters wide. And while the first few meters might be a meter deep, it rapidly dropped away, so that there was no sign of the riverbed beneath the brown, surging waters.

Clicking his tongue, he urged Tug down the bank and into the edge of the water. He was instantly aware, as the sturdy little horse arranged his footing and set himself more securely, of the power of the running current. He glanced down to where the water was lapping against Tug's belly and could see the water piling up against his upstream legs. Tug snorted as Will urged him forward. He stepped carefully, feeling out the uneven bottom, scoured into a series of ridges and channels by the fast-running water, as he went. Within a few paces, the water was up to his shoulders, well over the indicated depth of one meter. And with each pace, it rose higher.

And the far bank was still at least one hundred and forty meters away.

"We'll never do it," Will said bitterly.

I could make it. Even if I have to swim. Bumper too.

"Not with the cart," Will said. "And we can't leave that behind."

Tug's ears twitched and he shook his mane. He hadn't thought of that.

Wary of the fierce current battering against his horse, Will carefully turned him around and rode back out of the river. On dry land once more, Tug paused to shake himself, sending a brilliant fan of silver spray in all directions. Will turned back in the saddle to study the river. Of course, the water would recede in a day or two and the ford would be passable again. But that left the bridge farther along. Chances were, with flooding as violent as this, it could have been swept away, and that couldn't be rectified in a day or two.

"We're going to have to take the mountain road," Will said, and he urged Tug into a canter back toward their campsite. Aware that the mountain track would take a lot longer to negotiate, he was tempted to set the little horse to a gallop. But he desisted. It would only save him five or ten minutes at the most.

And Tug was going to need all his strength for the mountain track.

The track was a nightmare. In fine weather, it would have been difficult. But after the heavy rain, it was a mass of slippery, steep and unstable mud that wound its way up the side of the mountains.

Will and Maddie dismounted from the cart and took it in turns leading the horses as they struggled up the path, pulling the cart behind them. Their usual practice had been to let each horse pull the cart for an hour, changing them over at the end of that time. Now Will reduced that to half an hour, keeping a watchful eye on the willing little beasts as they fought their way upward in the gluey, uneven mud.

At the end of each half-hour shift, he praised and patted the horses as he unharnessed them. They were amazing animals, he thought, willing to give their all for their masters, never flinching or refusing or backing off from the task in hand. They simply put their shaggy heads down, braced themselves and heaved against the harness as they dragged the cart up the winding, steep path.

At times, the track was so steep and slippery that Will and Maddie had to lend a hand, putting their shoulders against the rear wheels, or the back tray of the cart, and heaving and shoving while whichever horse was in the harness pulled. On one occasion, when Bumper was harnessed, they even had to rope Tug to the cart for extra purchase. Such was the training and dedication of the Ranger horses that Tug needed no urging or driving. Sensing what had to be done, he added his considerable strength to the task.

Finally, after hours of hauling and heaving and shoving, covered in mud and panting heavily, they reached the top.

The mountain here widened into a large plateau, where the descent was more gradual. The track led them across the plateau, angling north, then northeast as it slowly descended by gentle stages to the plain below. They could see the river curving away beneath them, and at one point Maddie plucked at Will's sleeve and pointed.

Following the direction she indicated, he could make out the wreckage of the bridge.

"Even if we'd got across the ford, we'd never have made it past there," she said.

Will grunted in reply. His concern that the bridge might have been washed away was proven correct. That was some consolation, even though the mountain track had added kilometers to the distance they would have to travel.

Halfway down to the plain, he saw smoke rising from among a grove of trees. He checked the map once more and pointed it out to Maddie.

"There's a village there, called Entente," he said. "The map says there's an inn. We might stop and clean up a little, and give the horses a break."

"That sounds agreeable," Maddie said, and he looked suspiciously at her, wondering if she had just made an outrageous pun. She returned his look with such an air of innocence that he was sure she had.

Mud spattered and bone weary, they rode into the village, a collection of around twenty buildings. They were mostly residences, although there was the usual selection of commercial businesses: a mill, a tannery and a smithy among them.

And there was the inn. It was the largest building in the village and it was set at the far end as they rode in. It was the only two-story building, and it had the usual open space with tables and benches under an awning outside the main entrance, where customers could relax and eat and drink in fine weather.

Not that there'd been too much of that lately, Will told himself, noting the preponderance of deep puddles along the road surface and in the stamped-down fine gravel that covered the open space outside the inn. He brought their distinctive cart to a halt outside the inn. A second or so later, the door opened and a man emerged, wiping his hands on a long apron tied around his waist—the standard badge of office of an innkeeper.

"Good afternoon," he said cheerfully. "Always glad to see jongleurs passing through. Were you planning to entertain us tonight?"

Will grimaced. He was weary and muddy and didn't feel like performing after their difficult day on the road.

"I was planning more on a bath and a soft bed," he said. "It's been a difficult day."

The innkeeper nodded shrewdly. He gazed back down the road that had brought them here. "Came up the mountain, did you?" he asked.

"That we did. The ford at the River Cygnes is washed out. And the bridge is washed away too."

"That would happen after that storm last night," the innkeeper averred. He paused, then went on in a persuasive tone. "Still, if you'd agree to entertain the customers tonight, that hot bath and soft bed would be on the house."

Will considered the offer for a few seconds. His neck was still stiff after sleeping in the cramped interior of the cart the night before. The temptation to stretch out in a real bed, and the luxury of a hot bath, was too strong to resist.

"You've just about talked me into it," he said. "If there was a pot of good coffee included?" He let the sentence hang and the innkeeper smiled.

"Of course. You can leave your wagon there. It'll let people know you're in town." He indicated a side alley. "There's a stable behind the inn. You can put your horses in there. I'll get one of the girls to start heating water for the bath. The bathhouse is in the back as well."

Will clambered down wearily and began unharnessing Bumper, whose turn it was between the shafts.

"I'll take the first bath," he told Maddie.

"I expected no less," she replied, smiling.

26

THE STEAMING-HOT BATH, FOLLOWED BY THIRTY MINUTES' real sleep in a proper bed, did wonders for Will's sense of well-being. There was only a vague memory of his stiff neck remaining as he washed out his mud-spattered clothes, ran them through a mangle, then spread them on a line in the stable yard to dry.

He and Maddie ate an early supper—a fragrant vegetable stew with fresh, crusty bread and a jug of excellent coffee sweetened, as was their habit, with honey. The innkeeper eyed them curiously as they stirred the honey into the coffee.

"Can't say I've seen that done before," he said.

Will gestured to the coffee jug and honey pot. "Try it," he said and the innkeeper complied. His face lit up with a gratified smile as he tasted the fragrant, sweet brew and he quickly took another sip.

"Excellent!" he said. "I'll be recommending that to my customers from now on."

"And charging them for the honey, I imagine," Will said.

The man grinned. "Of course. Have you been in the innkeeping trade then?"

Will shook his head. "No. Just a lot of inns. Never knew an innkeeper who didn't know how to squeeze a few extra coins out of his customers."

He said it in a lighthearted tone and the innkeeper took no offense. Rather, he saw it as a compliment, of sorts. He offered his hand. "My name's Michel du Mont, by the way."

Drawn by the cart parked in front of the tavern, customers began arriving and filling the tables. As they ordered food and drink, sending the two serving girls scurrying back and forth from the kitchen to the taproom, Michel viewed the busy scene with a smile.

"Good business for early in the week," he said, then stopped Giselle, the prettiest of the two serving girls, as she hurried past with a jug of coffee for one of the tables. "Don't forget to serve them a pot of honey with that," he said. He had already told the girls about Will and Maddie's innovation.

Will waited until most of the crowd had finished eating, then he uncased his mandola and made a few adjustments to the tuning. An expectant buzz ran round the room and he affected not to notice that all eyes were on him. Finished tuning, he began to put the mandola away. A small cry of protest came from the middle of the crowd and he turned, pretending to be surprised as he saw the roomful of people watching him.

"Oh," he smiled. "Did you want to hear a song?"

There was a chorus of assent from the room, and a few hand-claps. He slung the mandola over his shoulder and launched into a bouncy, lighthearted version of "Sunshine Lady." It was one of his favorites, a popular folk tune about a redheaded girl with sunshine in her hair and happiness in her eyes. Few audiences could resist joining in and this one was no exception. The room echoed to the sound of eager, if occasionally tuneless, voices singing along while several dozen pairs of hands clapped in time.

In remote, sleepy villages like this one, it was relatively easy for a good jongleur—and Will was definitely a good one—to involve and excite the audience. Their lives were a repetitive sequence of work, eat, sleep and work again. The work was hard and there was little to divert them as the days and months passed and the seasons rolled around in a predictable and inevitable sequence.

Added to that, there was a certain glamour in Will and Maddie being foreigners, and Will salted his performance with tales of events and misadventures in exotic locations. Not all of them were strictly true, of course. But all of them were highly entertaining.

As Will neared the end of his set of songs, Maddie took the large sack around among the tables, and held it out while coins clinked into it. Within a few minutes, it had grown agreeably heavy. Satisfied that she hadn't missed anyone, she hurried outside and deposited the coins in the locked strongbox at the rear of the cart, snapping the heavy padlock back in place once she had done so. There was a lot of money in there by now, she noticed with some satisfaction.

Inside the tavern, Will was already announcing her act, billing her tonight as the Mistress of the Flashing Blades of Peril. She wondered idly when he would run out of hyperbolic ways of describing her to audiences. As two of the stable hands lifted the target wheel out of the cart and set it up, and the audience started pouring out of the tavern to the tables and chairs in the square outside, she fetched her knives and began her act.

It went well, very well indeed. To her surprise and gratification, she finally convinced an audience member to be strapped onto the target board—the wheel of a thousand deaths, as Will described it this night.

The person in question was the village blacksmith, a strapping young man named Simon, who had his eye on Giselle, the serving maid, and was eager to impress her with his courage and bravado.

The bravado faded somewhat as the wheel began to turn and he saw Maddie preparing to throw the first knife.

As it thudded into the wood beside his head, he let out a startled *eek!*

It was such an unlikely sound from such a big, muscular fellow that the audience broke out in peals of laughter, which became more infectious as each successive knife was greeted by the same high-pitched squeak of fright.

It made a superb climax to Maddie's act. She almost wished she could offer Simon a permanent job traveling with them as her target. As the wheel came to a halt, she skipped forward to help Will unstrap the blacksmith, kissing him on the cheek as he stepped down, his legs a little unsteady. She glanced around for Giselle and saw the girl was pointedly ignoring the young man, going to great lengths to look unimpressed—which told Maddie that she was very impressed indeed. As coins showered around Maddie, thrown by the laughing patrons, she took Simon's hand and held it high.

"Please, ladies and gentlemen, show your generosity for a courageous young man! Let's have some coins for Simon!"

But as the coins began to shower down once more, a voice from the back of the crowd interrupted.

"And let's have some coins for the Black Vultures!"

An ominous silence fell over the crowd as the speaker strode forward into the light. He was a man of average height and build, with long black hair tied in a queue at the back of his head. He had a full beard and, above it, a hawklike beak of a nose, surmounted by dark eyes, set close together. A horizontal scar ran across his forehead. He wore a ragged black jerkin and leggings and a short black cape that reached to his waist.

And he carried a loaded crossbow, resting in the crook of his arm.

The silence that had fallen over the crowd was replaced by a low hum of recognition. As the man stepped farther into the light, Will became aware of movement at other points around the fringe of the crowd. Seven more men, similarly dressed and armed with a variety of clubs, axes and short swords, moved out of the shadows, where they had been watching the performance.

The leader nodded at Simon, who was still swaying uncertainly. He hadn't yet recovered his balance from the time he had spent on the rotating target wheel.

"You! Start picking up those coins and bring them to me!"

But Simon, aware that Giselle was watching the confrontation, squared his shoulders and snarled in reply.

"The blazes I will! You can—"

He got no further. The bandit leader stepped in close to him and swung the butt of the crossbow so that it slammed into Simon's forehead. The blacksmith staggered and fell, hitting the gravel with a heavy thump. His head bounced off the hard ground and he lay stunned.

Maddie ducked involuntarily. The heavy impact could well have triggered the crossbow, she knew, sending the wicked-looking bolt who knew where. As she regained her composure, a figure darted across the square and fell to her knees beside Simon, cradling his head in her arms. It was Giselle. Blood ran freely down the blacksmith's face from a deep cut above his eye. She mopped at it gently with her apron.

His eye drawn by Maddie's involuntary movement, the bandit chief now pointed at her. "You! Girl! You fetch me those coins!"

Maddie hesitated, ready to defy him. Her blood was up, and she was angered by the cruel and unexpected attack on the young blacksmith. But Will touched her arm and said quietly, "Better do as he says. This isn't the time."

She took a deep breath, gaining control of her anger, as she realized Will was right. They were unarmed, facing a group of eight armed men—men who were obviously ready to use their weapons without further warning. The villagers couldn't be relied on for help. They were cowed by the dark-clad intruders. She couldn't blame them. They were farm folk. They were unarmed, as well, and unaccustomed to fighting.

She took the money sack from inside her jerkin and began to move around the open space of the square, collecting the money strewn there and dropping it into the sack. She moved past the sobbing Giselle. Simon was beginning to regain consciousness, groaning softly and moving his head from side to side.

More coins went into the sack and she moved to collect another pile that had rolled farther than the rest. Moving casually, bent over to retrieve the coins, she edged closer to the target wheel, where her five knives were buried point-first in the soft wood. She studiously avoided looking at the wheel as she moved closer and closer.

"Not another step." The harsh voice stopped her in mid-stride.

The target wheel was only two meters away and she looked up to see the gang leader had the crossbow trained directly at her, held at waist height.

"Get away from that," the man ordered, jerking the crossbow to one side to emphasize the order. Reluctantly, she backed away from the target wheel, standing in a half crouch. "Now move among the tables for more donations," he said, smiling sardonically. Then he addressed the people at the tables as Maddie approached them. "And I advise you to be generous, ladies and gentlemen."

Michel, the publican, stepped forward now to plead on behalf of his customers.

"Please, Vincent. These people aren't wealthy. They're poor farmers and they've already given plenty." He indicated the ground, where Maddie had collected the money thrown by the audience.

"Vincent?" the bandit said. "So you know my name, do you?"

Michel shrugged and lowered his eyes. "Everyone knows the leader of the Black Vultures," he said, hoping that an ingratiating manner might mollify the bandit and convince him to show a little mercy. But the ruse, transparent as it was, didn't work. The bandit's eyes flashed with anger.

"Then you should know that you address me as *Monsieur* Vincent," he snarled. Then he jerked his head at Maddie, who had stopped when Michel intervened on behalf of the villagers. "Keep going!" he ordered, and she held out the sack to the nearest table of customers, feeling it twitch as the coins clinked into it.

As she threaded her way among the tables, Vincent called out a further warning. "Don't hold back. I'll be searching a few of you when we're finished and if I find you've kept anything back, it'll go badly for you."

Finally, she collected the last of the coins from the villagers. The sack now held a considerable weight of money. She took it to Vincent and dropped it onto the table beside him, where it gave off a pleasing chink. He nodded, then gestured toward the cart.

"I'll have the cashbox from the cart as well," he said.

Maddie's heart sank as she realized he must have been watching her for some time, and had seen her deposit the takings into the cashbox earlier in the evening.

"Please, sir!" Will stepped forward a pace, then stopped abruptly as the crossbow swung toward his stomach. "We've been working and traveling all week for that money!"

Vincent smiled cruelly. "Then there should be plenty in it," he said. He jerked his head toward the cart and ordered Maddie. "Go get it."

"Sir, I beg of you!" Will pleaded. "That's all our money in the world! Leave us something!" Beneath the pleading, he wanted nothing more than to smash the superior grin off the bandit's face. But he knew it would be more in the character of a traveling jongleur if he seemed to beg.

"I suppose you're right. I shouldn't take it all," Vincent said. His eyes fixed on the pleading jongleur, Vincent reached into the sack on the table. Working by feel, he selected the smallest coin he could find and flicked it into the dust at Will's feet.

"Now get that cashbox," he told Maddie.

27

"IT'S MY FAULT," SAID THE INNKEEPER THE FOLLOWING MORN-
ing. "I should have known they were back in the area."

"Who are they?" Will asked, harnessing Tug between the
shafts of the cart as they prepared to be on their way.

"They call themselves the Black Vultures," Michel told him.
"They've been preying on the farms and villages in this area for
the past two years. I thought they'd gone south, or I would have
warned you to keep your money hidden somewhere safe."

"Could have used a warning," said Will, but without any
sense of recrimination. "He got all our savings—and we'd
worked hard for them. We'll be on short commons for a while
now."

Michel shrugged. "I'd help out if I could," he said. "But he
cleaned me out too."

Will glanced quickly at him. He doubted that last statement.
Innkeepers were experts at keeping their takings safe from
marauding bandits. Inns were a prime target, after all. Vincent
and his thugs may have taken some of Michel's cash, but Will
was sure there was a lot more hidden somewhere—probably
buried in the woods or under the flagstones of the bathhouse.

Still, it wasn't Michel's responsibility to recompense them.

Will snorted derisively now as he thought about the gang's name. "Black Vultures," he said. "Why do these ragged bandits always give themselves such fierce-sounding names? Black Vultures, Bearkillers. Why don't they call themselves the Turtledoves or the Puddle Ducks?"

Michel looked at him curiously. "Who are the Bearkillers?" he asked.

Will shrugged dismissively. "They were a bunch of thugs we ran into in Araluen," he said. He glanced up as Maddie emerged from the inn, carrying their luggage.

"Load that into the cart and we'll be away," he told her.

Maddie nodded and glanced at Michel. "How's Simon this morning?" she asked.

"He has an aching head," Michel told her. Then he added, with a smile, "But Giselle is looking after him so he probably thinks it's worth it."

"Give him my thanks for his help last night," she said, and he nodded.

Will finished buckling the harness around Tug's stout body, tugged at it once or twice to test the tension, then clambered up onto the driver's seat. Bumper was tethered to the rear of the cart, although that was only for appearance's sake. As a Ranger horse, he would follow wherever they went without the need for a lead rein.

"We'll be off then," Will said, as Maddie climbed up beside him. "Thanks for your hospitality."

Michel spread his hands in a helpless, unhappy gesture. "Sorry about the way things turned out," he said.

"Not your fault," Will told him. Then, as an afterthought,

he said, "By the way, any idea where those thugs might be? I wouldn't want to run into them again."

Michel paused uncertainly, looking up and down the road that ran through the village. "If they run true to form, they'll have a camp somewhere in the forest. But they'll stay away from the main road. You'll see a fork in the road about half a kilometer out of town. The right fork leads into the forest proper. I'd wager they'll be somewhere there. But you'd be wise to avoid them, as you say."

Will raised a hand in thanks, then clicked his tongue at Tug. The little horse leaned forward into the traces and the cart moved off at a brisk walking pace.

They sat in silence for some minutes. They reached the fork in the road that Michel had mentioned. Will brought Tug to a halt. He looped the reins over the brake handle and climbed down, gesturing for Maddie to follow him.

"Let's take a look around," he said. He was stooping, his eyes studying the surface of the road, still soft after the recent rain. After a few moments, he dropped to one knee and studied the road surface more closely. In a muddy patch where a puddle had dried only recently, he saw two distinct footprints. They were clearly delineated, which told him they were relatively new—they hadn't had a chance to deteriorate and lose definition.

Maddie, a few meters farther away, also dropped to one knee. She was looking at a patch of damp ground that spread from one side of the track to the other.

"Tracks here," she said. She traced the marks in the clay with one forefinger. "At least half a dozen men. I'd say it's our friends the Black Vultures."

"That's what I thought," Will said, straightening and looking off down the narrow road in the direction the tracks were leading.

"I take it we don't plan on avoiding Vincent and his cronies?" Maddie said, with a half smile on her face.

Will shook his head. There was no answering sign of amusement in his expression. It was grim and determined. "Not in the slightest," he told her. "I don't like being robbed. And I don't like bandits who prey on defenseless villagers."

He took hold of Tug's harness and led the little horse into a small clearing five meters off the road. He unharnessed Tug, then retrieved their saddles and bridles from the cart. Maddie joined him and they quickly saddled the two horses. Tug and Bumper shook themselves, pleased at the prospect of becoming saddle horses again. Pulling a cart was demeaning work, after all.

Maddie grinned at Bumper and rubbed his soft nose affectionately. "Happy now?" she asked, and he shook his mane at her.

"Time we changed too," Will said. They exchanged their gaudy jongleur's outfits for their drab gray, brown and green Ranger uniforms. Their weapons were in a concealed compartment under the tray of the cart. They strung their bows, hooked their quivers to their belts and buckled on their double scabbards. Maddie also had her sling wound loosely beside the hilt of her saxe, and she took a small but heavy chamois shot bag and hooked it onto the knife belt opposite the two knives.

Last of all, they slung their green-and-gray-mottled cloaks around their shoulders and pulled up the cowls, so their faces were in deep shadow.

In less than five minutes, the brightly colored, flamboyantly dressed jongleurs had transformed themselves into two heavily armed, grim figures, who merged into the dark tones of the forest background.

"I know just how Bumper feels," Maddie said, a satisfied note in her voice. Being a jongleur was all very well, but it was good to be back as a Ranger, she thought.

The trail left by the Black Vultures was easy to follow— particularly for two such skilled trackers. The road surface was soft clay and sand, and the recent rain had left a lot of water lying in puddles. The boots of the eight bandits had left deep, clear impressions, particularly as the bandits tended to walk on the side of the road where most of the water gathered. Maddie queried this and Will explained.

"Makes it easier for them to take cover in the forest if they're pursued. Or if they see a traveler coming toward them and decide to ambush him."

By contrast, the two Rangers rode down the center of the road, where the slight camber meant the surface was drier, as the rain drained off to the edges. That way, they left minimum sign of their passing. It was a habit deeply ingrained in them by years of practice and experience. Rangers, expert trackers that they were, left little sign for others to track them.

By the same token, they didn't ride side by side. They were stalking a dangerous foe and while Will led the way, keeping an eye on the tracks left by the Black Vulture gang, Maddie stayed back thirty to forty meters, ready to support Will if there was any sign of an attack from the trees beside the road.

They had been on the side road for two hours when Will drew rein and gestured for Maddie to catch up. She rode along- side him and stopped as he pointed to a faint track leading off into the trees. It was barely discernible. Most people would probably have overlooked it. But Will wasn't most people. And he'd seen that the jumble of boot prints they had been following went no farther down the road.

"They left the road here," he told her in a quiet voice. "I'd say we're getting close to their camp."

He dismounted and followed the narrow trail through the trees for a few meters. Then he stopped and pointed to the ground, where a small puddle of water had formed in an irregularity in the forest floor. On the edge of the puddle, there was a clear imprint of a boot. He beckoned to Maddie to join him.

"We'll leave the horses here," he told her, "and follow this trail. Keep your eyes and ears open. Vincent is an overconfident type and I'll wager he doesn't expect to be followed. So they won't go any great distance from the road before they make camp."

Maddie nodded. She glanced around at the closely set trees surrounding them. There wasn't a lot of room between them, which would make it awkward for her to use the sling—her preferred weapon. She unslung her bow, selected an arrow and nocked it to the string. Will did the same.

"Five-meter leapfrog," he said. "I'll go first."

Again she signaled her understanding. It was a standard Ranger drill for moving through cover. Will went first, while she waited, her bow half raised, ready to draw, aim and shoot if there was any sign of danger. Then he stopped after five meters and readied his own bow while Maddie slipped forward silently, passing him and moving on another five meters before stopping in her turn. Once she was settled, Will moved again, leapfrogging her position and moving another five meters into the forest.

And so they progressed through the thick growth of trees, barely visible when they were moving, almost invisible when they stopped, as their cloaks merged into the shadowy forest background. It was the sort of maneuver that had given the Rangers their reputation for becoming invisible to other people, a skill they had practiced again and again until they had it perfected.

The fourth time Will ghosted past her, he stopped and turned to look at her. When he saw he had her attention, he tapped one forefinger to his nose, then slid into cover behind a tree.

Maddie sniffed experimentally, and caught the faintest whiff of woodsmoke. There was a fire somewhere up ahead. And in this damp woodland, it wouldn't have just happened by accident. Someone would have lit it on purpose.

They were closing in on the Vultures' campsite.

28

WILL LEANED BACK AND PEERED UP THROUGH THE TALL TREE cover, looking for some sign of the sun. The light filtered down through the trees, and judging by the angle it took, it was early afternoon.

"We'll take a look at their camp," he said softly, his head close to Maddie's. "Then we'll come back here and wait for darkness."

After their successful raid the night before, it was most likely that the bandits would stay in camp this evening. There were no villages marked on the map in this direction, and if they had planned to raid another one farther along the main road, they would hardly have come all this way down the side track.

They set off again, maintaining the same five-meter-leapfrog pattern. Maddie was in the lead when she heard the low murmur of voices coming from ahead of her. She raised a warning hand and Will, instead of bypassing her, slid into cover beside her. She cupped a hand behind her ear and he pulled his cowl back and turned his head slightly.

There it was again. A low murmur, then a sharp burst of laughter. It sounded to be no more than twenty meters away. Will leaned toward her and whispered, "Stay here. I'll take a look."

She was content for him to do so. Skilled as she was at silent, unseen movement, Will had the benefit of many more years of experience. He left his bow with her and slipped away from the tree that sheltered them both, moving on his belly in a swift, silent serpent crawl. Maddie waited, staying low, keeping her face and eyes down. She pulled her cowl forward so that her face was in shadow. Lying inert as she was, and concealed beneath her cloak, she wouldn't be spotted unless someone trod on her. She smiled grimly at the thought. That had happened before, and more than once.

It was some minutes before Will slid back beside her, his movement barely audible. He didn't speak, but gestured with his thumb for her to follow him, then began to snake his way back the way they had come. She waited half a minute, then followed.

After twenty meters or so, Will rose from his belly and, moving in a crouch, continued to ghost his way through the trees. Maddie followed his lead until he stopped, near the point where they had first noticed the smell of woodsmoke. They knelt on the ground as he spoke. Even though they were well out of earshot, Will kept his voice low.

"It's them, all right. They've got a camp there. The fire is a small one. My guess is that it's a cook fire but they'll build it up once it's dark. They seem pretty confident. They haven't posted any guards and they don't seem worried that anyone will have smelled their woodsmoke."

"Probably not used to being followed," Maddie said.

Will nodded. "I suppose that's it. They've been preying on ordinary villagers and farmers for years. I doubt anyone has ever gone after them. People just seem to pay up and take it as part of the cost of life. It's what keeps bandits in business."

"Are they all there?" Maddie asked.

"Yes. All eight of them. They're sprawled around the camp. They stole some wine from the tavern last night and they're all drinking." He smiled fiercely. "That'll be handy for us later." He moved to one side, found a convenient tree and leaned back against it, pulling his cloak around him.

"For now, I'm going to get some rest. You can take the first watch. Wake me in an hour."

She smiled to herself as his head dropped onto his chest and he began to breathe deeply and evenly. Vincent and his gang might not bother to set a guard. But that wasn't the Ranger way.

Darkness fell over the forest. Once the sun had dropped below the treetops, the shadows crept quickly in. There were only occasional glimpses of the stars when Maddie peered up. With Will leading the way, they moved silently through the trees, back toward the camp. In the darkness, there was no need to serpent crawl. They walked carefully, placing their feet delicately and feeling with each step for any twigs or fallen branches that might snap underfoot and give their presence away.

Not that there was much chance of that, Maddie thought scornfully, as she listened to the noise coming from the bandits' camp. Their voices were loud and careless, as they talked over one another and shouted each other down. From time to time, they joined in the chorus of a raucous song. Then the singing would die away and they would laugh loudly.

Will caught her eye after one particularly loud chorus and mimed drinking from a glass. The meaning was obvious. The wine they had consumed over the afternoon was having an effect.

They had built up the small cooking fire as well. Now the flames rose high among the trees and the flickering light was visible through the close-set but narrow trunks for thirty meters or so.

The two Rangers moved closer, still making no sound and staying in the uneven shadows. As they reached the edge of the small clearing where the camp was situated, Will did a quick count of the figures sprawling and sitting round the fire. He turned to Maddie and held up eight fingers. All of the band were here. Nobody was on sentry duty.

Will pointed to himself, then made a semicircular motion with his hand, ending up pointing to the far side of the clearing. Maddie could tell what he meant, even if they hadn't discussed this before setting out. He was planning to circumvent the camp and approach from the other side. Maddie would stay where she was and provide cover for him if he needed it. And with eight armed men in the camp, she thought he might.

Maddie took stock of her position. She was at the edge of the clearing, and with the darkness of the forest behind her, she was able to move into the open, which gave her room to use her sling. She slung her bow over her left shoulder and loaded a lead shot into the pouch of the sling, letting the leather thongs dangle down from her hand.

She nodded once to let Will know she was ready and he set off, gliding through the trees like a wraith. Even though she was watching him as he set off, she soon found it difficult to see him. Then she realized that she was supposed to be watching the noisy, drunken group around the fire, making sure that none of them had noticed Will moving through the trees.

Not that there's any chance of that, she smiled to herself. When she darted a quick glance in the direction he'd taken, she could see no sign of movement.

She set her attention back on the gang of bandits, letting her eyes rove over them, taking care not to stare directly into the glare of the fire, and making sure none of them was about to raise the alarm or reach for a weapon. Vincent was sprawled on the soft ground opposite where she was concealed among the trees. He was propped up against a fallen tree trunk. She noticed his crossbow was close by, already cocked and with a bolt set in place. She sniffed derisively.

Your string's not going to last long if you leave it cocked and loaded all the time, she mentally told the robber chief.

Not that Vincent seemed to have any concern in that area. He hoisted himself up against the log so that he was sitting upright, and took hold of a half-full bottle of wine that had been standing on the grass by his elbow. He raised it now in a mock toast.

"Here's to our good friend Michel!" he said, and the Vultures responded with an ironic cheer. "So kind of him to insist on giving us all these bottles of his very finest wine."

The drunken group laughed at his words. Several of them had bottles of their own and they reached for them now to join him in his sarcastic toast. He held his bottle up prior to drinking from it.

Will's arrow smashed through it, showering the drunken bandit chief with wine and shattered fragments of glass, before thudding, quivering, into a log lying ready by the fire.

Vincent let out a yelp of fear, quickly followed by an angry snarl as he saw the arrow and his foggy wits worked out what had just happened. He whirled clumsily around, his hand reaching for the crossbow.

"Don't touch it."

Will's voice was low, but it carried clearly across the open space of the campsite. Vincent, his night vision blinded by the fact that he had been staring into the heart of the fire for the past hour or so, squinted and shifted his head from side to side as he tried to make out who had spoken. Whoever it was, he reasoned, was armed. Moreover, the interloper was at an advantage as he could clearly see Vincent, whereas the robber couldn't see him. His hand stopped moving toward the crossbow and he lurched up onto his knees, still peering into the shadows.

The other seven bandits were silent and frozen in place as well. Then Will stepped out into the clearing, at the fringe of the circle of firelight. He appeared to Vincent's blurred, drunken vision as a spectral, indistinct figure. His face was hidden in the shadows of his cowl and the cloak, with its irregular pattern and woodland colors, caused him to merge into the background in the flickering firelight, so that one moment he was visible and the next, he seemed to fade away.

Vincent felt his muscles freeze with fear. To his superstitious mind, the indistinct figure seemed to be some spirit of the forest—otherworldly and supernatural. The bandit chief opened his mouth to speak, but his throat was dry and no words came. The only distinct thing about the ghostly figure facing him was the massive longbow, and the deadly iron warhead that caught the firelight and glittered evilly.

"Who are you?" he croaked, finally finding his voice. The figure didn't move or reply. Vincent tried again. "What do you want?"

This time, he had more success. That calm, quiet voice replied.

"I want you to pay back the money you stole last night. You picked the wrong village to rob."

There was growl of anger from the other bandits and Vincent came up onto one knee. Will had picked the one emotion stronger than the robber's superstitious fear—his greed.

"Pay it back? Why should I pay it back?" he challenged.

"Because if you don't, things will go badly for you."

Vincent's mind was working fast, forcing him to think rationally in spite of the befuddling effects of an afternoon spent drinking. So far, the cloaked figure had threatened. And he had put an arrow through the wine bottle Vincent was drinking from. But he had done Vincent no actual harm. In his place, Vincent would already have shot him, without further warning. Coming to the conclusion that the stranger was unwilling to shoot, he grabbed for the crossbow on the ground beside him and stood, bringing it up to his shoulder.

And realized he had made a mistake.

Maddie whipped the sling up and over and the lead shot hissed through the air across the clearing, striking Vincent's skull behind the ear with an ugly thud.

The bandit's eyes glazed and he let out a sickly little moan. Then his knees gave way and he crashed to the forest floor, stunned. A slow trickle of blood ran down the back of his head.

"I warned you," Will said.

29

~~~~~~~~~~~~~~~~~~~~~~~~~~~~~~~~

It said a lot about Maddie's training, and her intelligence, that she continued to scan the campsite, watching for any sign of rebellion or danger from the other bandits.

Nine out of ten people, in that situation, would have had their attention riveted on Will and the fallen bandit leader. But she knew her task was to protect Will, to forestall any attempt to defy him. And with seven men capable of offering such defiance, the task was an important one. She had already loaded another shot into her sling and the weapon dangled loosely beside her, swinging gently back and forth, ready for instant action.

So while Vincent lay facedown and semiconscious, moaning softly on the forest floor, she kept her gaze moving quickly over the other figures spaced around the campsite.

Will himself, trusting in her to cover him, had his attention fixed on the bandit leader. On his right, across the clearing, one of the other bandits was also armed with a crossbow.

Out of the corner of his eye, Will saw a flicker of movement as the man rose onto one knee and leveled the crossbow. Maddie saw it too. She realized that Will was a second away from death and her arm went back, preparing to whip the sling over and send its missile humming across the clearing.

But Will was too fast for her. Before she could launch the projectile, his right hand flew to his double scabbard and in one smooth movement, he drew his throwing knife and sent it spinning across the clearing. The bandit's hand was beginning to tighten on the trigger when the knife hit him in the center of his chest. He gave a strangled grunt of pain, then everything went black for him and he fell to one side. His hand convulsively squeezed the trigger lever. The crossbow released with an ugly thump and the bolt flashed upward. Maddie heard it glancing off tree trunks as it went, until it finally lodged in the thick canopy of one of the trees.

The rest of the gang were silenced for a moment, staring at his crumpled form. Before they could act, Will's voice cracked out like a whip.

"Everybody stay exactly where they are. Anyone who moves, anyone who reaches for a weapon, will get the same treatment from my companion." He nodded toward Maddie, who had moved forward a few more paces and was now standing clear of the trees. Six pairs of eyes now swiveled in her direction. She had replaced the sling with her bow, with an arrow ready nocked, as it was more visually threatening. The sling, after all, looked like two leather thongs hanging from her hand. The bow was a weapon they could recognize, and the iron point of the arrow's warhead gleamed in the firelight.

Like Vincent, the bandits had spent the evening staring into the bright light of the campfire and their night vision was ruined. They saw a dark blur of movement as Maddie trained the bow back and forth across them.

"Perhaps you might demonstrate, Matthew," Will said.

They had discussed this deception earlier in the evening, before approaching the camp.

"We need to subdue them quickly. And that means they have to fear us. If they realize you're a girl," Will had said, "they'll feel a little less threatened."

Maddie had opened her mouth to remonstrate and he raised a hand to forestall her.

"You know it's nonsense, and so do I," he said. "But their tiny brains have been conditioned to think like that, so let's not take the risk. Otherwise, we may have to shoot three or four of them to make the point."

He'd paused and looked meaningfully at her. She nodded. It was annoying, but she realized he was right. Men like these would not have the intelligence to credit a girl with the skill or courage to face them and defeat them. And Will was right. If they showed any sign of defiance, he and Maddie would proba-bly have to shoot several of them—an outcome neither of them wanted.

But now she had been called on to demonstrate her accuracy and speed, and Will's life wasn't in immediate danger. She shot three times, in quick succession.

The first shot smashed through another wine bottle, bal-anced on a tree stump beside one of the gang. As wine and glass splinters exploded in all directions, the man flinched violently away.

Before the startled bandits had time to react, Maddie's second shot smacked into the sleeve of a gang member, pinning his right arm to the log he was leaning against. The third arrow buried itself into the soft earth between the knees of a bandit who was sitting with his legs sprawled out. With a shrill cry of fright, he scrabbled his way backward away from the deadly shaft, even though he was reacting way too late.

Will laughed grimly. "Bear it in mind. Anyone who doesn't do exactly as I tell them will be part of a further demonstration. But next time, Matthew won't aim to just miss you."

The bandits cast wary, nervous glances toward the indistinct figure who had just shot three arrows in quick succession. There was a clear message here. They were at a complete disadvantage, covered by an archer of fearsome skill, their own weapons well out of reach.

These were not fighting men. They were bullies and thieves, used to preying on simple, unarmed farm folk and villagers, striking without warning, using their numbers and their lack of compassion to instill fear into their victims.

Now they were confronted by two skilled warriors—warriors who wouldn't hesitate to shoot if they had to. It was not a situation they were familiar with. And it definitely wasn't one they liked. Will paused to let the message sink in—to let them ponder the possible results of any sign of defiance. His next words jerked them back to reality.

"We'll start with you in the green shirt," he said. "On your feet. Now!"

He spat the last word violently as the man hesitated. Slowly the bandit rose to his feet, looking warily around him, not sure what was coming next. He didn't have long to wait before he found out.

"All right, strip. Off with your clothes, down to your underwear."

Startled by the order, the bandit hesitated further. Will took half a pace forward and drew back on the arrow nocked to his bow.

"You have three seconds," he said.

The bandit responded quickly, stripping off his shirt and trousers so that he was standing, shivering, in just his undershirt and breeches. He watched Will uncertainly, wondering what was coming next.

"And your undershirt and boots," the Ranger ordered, and the man complied, stripping off his vest, then hopping on one foot as he pulled one boot, then the other, off his feet. The socks that he wore underneath were grubby and tattered. One big toe stuck out through a large hole.

"Now lie down. Facedown on the ground, hands behind your back."

The bandit did as he was told. When he was lying in that helpless, vulnerable position, Will leaned his bow against a tree and drew his saxe. Stepping forward and kneeling quickly beside the bandit, he drove the saxe point-first into the soft ground, then quickly whipped a pair of leather thumb cuffs around the man's thumbs, pulling the thong tight to secure them. Too late, the bandit tried to struggle against the restraints. But they were firm and his hands were secured behind his back.

Will retrieved his saxe and stood quickly, moving away from the now-helpless bandit. He gestured with the big knife to another member of the gang.

"You! You with the red cap. On your feet and off with your clothes."

The second bandit did as he was told, submitting meekly, then lying facedown and allowing Will to tie his hands.

Within the space of ten minutes, Will had five of the group

stripped, trussed and helpless, lying facedown and shivering in the cold. He ordered the sixth man to strip, then waved him over to where Vincent was still lying on the ground, groaning and crying softly, his wits still scattered by the savage impact of the shot. Blood seeped from the wound, soaking the hair around it. Head wounds usually bled profusely, and this one was no exception.

"Bandage him," Will ordered. "Tear up your shirt to do it."

The bandit wound strips of his torn shirt around Vincent's head, staunching the flow of blood. Then he helped his leader into a sitting position. Vincent was beginning to regain consciousness, but he was still in a bad way. He stared around the clearing, confused and bewildered, his vision fuzzy and his head throbbing.

"Wha's happened?" he asked, his voice thick and indistinct. He frowned as he looked at his companion. "Is tha' you, Pierre?" he asked groggily.

Moving swiftly, Will thumbcuffed Pierre, then Vincent.

Will pulled Vincent into a sitting position and, putting his hand under his chin, studied him carefully for several seconds, making sure he wasn't foxing. But he could see Vincent's eyes were wide and unfocused, and he knew that any form of defiance was well beyond him. Then he dragged him and the other bandits to their feet and quickly tied them together with a long cord, passing it around each man's throat. He ran the rope around four substantial trees and tied it securely. The Black Vultures were now fastened in a loose circle around the trees, their hands secured behind them. He gave a satisfied nod as he looked at them. They'd stay this way for hours before they could work their way free.

"Gather up their clothes, boots and weapons," he told Maddie, and assisted her in the task. Then he heaved the pile of clothing, boots and their assorted knives, swords, crossbows and other weapons onto the fire in the middle of the clearing.

For a few minutes, the flames died down and the fire emitted an acrid cloud of smoke. Then, as he piled more brushwood and logs on, the flames flared again. He added their blankets and sleeping bags to the blaze, then more firewood. He watched as the crossbow, spear shafts and ax handles began to burn, and the wood and leather handles of their swords burned away. The blades turned bright red and began to distort, their temper ruined by the intense heat.

Will searched the campsite and found a large, heavy sack full of coins. He hefted it over one shoulder.

"Looks like the money they stole last night." he told Maddie. "And a bit extra. I'm sure Michel and his friends will be glad to have it back. Let's be on our way."

As he and Maddie turned away from the pathetic group of former brigands, one of them called out.

"Wait! You're not leaving us like this?"

Will nodded. "Apparently, that's just what we're doing," he said. The bandit tried to plead with him, the effort hindered by the fact that his hands were secured behind his back.

"But we'll freeze!"

Will glanced at the sky, where clouds were once again gathering. "That is a possibility," he said cheerfully. "It does look like there's more rain on the way."

"We'll starve," the bandit cried, trying another tack.

Will nodded. "That, too, is a distinct possibility. You should have thought of that before you took up a career preying on defenseless villages." He gestured to Maddie and led the way into the forest, heading back to where they had left the horses. The bandit's pleading cries faded as they moved farther away.

"He's right, of course," Maddie said. "They could starve."

"A prospect that doesn't break my heart," Will replied. "But I doubt it. They'll work their way free in a few hours. They'll be unarmed and helpless. They won't be bothering the villagers again for some time."

Maddie was silent for a few minutes. Then she spoke again. "You didn't want to hand them over to the authorities?"

Will shrugged. "I don't know who the authorities are. Chances are, it's Lassigny and his men. If I take in half a dozen criminals to him it will ruin our cover as jongleurs, won't it?"

"I suppose so," she said. Then she asked a final question that had been bothering her. "This business of taking away their clothes and boots—I know we've done it before and I know it makes them more vulnerable and less threatening. But who thought of it in the first place?"

Will smiled. "See if you can guess."

She paused for a few seconds, then said: "Halt?"

He nodded once. "Right first time."

30

MICHEL DU MONT, INNKEEPER IN THE MOUNTAIN VILLAGE OF Entente, was disconsolately raking the fine gravel in the plaza in front of his inn. Vincent and his Black Vultures had cost him dearly. They had stolen a week's takings from the inn, including the larger-than-usual amount that had gone into his cashbox on the night the two jongleurs had performed.

Fortunately, they hadn't managed to get their hands on his main savings, which were buried in an iron strongbox in the stable yard behind the inn. But still, the loss was a serious one.

In addition, the bandits had taken all the ready cash held by the customers at the inn, and that meant that the village would be on short commons for some days. And that, in turn, meant that people would have no money to spend at the inn until they managed to restore their funds at the next market day, which was two weeks away.

All in all, things looked grim for the next ten days or so, and Michel quietly cursed under his breath. Vincent and his gang had robbed the village, and the inn, before this. But this had been a more serious matter than most. The inn had been full and most of the villagers had lost money in the raid.

So too had the jongleurs, he thought gloomily. But he couldn't be too concerned about that. They weren't locals. They weren't his neighbors or friends. And their way of life, traveling alone through the countryside and carrying substantial amounts of money with them, more or less ensured that they would be targeted by robbers from time to time.

Still, they had been a pleasant pair, and good entertainers, and he felt a degree of sympathy for them. It was particularly bad luck that Vincent had observed the girl storing their takings in the cashbox at the back of the cart. They hadn't just lost a night's pay, they had lost everything they had earned in the past week.

"Innkeeper!"

He started at the voice, which came from behind him. He looked quickly over his shoulder and saw a mounted figure just ten meters away. Michel, cautious now of strangers, measured the distance to the door of the inn, and the long cudgel he kept behind the door. He decided it was too far. The mounted man could ride him down in a few meters, if that were his intention.

Still, Michel had something nearly as good at hand. The gravel rake was long and heavy and its head was studded with a line of large nails. It would make an effective, if clumsy, improvised weapon if he should need one. He turned and faced the stranger, holding the rake ready in both hands, at an angle across his upper body.

The rider clearly recognized his intent.

"You won't be needing that," he said, gesturing at the rake. "I don't wish you any harm."

Michel frowned. There was something familiar about the figure but it was hard to ascertain what. He was wearing a strange cloak that broke up the outlines of his body, so that Michel had to peer closely at him to focus on him. And his face was hidden in the shadow of his cowl. A massive longbow, strung and ready for use, rested across his thighs.

His voice was vaguely familiar, but he spoke with a trace of an accent—Hibernian, Michel realized.

"I think this belongs to you and the rest of your village," the rider said. As he spoke, he unhitched a heavy sack from the pommel of his saddle and tossed it onto the raked gravel yard. The sack gave off a weighty chink of coin as it hit the ground. Michel started forward, a smile widening on his face as he realized that the village's fortunes, and his own, had just been restored. Then, driven by his innate sense of fairness, he hesitated.

"Some of that belongs to a pair of jongleurs who performed here two nights ago," he said.

The cowled figure nodded. "We've already given them their share. We saw them on the road."

Michel nodded, beginning to understand. The jongleurs must have encountered this mysterious warrior and his band— after all, he had said *we saw them*—and recounted the story of the robbery at the Entente inn. Then, for reasons best known to himself, the cloaked rider had decided to wreak vengeance on the Black Vulture gang. Michel didn't know why, and he wasn't about to question the man's motives. He reasoned that the warrior must have a sizable band working for him. After all, he had obviously overpowered the Black Vultures.

Had Michel been a more observant man, he might have recognized the shaggy gray horse that the stranger was riding as one of the two horses who had pulled the jongleurs' cart. But he wasn't a man who took much notice of horses. Cart horses were cart horses. They weren't well groomed or particularly remarkable.

"I'll bid you farewell," said the rider, and turned his horse back the way he had come.

"Yes . . ." said Michel uncertainly. He looked down at the bag of coins at his feet. "And . . . thank you, whoever you are."

But the rider didn't reply. He tapped his horse with his heels and cantered off down the road leading to Chateau des Falaises.

"He didn't recognize you?" Maddie said when Will rejoined her in the trees on the outskirts of the village.

He shook his head. "No reason why he should. I'm dressed differently and I changed my voice. I added a bit of Hibernian accent to it. And he was more interested in the bag of coins that I gave him." He scratched his chin thoughtfully. "You know, he's an honest man—not something you usually find in innkeepers. He told me that some of the money should go to the two jongleurs who performed at the inn last night. I said we'd already taken care of them."

"So what do we do now?" Maddie asked.

"We'll press on for Chateau des Falaises. It's about a day's ride from here. But I want to leave the cart hidden in the forest along the way."

Maddie glanced at him in surprise. "Really? Why's that?"

"I've been thinking about it and it's time we assumed a lower profile. I want to attract less attention. We'll go to the castle as a simple jongleur and his daughter. We won't put on a formal show for Lassigny and his court. We'll play informally for the staff and the garrison in the common rooms. That'll mean we can stay around for a longer period. If we perform for Lassigny in the great hall, we'll be hired for one night and then we'd have to be on our way. This way, nobody will take much notice if we stay for four or five days. And you'll have a chance to look around while I'm performing."

"Look around for what?" Maddie asked, although she was confident she knew the answer.

"Not what. Who. You can scout around and see where they're holding Philippe's son."

31

THEY CONTINUED ON THE ROAD LEADING TO CHATEAU DES Falaises. Around the middle of the day, they found a secluded glade some twenty meters off the road. Will carefully guided the cart through the trees until it was in the middle of the glade, and well hidden from the road. Maddie unpacked the large net they carried with them to conceal the cart. It was festooned with green and brown strips of cloth, and when it was loosely draped over the cart, it helped it blend into the forest background.

She retrieved their bows from the hidden compartment under the cart tray. The bows and the knives they wore in their double scabbards went into a long leather tube—of the kind fishermen used to protect their rods. Two slender quivers, each holding fifteen arrows, were also added.

Maddie indicated the knives. "We already have knives," she said. Each of them was wearing a saxe in a simple scabbard, and had a throwing knife in a concealed spot as well.

Will glanced up. "Doesn't hurt to have spares," he said. "Our knives might be confiscated when we go into the castle."

While Maddie was rigging the camouflage net over the cart,

Will set about transforming his jongleur's outfit. He selected the second-best outfit, and smeared it with dirt and dust from the road. Then he sewed several unmatching patches onto the jerkin, so that it looked old and worn. Maddie glanced across as he was doing this.

"What's that for?" she asked.

He paused to bite off a length of thread from his latest patch. "As I said, I want to keep a low profile. With the cart and its decorations, and your equipment, we look like top-of-the-line performers—the sort who would seek to appear in the castle lord's hall. This way, we look a little down at heel and Raggedy Andy—as if we'll be glad to sing for our supper in the common rooms of the castle, without bothering the quality folk."

He said "quality" with a slight sneer. He believed Lassigny to be anything but.

When he had finished, his smart, brightly colored jongleur's outfit was transformed into a rather dull, stained and patched version of its former self.

Maddie had donned a plain outfit as well—a green jerkin over brown leggings. She left her Ranger cloak tied behind her saddle and wore a waist-length cape made of gray wool.

Will eyed her approvingly. "Just the thing," he said. Then he spread his arms to display his stained, patched tunic, the once-bright colors now dulled by dirt and some grease from the cart's axle. "How do I look?"

Maddie eyed him with disapproval. "Like I shouldn't be seen traveling with you," she said at length.

Will took the cashbox from the back of the cart and buried it beneath a tree with a distinctive fork two meters from the ground. Then he marked the trunk with two parallel slashes from his saxe—easy enough to find again but not so conspicuous as to catch the eye of a casual observer.

"Be a pity if someone stumbled on the cart and decided to steal it," he said. "Along with all our earnings to date."

Then they mounted and rode out of the little clearing, continuing down the mountain road to Lassigny's chateau.

Chateau des Falaises was named for the steep cliffs that tumbled away below it on all sides—*falaise* being the Gallic word for "cliff." It was set on a rocky outcrop rising out of a lake. A raised causeway, some eight meters high and forty meters in length, connected it to the shores of the lake. The causeway was steep-sided and unfenced. It started out wide enough for eight or nine people to walk abreast. But as it snaked toward the castle entrance, it narrowed considerably. By the time it reached the castle, there was barely room for four people to stand side by side.

The situation for those traversing the causeway was made more precarious by the fact that the edges were unsealed and had crumbled away at several points, so that it looked as if a giant had taken huge bites out of the edge of the path.

At the base of the cliffs, to the left of the causeway, their attention was taken by a flock of gulls, screaming and wheeling in the sky over a pile of rubbish, obviously dumped from the castle high above.

Will sniffed disdainfully. "I imagine that gets pretty ripe in hot weather," he said.

The castle itself was a fairly standard design. After the graceful beauty of La Lumiere and Araluen castles, it was disappointingly plain. But it was solidly built and would be difficult to assault, even without the awkward approach path formed by the causeway.

There were four main towers, joined by curtain walls that reached halfway up each, the whole structure forming a square. The towers were surmounted by turrets that jutted out past the width of the tower itself and were enclosed by crenelated walls to form defensive positions. The design allowed defenders to shoot missiles or drop rocks and stones on attackers clustered round the base of the towers.

A massive gatehouse, containing the operating mechanism for a heavy iron portcullis, guarded the entrance to the castle. It was fitted with a fighting platform that provided room for more defenders, giving them a vantage point from which they could rain missiles down on enemies clustered around the heavy gates.

Inside the square formed by the towers and the curtain wall stood a fifth building. Wider and lower than the corner towers, it was a squat, solidly built structure that stood several stories higher than the curtain wall. Its roof was flat and the wall running round the roof was also crenelated, providing a further defensive line.

This was the keep—the central building of the chateau, where the staff and garrison were housed and fed. The higher levels would be devoted to administrative offices for the castle hierarchy, and private apartments for the castle lord and his senior advisers and officers. It was also the refuge of last resort in the event that the outer walls were breached and an enemy gained entry to the chateau.

A steady stream of traffic moved across the causeway to the chateau's gates. About half were pedestrians, some pushing handcarts, but there was a fair representation of people on horseback, and carts drawn by horses and donkeys as well. A mixed stream of goods made its way into the castle: sides of beef and sheep carcasses, vegetables, firewood, casks of ale and wine. Some carts were loaded with wooden cages of ducks and chickens. Each cart or traveler would be stopped at the gate, examined and questioned, then allowed to pass through the gate into the courtyard.

As the carts reached the narrow end of the causeway, they moved with extra caution, the drivers ensuring that the wheels stayed well clear of the crumbling edges of the path. A team of eight or nine soldiers, armed with short swords and long-shafted halberds, conducted the examination of would-be visitors to the chateau. As Will and Maddie watched the steady procession, they saw nobody turned away.

"That looks promising," Maddie said.

Will grunted. "So far, so good."

They had drawn rein on a small hill overlooking the start of the causeway. Now they urged their horses forward and found a gap in the stream of traffic moving toward the castle.

It took them some time to traverse the path, with the constant interruptions to the traffic flow caused by the interrogation and inspection of each person or group looking to enter the castle. Finally, it was their turn. One of the soldiers motioned them inside, leaving room for a cart full of sides of freshly slaughtered beef to be inspected outside the gate.

They clip-clopped through the dim interior of the gatehouse, then out into the bright sunlight again, where the soldier motioned for them to stop. He eyed Will's grubby finery, noting the leather mandola case strapped to his saddle bow.

"Jongleur, are you?" he asked.

Will smiled. "Yes, sir. I'm a musician, and this is my young daughter who's traveling with me."

The soldier frowned as he noted Will's accent. "Where from?"

"Araluen, sir. We've been traveling in this country for a month." Will had dropped the Hibernian accent he had assumed for Michel at the inn.

"And what do you want here?" the soldier asked. He was only half interested. It was fairly obvious what the down-at-heel performer would be looking for. But he had to go through the motions.

"I was hoping for food and lodging for a few days, sir. I'll be happy to perform for the castle staff in return."

"Why not stay at the inn in the village?" the soldier demanded. The village protected by the castle was a quarter of a kilometer back along the road. Will hesitated, looking embarrassed.

"It's only a small village, sir—not many to entertain. And the inn is rather . . . expensive."

The soldier gave a harsh laugh. He knew the local innkeeper's parsimonious reputation. "I imagine it is." He glanced at the long leather tube, strapped upright behind Will's saddle. "What's in there?" he demanded.

"Fishing rods and reels, sir," Will told him.

The soldier frowned a warning. "All fish in the lake and rivers in this fief are property of the Baron. There's no fishing for strangers."

"Of course, sir." Will bowed from the waist in acknowledgment. "I understand. No fishing."

The soldier eyed them for a few seconds, then shrugged.

"Very well," he said. "You'll have to get the seneschal's approval. His office is on the third floor of the keep. Leave your horses at the hitching post there."

He indicated a weathered post set into the cobblestones of the courtyard a few meters from the entrance to the keep. Will bowed again and urged Tug forward.

"Come along, daughter," he said, and led the way inside the castle yard.

The seneschal—the knight responsible for the administration of the castle and its staff—questioned them briefly, then he gave permission for them to take up two sleeping spaces. These were curtained-off recesses set around the walls of the great hall and the other common rooms of the castle. The lower-ranking castle staff—servants, kitchen hands and cleaners—slept there, as did casual visitors.

"Four coppers a day," he told them briskly. "That'll give you two meals a day—a cold breakfast and a hot supper—and a sleeping space each. Fresh straw every two days. How long did you plan on staying?"

"Perhaps a week, sir," Will said.

The man nodded, eyeing Will's clothing. "I assume you'll be performing?"

"Yes, sir. With your permission," Will told him.

The seneschal thought for a moment. "Very well. I'll make it three coppers a day. That's twenty-one but we'll round it down to twenty. If you decide to stay longer, come and see me again."

Will paid him and received two round leather medallions in return, with numbers burned into the leather.

"Eighty-two and eighty-three. They're your sleeping spaces," the seneschal said. "Your horses can go into the stables. They're on the eastern wall of the courtyard. But you'll look after them yourselves."

"Yes, sir. Thank you, sir." Will bowed several times. But the seneschal had lost interest in them already. He dismissed them with a brusque wave of his hand as he pulled a stack of invoices toward him.

32

They led the horses to the stables, which were in a two-story building set against the curtain wall on the eastern side of the castle bailey. The upper story was clearly a hay loft. There was a hoisting beam and pulley set in a wide double doorway, by which bales of hay could be lifted up and stored. The ground floor was a long, dimly lit building lined with horse stalls on either side. Just over half of them were occupied and the two new arrivals were met by a dozen or so curious noses peering over the stall doors as they clopped inside the building.

The stablemaster greeted them as they entered. He was a surly-looking man, thin as a rake and with a head cold that had him sniffing constantly. He eyed the two new arrivals and their apparently unimpressive horses.

"What do you want?" he demanded, although Maddie thought the answer was pretty obvious.

Will, however, maintained a subservient tone as he replied. There was no need to antagonize the man. He knew from long experience that people like this, with their own little domain and sense of self-importance, could be tyrants if not treated properly.

"The seneschal said we could stable our horses here, sir," he said.

"Did he now? And I suppose he expects me to look after them for you, does he?" the man challenged.

Will spread his hands in a placating gesture. "No, sir. He said we should look after them ourselves. We're happy to do that."

"So you should be. I don't have time to be chasing after a pair of shaggy nags like these two," the stablemaster said. Behind Maddie, Bumper raised his head and snorted indignantly. She quieted him with a quick touch of her hand.

"Put 'em in two of the stalls at the back there." The stable-master waved a vague hand at the row of unoccupied stalls at the rear of the long, low room.

"They can share one stall," Will told him. "They're small horses and they're used to each other's company."

"How lovely for them. Well, that's your choice but you'll still pay for two. There's water in the trough there, and hay and oats for them. One bin of oats every three days," he added shrewdly.

Will shrugged in acknowledgment.

"And that'll be six coppers for their feed for the week," the man said. There was a challenging note in his voice, as if he were waiting for Will to dispute the price.

Will looked at him for a long moment. He was sure that the cost of the horses' feed was covered by the fee he was paying the seneschal. But there was no point in arguing.

"Of course," he said. He rummaged in his belt purse for the six coppers and handed them over.

Perversely, the surly stablemaster looked a little disap-pointed, as if he had expected an argument. He waved a hand toward the stalls, and they led the horses into the long building.

They settled the horses into a stall, filling the feed bin with hay and the drinking trough with fresh water. Will leaned the bow case against the wall in the shadows at the back of the stall. Tug and Bumper would prevent anyone from looking at it more closely.

Then, carrying their saddlebags, and their rolled Ranger cloaks and bedding, Will and Maddie headed for the keep. Maddie waved goodbye to the stablemaster, who was repairing a harness. He scowled in reply.

"Friendly type," she said to Will as they emerged into the afternoon sunlight in the courtyard.

He shook his head. "Before we leave, I might take the time to smack him over the ear," he said.

Maddie smiled at the thought. "I'd pay you six coppers to see that," she said.

The common room on the ground floor of the keep was where they would eat and sleep while they were here. The vast room, set with tables and benches, could seat between fifty and seventy people—the less important members of the castle staff. The sleeping spaces were set in niches around the walls, each with room for a straw-filled mattress and with hooks set into the wall to hang clothes and belongings. A waist-high wooden platform served as a bed. It was covered with a thinly packed straw mattress and a coarse linen pillow. The spaces were curtained off from the main room to provide a modicum of privacy for the occupants.

They found their allotted spaces and spread their bedding

out on the straw mattresses. Will studied his and sniffed it once or twice.

"Seems clean enough," he commented.

They concealed their saxes under the bedding. Their throwing knives were in concealed sheaths—Will's strapped to his left forearm and Maddie's inside the back of her collar.

Will had shaken his head when she had selected that hiding place. Years ago, he had nearly died as a result of his knife snagging as he tried to draw it from a collar sheath. But there was no such thing as an ideal hiding place for a knife—there was always the possibility that a hidden blade could snag or catch on clothing if the owner tried to draw it too quickly.

He glanced around the room. There was a low buzz of conversation from the other people seated around the walls. There were about twenty of them in all. The rest were doubtless still on duty in the castle. They'd arrive as the day drew on and the evening mealtime approached.

"I'll play a little after we've eaten," Will told Maddie. "Once I've got their attention, you slip away and check out the higher floors of the keep. We need to know where Lassigny is holding the prince."

"Is there anything specific I should be looking for?" Maddie asked.

"Look for any rooms where there are guards on duty. Anywhere they seem to want to keep nosy strangers out."

"Do you think he'll be in the keep?"

He shook his head. "Probably not. But we might as well start here."

Some twenty minutes later, the serving staff from the basement kitchen brought the evening meal in. They placed half a

dozen big cauldrons on the tables, spacing them out. Other servers brought stacks of wooden bowls and spoons. The numbers
of people waiting in the room had doubled as the mealtime grew
closer. Will glanced at one of the high-set windows in the wall,
above the row of sleeping spaces. It was still daylight outside.
Obviously, the staff ate at an earlier hour than the knights and
nobles in Lassigny's dining hall.

He and Maddie found places at one of the tables and he
ladled food from one of the big pots into two of the wooden
bowls. He dipped up a spoon and tasted cautiously. The meal, a
lamb and vegetable stew, was surprisingly good, although a little
over-flavored for his taste.

"Heavy on the garlic," he muttered. "Typical Gallic cooking."

Maddie had no such reservations, and she ate quickly, dipping a broken-off piece from a long bread loaf into the stew.
There was more vegetable than lamb, she noted. But the food
was hot and well flavored. The gravy was rich and the bread was
light and airy—unlike the flat, heavy loaves she was used to in
Araluen. She finished her bowl in quick time and glanced around
the room. Seeing other diners helping themselves to additional
servings, she spooned more of the stew into her bowl and continued eating.

"Slow down," Will cautioned her. "You'll give yourself a
bellyache." But she noticed that he too had a second helping,
then pushed his bench back from the table, a satisfied look on
his face.

"Not bad," he said contentedly. "Not bad at all."

The servers had set out jugs of water, ale, wine and coffee on
the tables. Will tasted the wine and pulled a face. It wasn't to his
liking. He poured himself a mug of coffee instead, looking round

hopefully for a bowl of honey. But there was none and he shrugged, drinking the coffee unsweetened. He would have preferred to have it sweetened but it was good coffee, with a rich flavor, and eminently drinkable, he thought.

Gradually, the other diners finished their meals and the servers took the pots and bowls away, leaving the coffee and wine jugs on the tables. The people seated at the tables broke up into smaller groups, placing their stools in circles and leaning forward toward each other as they conversed in lowered tones.

Will rose and moved to his sleeping space, where his mandola was on his bed. He opened the leather case and removed the instrument, checking its tuning as he did so. Maddie, who had gone with him, noticed several of the people sitting around the room glancing at him curiously.

"You're going to perform?" she asked.

He shook his head. "I'm going to sit quietly to one side and provide a little background music," he said. "People don't always want their conversations interrupted. Those who want to listen rather than talk can gather round me."

He settled his mandola's strap around his shoulders and turned toward the tables once more. "You wait here," he said. "Once I've drawn a bit of attention away from you, slip away and see if you can find where they're holding Prince Giles."

Maddie waited by her sleeping niche, pretending to store her clothes on the hanging hooks and shelves provided. Will moved across the room, hooking a stool with his foot, then carrying it to a spot against the far wall.

He sat down and began quietly strumming a few chords. There was a brief lull in the various conversations around the room as people turned to look at him. Most resumed their conversations, but some turned their stools in his direction as he began to sing quietly. After the first song, half a dozen moved their stools into a small semicircle around him. He smiled at them and struck up another song.

Maddie glanced around. Nobody seemed to be paying any attention to her. Quietly, she slipped away along the row of sleeping spaces and out the big double doors.

33

From the ground floor, there was a wide central stairway leading to the higher levels of the keep. Maddie clung to the walls of the big room, staying out of sight as far as possible. Once she started upward, she would be open to challenge. She had no excuse for being in this part of the castle, other than curiosity—and she didn't think that would be a particularly valid excuse if she were spotted.

Fortunately, the daylight was nearly gone and the interior of the building was poorly lit. What windows there were were small and narrow—tall, wide windows didn't make for a good defensive design. Still, as she mounted the wide stairway, she felt horribly exposed and visible. She stayed close to the balustrade, her soft-soled boots whispering on the timber stairs, and ghosted her way upward. Her skin crawled as she imagined dozens of unseen eyes watching her progress.

The first floor was the site for Lassigny's office and living quarters. The door to the office was open and she could see the massive desk, strewn with papers and notes. There was no sign of the Baron, or any of his staff. She assumed he would be in his living quarters, preparing for the evening meal.

She edged around the stairway. The wide timber stairs continued from this level up to the third. She paused at the foot of the second flight of stairs, peering upward, exposing as little of her body as possible to any observer who might be looking down from the third floor. Seeing nothing, hearing nothing, she went upward again, moving more quickly in her eagerness to be finished with this exposed position.

She stopped at the top of the steps and took stock. This was obviously the dining hall for the Baron and his senior staff. As she watched, servants were moving among the long tables, setting places for that night's meal. None of the serving staff paid any attention to her, if they noticed her at all. She quickly continued up to the next floor.

As she reached the top of the stairs, the seneschal's office, where she and Will had requested accommodation, was directly ahead of her. The large brassbound door was closed and there was no sound of movement from within. She looked around the third floor. The other three walls were lined with heavy timber doors, all closed. Light was provided by a line of torches set in sconces on the walls. She quickly moved to a spot halfway between two, where the shadows were thickest. She paused, watching and listening.

There was no sound, although the beating of her heart seemed deafening to her. Crouched back in the shadows, she studied the layout of this floor.

The wide central stairway went no farther and she looked for access to the higher floors.

In two of the corners, the line of heavy timber doors was broken by narrower, open doorways. Inside one, she could see the first few rows of steps leading upward. She hurried toward the nearest doorway and peered inside.

A flight of steps spiraled around the interior of the narrow space. As was always the case in castles, the spiral ran from left to right. This meant that an attacker coming up the stairs would have to expose his entire body to use his sword, while a right-handed defender would only need to expose his right arm. Maddie peered upward. The light in the stairway was uncertain. There were no torches set in the wall. There was only the light reflected from the third and fourth levels to illuminate the stairs. She mounted them quickly, her ears alert for the sound of anyone coming down. If that happened, she'd have to turn and race back down the stairs and find a hiding place on the floor below. But there was no sound of anyone moving and she emerged onto the fourth floor.

This was a large, open space, with high windows set along two walls. The defensive needs weren't as important this high up, she knew. She stepped out into the open space and looked around. The two windowless walls were lined with racks of weapons and armor. This floor was obviously devoted to a weapons practice room and the castle armory.

The tall windows provided light for people practicing their weapon skills. Many of the weapons in the racks were wooden practice weapons, she could see.

She turned back to the stairway and continued upward.

So far, she had seen nothing that suggested the presence of a prisoner being held in any of the rooms, and the next two floors were similarly disappointing. A narrow corridor ran around each floor, pierced either side with doors. Those on the outer side were spaced farther apart and she guessed they would be apartments or suites for senior knights and nobles in Lassigny's court. The doors on the inner side of the corridor were spaced more closely together. She tried one and the handle moved under her touch. Heart pounding, she eased the door open a crack and cautiously peered around.

She heard a rustle of movement and froze, ready to run for the stairway. Then the silence was broken by an unmistakable sound—someone was snoring. She eased the door open farther and peered into the room.

A young man, half dressed, was lying on his back on a narrow bed set opposite the door. His eyes were closed and his chest rose and fell rhythmically. In addition to the bed, the room contained a table and chair and an armoire. A liveried jerkin was hanging over the back of the chair.

A squire, she guessed. The size of the room and the meager furnishing seemed to bear out the theory. Carefully, she eased the door closed, making as little noise as possible. The snoring continued, muffled now with the closed door between her and the young man. She studied the nearest door on the outer side of the corridor. She moved closer to it and laid her ear against it. From within, she could hear the faint murmur of voices—male and female. That seemed to confirm her theory that these were apartments kept for the senior knights and their families. Silently, she moved down the corridor and listened at the next door. This time, she heard nothing—no voices, no sound of movement from within. She tried the door handle and it moved easily, the latch slipping open with a soft click.

The door opened inward and she leaned her weight against it, holding the door handle and opening the door several centimeters. She paused. Her heart was thumping and her pulse was racing. She would have no excuse if she were discovered now. Taking a deep breath, she eased the door open a half meter and peered round the edge, ready to take to her heels at a moment's notice.

She was looking into a well-furnished living room. The floor was carpeted with several rugs. Two wing chairs stood either side of the fireplace and a wooden settle was ranged along one wall. A dining table set with four straight-backed chairs was by the window. Several doors led off to other rooms, confirming her guess that this was an apartment or suite. As she looked, she heard a door slam from farther inside the apartment, and a male voice speaking. Quickly, she closed the door once more and headed for the stairs.

The next floor, when she emerged onto it, was a similar layout—smaller rooms on the inner side of the corridor and larger suites on the outer side, where the inhabitants would enjoy views out over the lake and the surrounding countryside. It was possible that Prince Giles was being held in one of the apartments, she reasoned. But there was no sign of guards posted anywhere, which would seem to discount that idea. She hurried along the corridor, stopping at each corner to peer round and make sure nobody was watching.

The corridor was deserted, and in a few minutes she was back at her starting point. The tension was unbearable. She was continually keying herself up to round each corner, expecting every moment to run into someone, poised to run for her life. Then, as there was no sign of anyone, she found the adrenaline draining away from her. Her jagged breathing grew more relaxed. She paused, took several deep breaths to calm herself. It was time to leave, she thought.

"There's no one here," she told herself softly. "Just relax."

And as she said the words, the door beside her opened and a

burly figure, clad in green-and-yellow livery, emerged from one of the apartments and barged into her.

There was a moment's confusion as the two of them stumbled apart. The man uttered a surprised oath, then peered at her suspiciously.

"Who are you?" he demanded. "What are you doing here?" He grabbed hold of her arm in a powerful grip.

"Changing the bed linen," she replied immediately, and turned to go.

But the man wasn't satisfied. "Where's the linen cart?" he asked roughly.

She knew that the chambermaids would have pushcarts piled with fresh linen, with space underneath for the used sheets and pillows that they were replacing. She pointed down the corridor.

"There."

As he turned his head, she tried to pull free of his grasp. Catching him by surprise, she nearly made it. Her arm slipped from his hand. But he instantly snatched at her again, grabbing her by the wrist, and pulled her toward him.

He was expecting her to pull away from him again. Instead, she suddenly stepped toward him. Caught by surprise, he instinctively pushed back against her. As he did, she grabbed a handful of his tunic, bent her legs and shoved her backside into his body. With their bodies pinned together, she straightened her knees, using the strength of her legs to lift him from the floor, and heaved him up and over her hip in a whirl of arms and legs.

He hit the floor with a shattering thud. The breath was driven from him in a loud *whoof!*

Maddie ran.

She glanced back as she reached the stairwell. The knight was staggering awkwardly to his feet, supporting himself against the corridor wall. Then he lurched after her, breathing heavily.

She flew down the first flight of stairs, her soft boots making virtually no sound. She had reached the floor below when she heard his heavy boots on the steps above her. She went down the next flight two at a time. This time, when she reached the bottom, she darted out into the corridor and set off for the second spiral staircase, set at the next corner of the tower. She reached it and plunged into the dimly lit interior. Behind her, she heard the lumbering steps of her pursuer coming down from the next floor. She paused, listening as the footsteps went past the entrance to the stairwell and the man continued downward. Then, figuring he would assume that this was the last thing she would do, she went back up the stairs again.

This time, she kept going until she reached the top floor. It was used for storage. Old furniture, armor, boxes of clothing and bedding were piled in the center of the floor. At each wall, a doorway led out onto a balcony, which afforded a view over the surrounding countryside. She assumed that this floor would be used as a lookout in time of war. She finally relaxed, letting her breathing settle. She pushed a pile of folded curtains to one side to make a hiding place and crouched down behind them. She didn't think the knight would continue to hunt for her once he realized she'd given him the slip. But she waited for an hour until it was full dark, then crept down the stairs to the common room.

As she entered, she saw Will sitting to one side, talking to several of the kitchen hands. His mandola was on the table between them. He saw her enter and glanced at her, one eyebrow raised in a question.

She shook her head and made her way to her sleeping space. She dropped onto the bed, exhausted by the tension of her encounter and near capture.

Wearily, she pulled the curtain closed.

34

Behind the keep, in the northwestern corner of the bailey, there was a terraced garden.

It was intended to provide an outdoor recreation area for the castle inhabitants in those times when enemies might be attacking and the castle gates were kept closed. After all, Maddie thought, the staff and garrison could hardly spend all their time enclosed in their rooms or in the public halls of the keep. There would have to be some sense of normality maintained in their day-to-day living.

The gate and portcullis were both open today, of course. There was no sign of an apparent threat to the castle and the usual stream of traffic made its way across the causeway and into the bailey. But they came nowhere near the pleasant, grassy space. The kitchens and storerooms were located on the opposite side of the castle and access to the garden was limited to those staying within the castle.

Will and Maddie were sitting on one of the stone benches set under an arbor of trees. It was midafternoon and Will had been playing and singing to a small but appreciative group in the garden. Now he had set the mandola aside and the audience had drifted away, some of them tossing coins into the open mandola case on the grass between his feet.

He waited till the last of the audience had moved away, out of earshot.

This was the first chance he and Maddie had to discuss her exploration the previous night. The common room had too many people, and too many potential hiding places for eavesdroppers. Here, in the open, they could see if anyone came too close.

"Do you think he'd recognize you again?" he asked. Maddie had already told him about her encounter on the upper floor of the keep.

She shook her head. "I was wearing my cap and I had my hair bundled up under it. I doubt he even knew I was a girl."

Will smiled. "Even if he suspected it, his manly pride would hardly let him admit to it. You seem to have thrown him about like a sack of oats. Girls aren't supposed to do that."

"I'll bear it in mind next time I meet him," Maddie said. "Not that I'd recognize him, either. It was pretty dark in that corridor. Although I'd recognize his livery," she added as an afterthought.

"Odds are he's done nothing more about it. Probably thought you were sneaking around looking for something to steal. He may have reported it to the seneschal, but what can he do about it? You're long gone and nothing was stolen. That's hardly worth starting a hue and cry."

"At least we know that the prince isn't in the keep," Maddie said.

"I didn't really think he would be," Will replied. "Too much coming and going in the keep. Too many people around. He's probably in one of the towers—on a high floor. I'd guess that Lassigny would want to keep him out of sight as far as possible."

"Speak of the devil," Maddie said in a warning tone.

Will followed the direction of her gaze. Baron Lassigny was strolling through the garden area, accompanied by his seneschal. The two men were deep in conversation, their heads close together, which gave Will and Maddie a good opportunity to study him. They had seen him before, but only at a distance and only fleetingly.

He was taller than average, which meant he had to stoop to speak to the shorter man beside him. He was powerfully built, with broad shoulders. There appeared to be no excess fat on him. He was fit-looking and muscular. His hair was close cropped—black but with traces of gray at the temples. His skin was olive complexioned and he had no beard. Dark brown eyes, almost black, were set under heavy brows. They made Maddie think of a hawk's eyes and, like a hawk, they seemed not to blink. The nose was strong and the features were even. All in all, the Baron was a handsome figure of a man. He wore a green surcoat, emblazoned with a yellow hawk's body in plan form—stylized so that the wings formed a heart's shape. The hawk clasped a short spear in its talons.

As they strolled, the seneschal's eyes lit on Will and Maddie sitting on the stone bench. He said something to the Baron and pointed in their direction. Those dark brown eyes trained on them and studied them closely. Maddie shifted awkwardly. She had the feeling that Lassigny could see past her innocent exterior and read her thoughts.

Will seemed to sense her discomfort. "Relax," he said softly as the two men changed direction and strode across the grass toward them. As they came closer, Will rose from the bench, tipping Maddie's elbow to prompt her to do the same.

Baron Lassigny stopped a few meters short of them, feet apart, fists on his hips as he stared at them. It was an aggressive stance, a dominant one. It was the body language of a man who knew he was looking at his inferiors.

"My lord," said Will, bowing his head.

"You're the jongleur," Lassigny said. His voice was deep and resonant—courtesy of that heavyset body and broad chest.

"That's right, my lord. I'm Will Accord, of Araluen. This is my daughter, Madelyn."

The hawklike gaze switched briefly to Maddie, who dropped into a curtsey. She kept her eyes and face down so that Lassigny wouldn't see the twist on her lips. She hated curtseying. It was demeaning and submissive. If a man simply had to bow his head, as Will had done, why shouldn't a woman do the same?

Lassigny's gaze flicked back to Will, who straightened now from his bow. "I'm told you're quite good," the Baron said.

Will smiled ingratiatingly. "You're very kind, my lord."

Lassigny shook his head suddenly. His movements all tended to be sudden and abrupt. "*I* didn't say so," he said. "I said I'm *told* you're quite good. I'll reserve my opinion until I hear you perform."

Will said nothing. There was nothing to say, after all. He inclined his head once more.

Lassigny turned to the seneschal. "When can we hear him, Gaston?" he asked, then answered his own question. "Tomorrow night?"

The seneschal nodded. "You are dining your nobles and knights tomorrow night, sir. That would be a good opportunity."

"Tomorrow night then, at the ninth hour," Lassigny told Will. He stepped closer and flicked a disparaging hand at Will's soiled outfit. "Try to clean yourself up. You look like a beggar, not a jongleur."

"Yes, sir," Will said, maintaining his obsequious smile with an effort.

The Baron snorted dismissively and turned away, resuming his conversation with the seneschal as if Maddie and Will didn't exist. Again, Will bowed and Maddie curtseyed.

"So, Gaston, let's lean on that wine merchant. He's making a fortune from us. Time to make it a little less."

"Yes, my lord," the seneschal replied, and they moved out of earshot. The two Rangers straightened. They exchanged a glance.

"Tidy yourself up," Maddie said, in a fair imitation of Lassigny's bullying tone. Will rolled his eyes and they resumed their seats on the bench.

"At least we know most of his knights will be dining together tomorrow," Will said. "That'll give you a chance to take a look at the towers. That's where I'd guess he's holding Giles."

Maddie gazed around at the four towers that formed the corners of the chateau. They were identical, each with a heavy wooden door at the base giving onto the bailey. They rose to the level of the curtain wall without any break in their walls, other than a few narrow slits to allow archers or crossbowmen to shoot down into the interior. Above the level of the fighting platform around the top of the crenelated walls, there were larger openings, denoting rooms or suites of rooms.

"Where do I start?" Maddie said. One tower looked much the same as the others.

As she spoke, they heard the door to the keep open and then bang shut. Two kitchen hands were crossing the cobbled courtyard, heading for the southwestern tower. They carried a tray covered with a napkin and a large pottery flagon and several wooden goblets. As Maddie and Will watched, they paused at the heavy door and hammered on it three times. There was a short pause, then the door creaked open. Inside, the two observers could see several armed soldiers. The soldiers checked briefly to see who was outside, then opened the door farther to allow the kitchen hands to enter. A few seconds later, the door closed behind them. Even from this distance, Will and Maddie heard the metallic jangle of a key turning in the heavy lock.

"Let's see," Will mused. "The midday meal is just over, and a tray of food and wine is being taken to someone in the southwest tower. I'd say that's where you might find young Giles."

35

"I'LL NOSE AROUND TONIGHT," MADDIE SAID AS THEY HEADED back to the keep. "I need to work out how to get into the tower and up the stairs. Then, when you're singing tomorrow night, I'll get inside and see if I can find where they're holding Giles."

"I'd say you're going to have to climb the outside of the tower," Will said. "You need to get past the door guards and that seems to be the only way to do it."

Maddie paused and turned to look back at the tower. It was constructed from large granite blocks and, from this distance, they looked to have plenty of gaps for potential hand- and footholds. She was an accomplished climber and had no fear of heights.

"I wouldn't worry about the first three floors," Will said. "The ones up to the level of the curtain wall. They'll be ready rooms for defenders when the castle is under attack. Above the level of the curtain wall you can see there are apartments. That's where you'll find him."

"I think I'll take a closer look at the stonework," Maddie said, turning back toward the tower.

Will stopped her with a hand on her arm. "Don't go looking

at the southwest tower," he cautioned her. "If that's where they're holding Giles, you don't want to arouse any suspicions. Have a look at the northwest tower. They're the same construction. If one is climbable, the others will be."

She nodded and strolled back toward the garden where they had been sitting. Will watched her go for a minute or so, then turned away toward the keep.

Doing her best to look casual, Maddie strolled through the grassed garden area, angling toward the corner tower. Baron Lassigny and the seneschal had gone back to their offices, and there were only a handful of people still in the garden. The rest had gone back to their workplaces now that the lunch hour was over. She stopped to peer into a fishpond set under an outcrop of rock. Large carp nosed the surface of the green water, searching for errant insects that might have fallen in, leaving expanding rings on the surface as they sank back into the depths. She took the opportunity to look around, but nobody seemed to be interested in her movements. She resumed her casual stroll, moving closer to the northwest tower.

She checked her surroundings once more. The nearest people to her were a young couple standing under a low tree, holding hands and looking deep into each other's eyes. They definitely weren't interested in her, she thought.

She moved closer to the tower, studying the rough gray walls and the heavy, iron-reinforced door at the base. A few meters away, a wooden stairway led up to the fighting platform that ran along the inside of the crenelated curtain wall. She nodded thoughtfully to herself, turning to look back at the southwest tower. There was a similar flight of steps there. Obviously, the steps were intended to provide access for defenders to reach the walkway that ran along the inside of the wall. Additional access would come from the towers, she realized. She looked back at the one near her. At the level of the walkway above her, she could see another timber door giving access from the tower.

Considering Will's comment about the lower levels of the tower providing barracks for defenders, it made sense that they would be able to access the defensive walkways from within.

She checked around her again. Nobody was watching her. The young couple had withdrawn into the shadows of the tree and were locked in an embrace.

"Young love," she muttered derisively. Then she moved close to the tower, studying its construction.

The massive granite blocks were fitted together roughly. They were unevenly shaped, leaving substantial gaps between each one—gaps that had been loosely filled with mortar. Over the years, much of the exterior mortar had worn away. She slipped her right hand into one of the horizontal gaps. It was a firm handhold, with plenty of room for her hand. Tentatively, she slipped her toe into another gap at ground level and tested her weight on it. Again, there was plenty of room and plenty of support. She would have no trouble climbing the wall, she thought, although she would be exposed to view for the lower section of the climb, up to the walkway.

She stepped back from the wall—and not a moment too soon. The heavy door, only a few meters away, suddenly slammed open, and a guard stepped out. He looked at her, a mixture of surprise and suspicion on his face.

"What do you want?" he demanded roughly. "What are you doing here?"

"Just looking around," she said innocently. "Exploring the castle. I only got here yesterday." She smiled at him but there was no answering smile. He continued to glare at her.

"Could I take a peek inside?" she asked artlessly, gesturing toward the dark interior of the tower behind him. "I've never seen inside a real castle before."

"No!" he snapped angrily. "Do you think I'm running sightseeing tours here? Clear off out of it!"

He raised a threatening hand and she stepped quickly back out of reach.

"All right!" she said hurriedly. "I'm sorry!"

Making apologetic gestures, she hurried quickly back through the garden. She glanced back once when she was fifteen meters or so away. The soldier was still watching her. Then, as she looked back, he made a further threatening gesture and stepped back inside, slamming the door behind him. Despite the distance, she heard the rattle of a large key in a lock.

She slowly resumed her walk, rubbing her chin thoughtfully with her finger and thumb. Why was the guard so aggressive? she wondered. Why was he so keen for her to stay away from the tower? Was it because this was where Prince Giles was being held captive? That would certainly explain his overzealousness and his warning for her to keep away.

Then she considered further. They hadn't seen any food being taken to this tower, she realized. And the towers and ramparts were essential components in the castle's defensive structure. It was logical that the sentries would discourage random visitors and prying eyes. She had no doubt that if she approached any of the other towers, she'd receive the same short shrift and lack of welcome. But she wasn't about to test her theory. The southwest tower would seem to be the most likely place to find the prince.

"Besides, I have to start somewhere," she said to herself. "So it might as well be there."

Head down and deep in thought, she didn't notice the old beggar sitting under a tree in the garden until she was almost level with him.

"S'il vous plait, mam'selle?" he said in a gravelly voice, snapping her out of her distracted state.

She glanced quickly at him. He must have been among the many day visitors who streamed across the causeway each morning seeking entrance to the castle, she thought. He was bent over, not looking at her, but with a begging cup held out to her. His white hair and beard were long and unkempt and he was wearing a ragged blue-and-white-striped cloak. She reached into her purse and found a few small coins, dropping them into his cup and moving on.

"Thank you, miss," he called after her. She had gone another ten paces before it registered with her that he had used the common tongue, not Gallic—which he had used when he first spoke to her. Yet she hadn't spoken or given him any reason to believe she wasn't Gallican.

And there had been something vaguely familiar about him.

She turned quickly to look back at him but there was no sign of the blue-and-white-cloaked figure. She frowned.

Odd, she thought. Then she shook her head, dismissing the beggar from her thoughts. She had other matters to concern her.

"Better not do any more poking around," Will told her as they sat in a secluded corner of the common room. "You don't want people noticing that you're interested in the towers."

She nodded agreement. "I'll keep my distance," she said. "But I want to check out the sentries' schedule tonight. I plan to take the stairs to the walkway at the top of the wall, then move around to the outside of the tower and start my climb from there."

Will considered her plan for a few seconds. "Good idea," he said finally. "You'd be fairly conspicuous climbing from ground level. This way, if you move to the outside of the tower, you'll be pretty much out of sight." He paused, then added, "Just make sure you don't fall."

Maddie grinned. "That'll be the last thing I do," she said.

Will raised an eyebrow. "You might like to rephrase that," he said.

The following night, Maddie crouched in the shadows under the stairway that led to the top of the curtain wall.

She listened to the measured tread of the sentry's feet on the wooden platform above her. The current batch of sentries had been on duty for just over two hours now, with another hour to go before they were due for relief. She had timed their schedule and their patrol patterns the night before. In her mind's eye, she visualized the man on the ramparts above her. At this point, well into his scheduled three hours, he would be thinking more about his relief than about possible attackers approaching the castle.

It was only human nature, she thought. At the beginning of his watch, the man would be energized and motivated, ready to investigate or query any stray sound or perceived movement. But as the first hour passed, then the second, without any sign of a threat, inevitably, his alertness would be blunted, his motivation dissipated. His hands would grow cold in the brisk night air. His feet would begin to ache from the constant pacing in stiff boots on unyielding planks.

And worse than the physical discomforts of patrolling the ramparts would be the boredom that would set in. With no conversation—other than a few casual words with his opposite number as they met in the center of the walkway—his mind would begin to be dulled by the constant repetition and lack of mental stimulation.

She frowned as she thought about it. It was a useful lesson for the future, she thought: If you were assigning men to sentry duty, don't give them all the same start and finish times. Vary them so there were always fresh eyes and alert minds coming on duty.

Above her, she heard the boots scrape as the man reached the end of his section, close to the massive wall of the southwest tower. He paused, resting for a second or two, and she heard the distinct sound of his yawning. Then the boots started again, trudging now and dragging slightly on the rough timbers of the walkway.

"Time to go," she said.

36

SHE SWARMED UP THE STAIRS LIKE A WRAITH, STAYING LOW, a silent shadow against the dark shadows of the wall behind her. As she neared the top, she heard the sentry turning at the end of his patrol, his boots scuffing the boards, breaking the steady rhythm of his marching. Instantly, she dropped to the rough timber of the staircase, her cloak spread around her, masking her shape and turning her into an anonymous dark mass. She was still below the level of the walkway so she had no real fear that the sentry would see her. But her heart still beat faster as he came closer. Logic was all very well, but when you were only a few meters away from an armed enemy, it wasn't possible to stay completely unconcerned.

Again, the man stopped at the end of his patrol, close to the stone wall of the tower. He stepped closer to the crenellations and peered over the side into the darkness below. Obviously seeing nothing, he sighed and turned again to retrace his path back to the center of the wall. She let him go a few meters, then, on hands and knees, she slipped up the rest of the steps and moved across the walkway, crouching in the shadows at the base of the wall where it met the tower.

She glanced down the walkway after the sentry. He was twenty meters away, pausing to talk briefly to his opposite number. She would have to remain where she was until he had returned to his start point and turned away again. At that point, the other sentry, even though he would be facing her, would be forty meters away and her movements would be shielded by the uncertain light. But she would have no time to waste.

As the sentry approached again, she huddled at the base of the wall, her cloak pulled tight around her, her face masked by the deep cowl. She hoped that this time, the sentry wouldn't choose to peer over the wall. If he did so, he would be almost certain to tread on her.

She crouched, eyes down, listening to the footsteps coming closer, expecting any moment for them to stop and to hear the sentry's sharp exclamation of surprise as he spotted her. But he came on, his pace unvarying.

For a few seconds, she considered waiting until he had turned and then entering the tower at this level, using the large wooden door. She was certain it was unlocked—she had heard the sentry come through it when he began his vigil and there had been no sound of a key turning after he had closed the door behind him. That would get her out of sight much more quickly than if she clambered up onto the curtain wall and climbed around to the outside of the tower.

But she quickly discarded the idea. The tower room on the other side of the door would probably be a ready room for soldiers assigned to guard duty that night. The next shift were probably dozing on bunks in there at the moment, waiting their turn to take over the watch. That was how things were organized at Castle Araluen, she knew. And at Castle Redmont.

There was no reason to suppose things were any different here. If she went into the tower at this level, chances were she would be walking in on up to a dozen armed men.

Better to stick to the original plan. Go up a few floors, check to find an unoccupied room and then gain entry to the tower.

Again, the sentry was approaching. She controlled her breathing, keeping it smooth and steady and, most important, virtually silent. With her head and eyes down, she couldn't see the sentry. But she could hear him and actually sense his presence close to her. It seemed impossible that he wouldn't notice the dark shadow crouched at the base of the wall. He *must* see her this time, she thought.

But she was just a shadow among other shadows. The footsteps stopped. She heard him pivot and then begin to walk away. Incredibly, he had overlooked her, even though she was only a few meters away from him.

People see what they expect to see. She heard Will's voice in her mind. He had spent years dinning into her brain that utter stillness was the best form of concealment in a situation like this. The sentry didn't expect to see a small figure crouched in the shadow line at the base of the wall. Therefore, he *didn't* see her.

With a start, she realized she was wasting valuable time thinking about this. The sentry was already a quarter of the way along his beat. And that meant that the far sentry was getting closer, to a point where he might notice her moving.

Swiftly, she rose and vaulted up onto the crenelated wall. She took a few seconds to study the surface of the tower wall facing her, then selected two handholds and a gap in the stones for her right foot. She swung herself up and out over the dizzying drop, clinging to the tower wall like a giant spider.

Her left foot reached out, searching the uneven tower wall, seeking a crevice to support her. She found one and transferred the bulk of her weight to it, removing her left hand from its hold and reaching along the wall, to the left and upward. She found another sizable gap in the stones, tested it and found it was firm. Once her left hand was established once more, she removed her right foot from its purchase point and sought another.

Always keep three points of contact with the wall, Will had taught her.

As she set her right foot in a crack, she glanced back over her shoulder. She had moved out and around the curve of the tower a few meters but she could still see the sentry on his patrol path. He was turning now, having met his opposite number halfway along the wall, and heading back. She froze in place. It was unlikely that the sentry's eyes would be on the outside wall of the tower, but any movement now might catch his attention and give her away. She huddled against the rough stone of the tower, spread-eagled, with her hands and feet wide apart. Below her, she was conscious of the small waves on the lake tumbling against the rocks. The wind out here on the tower was stronger, and it sighed around her ears.

For a moment, she had a sensation that her hands were slipping and that she was about to topple backward and go crashing to the rocks below. But she fought down the treacherous feeling. She was firmly established on the wall, with secure hand- and footholds. There was nothing to fear—other than the fear of falling itself.

She knew some people, in fact most people, suffered from this false perception. It was why so many people would fall from a high place—as if the fall itself beckoned them.

She settled her breathing once more, pressing against the stone, feeling the security of her position until the sudden fear passed. She could hear the sentry, pacing slowly along his beat. He had almost reached the end of this pattern. She listened for the slight scuff of his boots as he turned, and when she heard them she began to climb again.

Left hand, right foot, right hand, left foot. She moved smoothly out and up, the only break in her rhythm coming when she didn't immediately locate a new foot- or handhold and was forced to search for one. She glanced back again. She had moved out around the curve of the tower wall now and the sentry behind her was obscured from her sight. If she moved farther around the wall, she would become exposed to the view of the sentry on the next section. Now was the time to simply move up.

She looked up. There was a window a few meters above her, the stone window ledge standing out from the wall. There was no sign of a light behind the window. Either the room behind it was in darkness or there were curtains drawn across it. She came closer, peering over the rough stone windowsill, and saw that it was the former. There were no curtains but the room behind the thick, uneven glazing was dark and still.

"Which is not to say there's not someone sleeping in there," she muttered to herself. She decided she was still too close to the guards' ready room—just one floor above it. She would go higher before attempting to enter the tower itself.

She looked up, leaning out slightly. It was a movement that would have sent another person toppling backward off the window ledge, but after that brief moment of vertigo, she had recovered her equanimity completely and was totally at home on her precarious perch.

There was another window, with a similar window ledge, four meters above her. As far as she could see, it too was unlit. She felt for handholds on the rough wall of the tower, found purchase for her right foot and pushed off once more, climbing steadily upward.

As she came closer, she saw that she had been mistaken. There was a glimmer of light showing through the window. She pursed her lips in a moue of disappointment and continued up to the next window, a floor above it.

This time, there was no light showing. The interior of the room was in darkness. She perched on the windowsill, framing her hands around her eyes and trying to pierce the interior darkness.

After several seconds, she gave up.

"Only one way to find out," she told herself. She shifted her position slightly and studied the window. It was in two halves, each one hinged and with a latch at the center. It was a simple tongue and socket lock. She could clearly see the handle that moved the tongue up and down into the socket. The gap between the two halves of the window was a narrow one—too narrow for the heavy blade of the saxe she wore at her belt. She reached behind her neck and felt for the hilt of her throwing knife. Its blade was thinner than the saxe's.

She carefully worked it into the gap between the two window halves. It was a tight fit but the more she waggled it and jiggled it, the more its movement freed. She placed the blade under the lock's tongue and levered upward.

For a moment, nothing moved. Then the tongue flew up with a loud *click!* and the lock was free. She put pressure on the blade, forcing the right-hand window—the one farthest from her—to open outward, catching hold of it before it could bang against the stone window frame.

She heard movement inside the room and the breath stopped in her throat as she listened. Then she relaxed. It was something moving with the wind, which was now coming through the open window—a wall hanging or a curtain. She waited a half minute to see if there was any further noise—any sound of breathing or the stirring of a body under bedcovers.

Nothing.

She slipped the knife back into its sheath behind her neck. Since the window opened outward, she couldn't open the half nearest her as she was blocking its movement. She took the simplest way through the open half, jackknifing her body over the sill so that she went through headfirst, reaching down with her hands to find the floor. She lowered herself to the floor, bringing her legs and feet smoothly through the open window after her, and rolled forward in a slow somersault, coming to her feet in the same movement.

She stood, waiting for her eyes to become accustomed to the darkness, poised and ready with her hand on the hilt of the saxe at her side.

The room was empty.

37

WILL FINISHED HIS PLANNED SET OF SONGS WITH A RINGING chord on the mandola. He bowed deeply from the waist as the room burst into loud applause, and the knights and their ladies seated at the lower tables began to shower coins toward him.

As has been noted, he was a good performer—a skilled musician and a singer with a pleasant voice and a good range. Moreover, he had learned many years ago from Berrigan how to structure a set of songs for an audience.

Don't give away your best songs too early, the older jongleur had told him. *You have to build an audience's interest, so your early songs must be good—rousing and entertaining—but not your best. They follow when the audience is captured and ready to participate.*

Added to the fact that he was a good performer, the audience here in Chateau des Falaises was somewhat starved for entertainment. The chateau was not on any of the main highways through the country. It was something of a backwater and traveling entertainers were rare here.

Baron Lassigny's reputation was another factor that kept travelers away. He was known to have an unpredictable temper and a sadistic mind if someone got on the wrong side of him.

That was enough to deter the majority of traveling entertainers from making the trip to this relatively out-of-the-way spot.

More fool them, Will thought as he bent and scooped the coins into his hat. There was a sizable weight of money in there when he finished. And he noted that few of the coins were copper. Most were silver, with a smattering of gold coins as well. There was something to be said for traveling to a chateau where entertainers were few and far between.

He bowed deeply to the room again, then transferred the contents of his hat to the purse hanging from his belt.

"Jongleur."

The word cut across the low hubbub of conversation in the vast room. Will turned to meet Lassigny's hawklike gaze. Once more, he bowed from the waist.

The Baron was seated at the top table, set crosswise to the long room on a raised dais. His seneschal sat on his left side and his wife on his right. The Baroness Lassigny was a tall, slim woman, with long, raven-black hair hanging down almost to her waist. She was quite beautiful, Will thought, but that was no surprise. A man with Lassigny's reputation would make sure his consort looked the part. Beautiful as she was, she had a disdainful attitude, looking down on Will, literally and figuratively, and the others in the dining hall, with a supercilious twist to her mouth. It was all too obvious that she considered herself to be superior to them all.

Two knights and the baroness's lady-in-waiting made up the rest of the table.

"My lord?" Will said, in response to the one-word summons.

Lassigny raised a hand and beckoned to him. "You may approach," he said. There was no warmth or welcome in the voice. No sense of praise for a job well done. Will set his mandola down on the nearest table and stepped forward to the base of the dais, looking up into those impenetrable eyes.

He stood, waiting. There was nothing for him to say and Lassigny looked him up and down, assessing, evaluating. Eventually, the Baron spoke again.

"Where is your daughter tonight?" he asked.

Will wasn't expecting the question, but he showed no sign of surprise or uncertainty. You don't miss much, he thought.

"She has a slight chill, my lord," he said. "She took to her bed early."

It was unlikely that the Baron would check the veracity of this reply, Will thought. He had more important matters to consider than the health of a young girl traveling with a lowly jongleur. In any event, Will and Maddie had placed a pair of pillows under her blanket and pulled the curtain shut across her sleeping niche. Any casual inspection would see a huddled figure beneath the blankets. If there was a more-than-casual inspection, questions might be asked. But if such were the case, Will's and Maddie's movements would have already aroused suspicion.

Perhaps, Will thought suddenly, Lassigny had heard about the young girl caught wandering in the upper floors of the keep. Lassigny's next statement seemed to discount this concern.

"So she missed your performance," he said. It was difficult to tell if this was intended as a statement or a question.

Will shrugged and assumed a self-effacing grin. "She has heard me sing before, my lord," he said.

Lassigny didn't return the smile. He simply nodded. "Of course. How long have you been in this country?" he asked suddenly.

Will was beginning to see a technique in his questioning: ask a series of questions and then suddenly switch tack to a new, unrelated topic.

"A few weeks, my lord. Nearly a month," he replied.

Lassigny considered the answer for several seconds. "Yet you have several Gallican songs in your repertoire," he commented.

Will nodded. "A good jongleur always prepares for a new audience, my lord. I've encountered several Gallican jongleurs traveling through Araluen. It's a close community and we tend to learn songs from one another."

Although we don't teach each other our best songs, Will thought with a wry smile. Those ones, we have to steal while our foreign colleagues aren't watching.

"A pity about your execrable accent, of course. It rather ruins the effect."

The hall was silent. The people at the tables had enjoyed Will's rendering of the Gallic folk songs he had included in his bracket. None of them had objected to his accent—although nobody was about to disagree with Lassigny's opinion. Once again, Will bowed his head in apology.

"I do my best, my lord," he said humbly.

Lassigny sniffed derisively. "If you plan to perform in my country, you should do us all the courtesy of pronouncing our language accurately," he said coldly.

There was no answer Will could think of that might not be seen as argumentative. He remained silent, meeting Lassigny's black, impenetrable stare.

Eventually, the Baron gave a small, derogatory snort and broke eye contact with Will, turning to look at the seneschal.

"Still," he said, "your performance was reasonable in spite of that shortcoming. Pay him, Gaston."

The seneschal produced a small leather sack and tossed it down to the lower level. Will caught it and glanced briefly at it while he weighed it in his hands. It wasn't very heavy. If the contents were gold, it wasn't an overly generous payment for his work. But then, he thought, *generous* was not a word one would associate with Baron Lassigny. He slipped the small sack inside his jerkin and touched his forehead with his right forefinger in salute.

"Your lordship is too kind," he said, making sure there was no trace of the sarcasm he felt in his voice. Lassigny stared at him, still unblinking. Will found himself wondering if he had actually seen the Gallic baron blink at any time. He couldn't remember doing so.

"Yes. I am." Lassigny turned to his wife, who had watched the conversation with a sneer twisting her full lips. "What do you say, my dear? Shall we have the jongleur perform for us again?"

She shrugged. "Why not? His singing is tolerable. And lord knows, there's little else to listen to of an evening."

That's a ringing endorsement if ever I heard one, Will thought.

"That's settled then," Lassigny said. "You'll sing for us again on the sixth day."

Will shifted his feet uncomfortably. "I had planned to leave on the sixth-day morning, my lord," he said. There was no harm in letting the Baron know that he wasn't planning on staying around indefinitely.

Lassigny's expression didn't alter. "You will perform for us here on the sixth day," he repeated, his tone unvarying. "Am I making myself clear?"

"Abundantly, my lord," Will replied, and bowed once more.

"And next time, make sure your daughter is with you," Lassigny told him.

38

Maddie crossed to the door and placed her ear against it, holding her breath as she listened.

There was no sound of anyone moving outside in the corridor. No sound of voices. She rested her hand on the door handle and slowly eased it down. There was a large key in the door, but as there was nobody in the room, she assumed that the door wouldn't be locked. She was right. As the door latch slid back—thankfully making very little sound—she let the door open a crack and listened again.

Again, nothing. That wasn't to say there weren't a dozen armed men in the corridor outside, waiting for her to emerge. She placed her eye against the narrow gap and tried to see out. Her view was restricted, but so far as she could see, there was nobody in sight.

"Here goes," she muttered, and eased the door fully open, moving as smoothly as she could, without rushing and making undue noise. She stepped out into the corridor, her hand on the hilt of her saxe, and quickly looked to either side.

The dimly lit space, illuminated by a row of oil lamps set on the wall, was empty. The staircase was in the center of the tower,

with rooms running round the outside wall. Quickly, she moved
to the stairs and glanced upward. These stairs didn't spiral like
the ones in the keep. They were constructed in a series of switchbacks, with two flights leading from one floor to another,
reversing direction halfway up.

The stairwell itself was square in shape, and as she peered
upward, it disappeared in darkness. Looking down, she could
see faint traces of light below her. There was no sound. She estimated she was on the sixth floor of the tower, high enough not
to hear the murmur of voices on the third floor, which was at the
height of the walkway around the curtain wall.

She stepped carefully onto the stairway, aware that such
stairs were often constructed so they moved when someone put
their weight on them, the resultant noise alerting people above
that someone was coming. Accordingly, she kept to the side of
the stairs, where any such movement would be minimal. There
was a faint squeak and she moved up another step, then progressed slowly, testing each step as she placed her foot on it. At
the fifth step, she felt excessive movement and an incipient
squeak of loose timbers rubbing together. She took her foot off
the step and placed it on the next highest.

There was no noise this time, so she continued upward, testing each step as she went. She reached the landing that marked
the switchback. It was likely that there would be more loose
boards here and she trod carefully, locating one and stepping
over it. Then she was on the second flight of the switchback,
leading to the seventh floor.

She reached the top with a minimum of noise and crouched
on hands and knees, listening. This floor seemed to be more
brightly lit than the lower floors, she noticed.

A sudden burst of laughter startled her, setting her heart racing. Two or three men, she estimated, farther along the corridor and suddenly laughing at a joke. The laughter died away and now she could make out the sound of voices talking. But they were muffled and she couldn't make out the words. Crouching low, she peered round the edge of the stairway, keeping her face as close to the floor as possible.

Five meters away, she saw four armed soldiers outside one of the doors. As she had noted, there was more light on this floor. In addition to the oil lamps, there were two large candelabra set on a table. Four canvas-and-wood chairs were ranged in a semicircle facing the door. There were a flagon and four goblets on the table. As she watched, one of the men took the flagon and filled the goblets. His companions took one each and they all drank deeply. One of them said something and there was another burst of laughter.

Seizing the opportunity, and realizing that the men's attention would be distracted momentarily, she slipped around the banister pole to the next flight of steps, and went up again. By now, she was accustomed to feeling her way and testing each step before she placed her full weight on it, and she moved more quickly. She reached the landing and the switchback and continued upward. As she did, the voices faded to a murmur once more as the stairway blocked the sound.

Four steps from the top, she slowed down. The light was dim above her and there was no sound of voices, other than the faint murmur from below, punctuated occasionally by bursts of laughter.

The eighth floor, the top floor of the tower, was a different arrangement from the lower floors. Instead of rooms set around the outer curve of the tower, it was an open space. There were no lamps here, and the only light came from the moon striking through the windows. She rose to her feet, moving into the space, and studied the room.

On one side was a large rack of crossbows and quivers, each full of quarrels. A ladder led to a trapdoor in the ceiling. She climbed quickly to the top, pushing the trapdoor open and peering out. The trapdoor gave access to a flat roof, surrounded by a crenelated wall, forming a fighting position from which crossbowmen could shoot down on enemies attacking the castle and trying to scale the curtain wall. Against the outer wall, there was a lifting beam, with several large cauldrons set beside it.

"Boiling oil or water," she muttered, glancing around and seeing a fireplace in the center of the space, where such liquids could be heated, then transferred to the lifting beam, hoisted up and poured on those below.

She lowered the trapdoor and climbed back down the ladder, studying the eighth floor once more. In addition to the rack of crossbows, there were spears in racks, a dozen bunks and several tables with benches. Obviously, in times of danger, soldiers would be stationed here to defend the castle. It was similar to the higher floors of the towers at Castle Araluen.

Orienting herself, she moved to one of the windows set round the wall, judging that it would correspond to the room below, outside which the guards were stationed. She leaned out and peered down. There was a window some four meters below her and she could see a gleam of light coming from it.

"That must be where they're holding Giles," she muttered to herself, and uncoiled the length of rope that was around her shoulders. She looked around for a point to anchor the rope and selected one of the bunks. She tested it, pushing against it to make sure it wouldn't slide across the floor when she committed her weight to it. She didn't want any noise to alert the guards who were directly below. But the bunk was solidly built from heavy timbers and she couldn't budge it.

Quickly, she knotted the end of the rope round the leg of the bunk and went to the window.

"He's on the seventh floor, in an outside chamber," Maddie said. Will glanced casually at the tower, scanning upward to the second-last floor.

"You're sure it's him?" he asked.

Maddie shrugged. "As sure as I can be. I climbed to the eighth floor and let myself down on a rope to look in the window. He's a young man, a little below average height and wearing expensive clothes. Who else could it be?"

"Does he look like the portrait the King showed us?" Will asked.

Maddie hesitated. "Who does look like their portrait?" she said finally. "It could be him, but I suspect the portrait painter erred on the side of flattery when he did that painting. For a start, he gave him a chin. But there is a strong resemblance to the King himself."

It was the morning after Maddie's exploration of the tower. They were strolling in the garden area once more—the best place to keep their conversation private. Aside from a few words when Maddie returned to the common room the night before, it was the first time they had had to compare notes.

"What's on the top floor?" Will asked.

"It's open space. I'd say it's intended to be part of the castle's defenses in case of an attack. There's access to the flat roof above it, and there are racks of crossbows and weapons and bunks for troops."

"And you didn't make contact with him last night?"

Maddie shook her head. "I didn't. I figured there'd be a risk we might be overheard by the guards outside. And I knew we'd have to contact him again to get him out. I thought this way I'd halve the risk."

Will considered this for a few seconds. "Good thinking," he said.

"How will we get him out?" Maddie asked.

Will rubbed his chin with thumb and forefinger. "I guess we can get him out of the tower easily enough. We'll take him back up to the top floor, then down the stairs and out through the window on the sixth. We can lower him on a rope if he's not up to climbing."

Maddie rolled her eyes. "He's a Gallic prince. I doubt he's up to climbing. Or much else."

"Getting him out of the castle is another matter. The only way out is the main gate and the causeway. We'll hide him in the stables until the sixth hour, when the gate opens each day. The kitchens don't start serving breakfast until the eighth hour, and we've seen that he's fed after everyone else's meals are served. Odds are, nobody will discover he's missing until his meal is delivered. So we'll ride out, saying we're exercising the horses. We can steal a horse for him and he can come a few meters behind us."

Will nodded toward the main gate. "I've been watching the guards at the gate over the past few days and, while they check on people coming in, they don't take too much notice of people leaving the castle. I guess they think if you're in here, you've already been checked. But if the worst comes to the worst, and we can't bluff our way out, we may have to fight. There are six guards at the gate, but if we take them by surprise, we should make it out. While we've distracted the guards, he can ride out. Then we ride as if the devil is after us."

Maddie pursed her lips. "That's one too many 'if's for my liking," she said.

Will shrugged. "Can you think of another way?"

She shook her head.

"Neither can I. And at least this plan is simple, which is all to the good."

"I suppose so," Maddie agreed.

"One thing," Will said. "We're going to have to do it in the next two days. I think Lassigny is getting suspicious about us. He was asking where you were last night and he's engaged me to sing again on the sixth day—and I don't think he liked my singing all that much."

"Suspicious? What does he suspect?" Maddie asked.

Will shook his head. "We're strangers. We're foreigners. And he's a man who's up to his neck in plots and treachery. Men like that are always suspicious."

"Then the sooner we get the prince out the better," Maddie said. "Let's do it tonight."

Will thought about it for several seconds, then nodded slowly. "That's what I was thinking," he said.

39

They planned the rescue mission for the third hour after midnight. The moon was due to set at the first hour, and there was a heavy cloud cover, so they would have ample darkness and shadow to conceal their movements.

This would be important if three of them were to make it down the outside of the tower and across to the stairs leading up to the ramparts without being seen by the sentries. It had been relatively easy for Maddie to manage this, but with three of them, the chances of being noticed were much higher—particularly as the prince was unused to moving without being seen.

The day passed slowly. They visited the stables in the early afternoon, on the pretext of feeding and watering their horses and cleaning out their stall. They took their few belongings with them and concealed them in the back of the stall.

Maddie forked extra straw into the stall, piling it at the rear. They would use it to conceal Prince Giles when he was in the stable. Will checked the leather bow case. It appeared to have been untouched since they had left it at the back of the stall. Both bows and quivers were still inside, as well as two double scabbards, each one with a saxe and a throwing knife.

The one item Will didn't take with him was his mandola. It hung on a peg outside his sleeping space in the keep, and it would be too obvious if he were to remove it to the stables—a clue that he was planning to leave.

"Pity," he said, regarding it as they returned to the common room. "I'll miss that mandola."

Maddie smiled sympathetically. "Just as well it's not your Gilet," she said. The Gilet was Will's pride and joy, a mandola made by one of Araluen's finest luthiers, which had been given to him many years prior. It was a very expensive instrument, and he had decided not to risk it to the rigors of travel.

The evening meal was served at the usual time. It was a rich vegetable stew, with fresh, crusty bread from the kitchen and jugs of ale, wine and water on the table. Maddie's stomach was churning with anticipation of the coming action and she picked at her food until Will admonished her.

"Eat up," he said. "You won't be getting breakfast and you don't know when your next meal is going to be."

She nodded, realizing the good sense of his statement, and applied herself to the task of finishing the bowl. The food served in the common hall was simple and the menu unvarying. But it was tasty and nourishing all the same—although this time, she might as well have been eating straw for all the flavor she found in her food.

They finished the meal with coffee, sweetened with honey as usual. Will had prevailed on one of the servers to provide a small bowl for them at each meal.

As the platters and bowls were cleared away, the people in the common hall broke up into small groups, pulling their stools into circles and talking and laughing together while they finished the ale and the wine. Will pushed back his stool from the table and rose.

"Let's get some sleep," he said. "It's going to be a long night."

Maddie yawned as he said it. She had been awake most of the previous night and had had no chance to catch up on her sleep during the day. But as they headed toward the sleeping niches set around the wall, a servant intercepted them.

"How about a few songs, jongleur?" he asked. His tone was friendly and he gestured toward a small group of his fellow workers who were gathered in a half circle, watching hopefully. Will hid his reluctance behind a smile. After all, no jongleur would refuse such a request, as it would provide an opportunity to earn a little extra money.

As he took the mandola down from its peg, he was glad he had decided not to take it to the stables with their other belongings. Its absence might have been difficult to explain. He moved to the small semicircle of expectant staff, hooking a stool with his foot as he went and positioning it in front of them. A few other people in the room, seeing he was preparing to sing, moved to join the audience. Maddie, deciding that her absence might be noticed, took a seat at the rear of the audience, where she could lean back against one of the long tables.

It's all right for you, she thought to herself as Will launched into his opening song. This gives you something to take your mind off things, while I'm sitting here thinking about all that can go wrong.

The tight knot of tension was back in her stomach. Waiting was always the hardest part, she thought. In spite of the tension, or perhaps because of it, she yawned hugely. She closed her eyes, hoping that the sweet sound of the mandola and Will's soothing voice might help her relax.

After several minutes, she sensed movement in the people around her and opened her eyes, looking around the room. The seneschal, Sir Gaston, had entered the room and was scrutinizing the occupants with his gaze. Seeing Will performing to a small but attentive audience, he watched for several minutes, his foot tapping in time to the music. Will looked up, caught his eye and acknowledged him with a slight bow of the head.

Sir Gaston nodded in return, then turned away and headed for the large doorway. Odds are, he was on his way to the dining hall on the next floor, where he would report to the Baron.

Just as well that servant asked you to sing, Maddie thought. Sir Gaston will report that all is normal in the common room.

Will sang another two songs after the seneschal had left, then brought the performance to a close. The audience clapped appreciatively and, one by one, they rose to drop a coin or two into his hat, which was laid on a bench beside him. Then they drifted away, breaking up into smaller groups.

Will scooped the money into his belt purse, then hung the mandola on its peg once more. Maddie noticed his hand lingered on its polished wood surface for a few seconds, as he stroked the instrument in a private gesture of farewell. Then he caught her eye and nodded meaningfully at her sleeping niche.

She rose and moved to the narrow bed, removing her boots and swinging her legs up onto the mattress before pulling her blanket up around her. Will peered round the end of her curtain.

"I'll wake you at three," he said.

She nodded. She knew he had an uncanny knack of waking himself at any hour he pleased. He pulled the curtain shut, cutting out the dim light from the common room. Maddie lay on her back, breathing deeply, listening to the muted conversations around the room.

She noted the strange phenomenon that, when a person is half asleep but conscious, they can hear the voices around them more clearly, and listen in on conversations that are being carried on in lowered tones some distance away.

She yawned again but sleep eluded her, even as the room outside her niche grew quieter and darker and people drifted off to bed, dousing their lanterns as they went. Her mind raced, going over their plan, listing the things that could go wrong.

The curtain wall sentry might see her, or Will, as they climbed the tower. What if Prince Giles cried out in alarm when they entered his tower room, alerting the guards outside his door? What if he lost his nerve and made a noise or fell, when they hauled him up to the top floor? What if they were spotted as they descended from the sixth floor to the battlements? What if the stable master woke when they entered the stables to wait for the morning?

What if, what if, what if? She had told Will there were too many "if"s involved in this rescue attempt. Now all of them crowded into her mind, dispelling any possibility of sleep, leaving her tossing and turning on the thin, straw-filled mattress.

The watch tower bell struck twelve. She counted the strokes. But her mind was racing and she couldn't sleep. Still wide-awake, she heard it strike one, then two. Then, perversely, in the last hour, she drifted off, waking suddenly when Will's hand shook her shoulder gently. As she did, she heard the bell finish striking three.

"Time to go," Will whispered.

40

THE MAIN DOOR TO THE KEEP WAS SUPPORTED BY RUSTY hinges that creaked loudly when the door was opened or shut. By day, this wasn't too big a problem, as the sound blended into the ambient noise of the comings and goings in the courtyard outside.

But now, in the still of the early morning, all was silent outside and the squeaking hinges would be audible around the courtyard and on the battlements. Will had brought a small bottle of thin oil with him and they paused inside the door as he poured liberal amounts over the three large hinges.

Maddie fidgeted impatiently as they waited for the oil to penetrate the crevices in the hinges and lubricate the metal. Will frowned at her and mouthed the words, *Be still.* She sighed quietly and tried to settle down. Finally, after what seemed like an age, Will nodded to her and took hold of the large metal ring that opened the door latch. He turned it and eased the door open several centimeters, testing the effect of the oil.

There was an initial squeak as the door first moved, then the hinges fell silent as the oil smoothed their movement. Will opened the door a few more centimeters. There was no further noise and he opened the door wide enough to let Maddie pass through.

"Go," he said softly.

She slipped through the narrow gap and, hugging the wall, turned left, away from the tower. They had planned this earlier. If they were seen crossing the courtyard, it was better that they weren't seen heading for the tower where Giles was kept prisoner. Will had decided that they should make for the stables first, then, keeping close to the base of the curtain wall, move around to the stairs leading up beside the southwest tower, staying in the deep shadows under the walkway.

He watched as Maddie's dark form crossed to the stables, then disappeared in the shadow. Then he slipped round the door, closing it gently behind him, and followed her.

The courtyard on this side wasn't completely empty, another reason for choosing this route. There were stone benches, a drinking trough for horses and several mounting blocks on the way, each of them providing cover to conceal their furtive progress from any eyes that might happen to look their way. Will slipped from one piece of cover, from one area of shadow, to the next. He moved swiftly, but without undue haste that might attract attention or catch a sentry's peripheral vision.

He passed the stables, sheltering for a few seconds in the deep shadow under its recessed main door. He waited, watching and listening, to see if there was any sign that their movement had been noticed. There was no outcry, no sound of alarm, so he continued, slipping across the last piece of open ground to the line of shadow under the walkway. As he ghosted his way into the concealing darkness, Maddie rose from a crouch in front of him. He nodded to her and jerked his head toward the stairway beside the southwest tower.

They could hear the measured tread of the battlement sentries on the wooden walkway above their heads as they made their way with virtually no sound around the inner wall to the stairway. Maddie crouched at the base, waiting for him, and he signaled her to go ahead. On hands and knees, she swarmed up the stairs, staying close to the wall. He watched from below, seeing her freeze as the sentry's footsteps approached. Then, as he turned away again, she continued to the top of the stairs, stopping just below the walkway level. Silently, Will followed her, reaching a spot just below her as the sentry returned.

They had planned the next sequence of movements earlier in the day. As the sentry began his return patrol, Maddie slid over the top of the stairs and moved to the battlements alongside the tower. Will waited. There was no time for two of them to make it to the battlements at the same time, and not enough cover for two of them to stay concealed if they did. He peered carefully over the top of the stairs. The sentry was halfway along his prescribed beat. His opposite number was still far enough away not to notice Maddie's dark form as she climbed onto the battlements, crouching low, then clambered onto the wall of the tower, moving out around the curve so that she was out of sight.

Will waited, crouching in the darkness, as the sentry returned. He was confident in his ability to remain unseen—after all, he had been doing this sort of thing for over twenty years now. But still, his heart beat at an accelerated rate inside his chest. There was always the chance that something could go wrong.

He counted slowly to himself, hearing the sentry come back, then turn away. He had to give Maddie time to climb to the higher level and lower a rope for him. He reached two hundred as the man was on his return path. He'd have to wait now until he reached the tower, turned again and headed back. He heard the footsteps grow louder. They stopped just above him and he heard the sentry yawn. Then his boots scraped on the walkway as he turned and headed off once more.

Will rose to a crouch and swarmed across the walkway to the wall.

In the chamber on the sixth floor, Maddie waited impatiently. She knew Will would have to time his movements to coincide with the sentry, but he seemed to be taking an interminable time about it, she thought.

She had gained entry to the same room with no problem. The window was still unlatched from where she had opened it the night before. Obviously, the chamber was unoccupied. Tonight she had brought with her a bent piece of wire, which would let her hook the latch behind them when they made their way back down. That way, there would be no evidence of the route taken by the escaping prince.

She peered out the window, looking down, waiting for Will to appear. There was no fear that she might be seen. She was halfway around the curve of the tower wall, concealed from the sentries' view. Then she saw the dark shape moving on the wall below her, scrabbling his way out and around the curve of the tower to a point where he too was concealed from the battlements. She gave a soft whistle and saw the pale oval of his face as he looked up, spread-eagled on the wall. She lowered the rope that she had ready until it reached him, then secured it to the leg of the bed in the room with a series of half hitches.

Taking hold of the rope, Will leaned back, placed his feet against the rough surface of the wall and began to climb.

"It's all right for you to go climbing up the wall like a giant spider," he had told her earlier. "But I'm older and heavier than you. I'll use a rope, thank you very much."

In spite of his protestations, he climbed quickly, and when he slid over the windowsill to join her he was barely breathing hard. He's very fit, she thought, and led the way to the door.

There was no need for them to speak. They had planned their movements meticulously during the day. As before, she eased the door open and checked the central space outside. There was no sign or sound of movement, so the two of them, moving like silent shadows, made their way across to the stairway and started up.

This was familiar ground to her now, and she had briefed Will thoroughly. As they went higher, they began to hear the mutter of voices drifting down the stairway from the seventh floor. The guards weren't as noisy as the previous night. But then, it was much later and probably some of them were dozing while the others kept watch. She signaled upward with her thumb and the two of them slid round the banister pole and started up to the top floor.

They wasted no time looking round the big open space but headed directly to the window she had used the night before. Will unlocked it while she fastened the rope to a bed once more. They stood together, peering down at the window directly below them. She seized hold of the rope and started to climb onto the windowsill but Will stopped her, with a hand on her shoulder.

"I'll go first," he said softly. "When you see me go through the window, you follow me."

She nodded and stood aside as he climbed onto the windowsill and let his legs dangle over the long drop. He took hold of the rope and, in a smooth movement, swung out, placing his feet against the wall and walking himself down the tower to the window below. She craned out, watching him as he settled on the window ledge. The clouds cleared for a few moments. She saw the gleam of starlight on his saxe and heard a faint click as he unlatched the window. Then he went through the open window and disappeared from view. She took the rope in both hands and lowered herself over the edge, going hand over hand down the rope.

One floor down, Will stood by the window, getting his bearings. The room was lit by the dim glow of a small lamp set on a table in the center of the room. Either Giles was a nervous sleeper or, more likely, the lamp was kept burning so the sentries could check on him from time to time. There would almost certainly be a spyhole in the door somewhere.

Giles himself was flat on his back in a narrow bed set against the wall. The soft sound of his snoring indicated that he was fast asleep. A faint slithering sound from the window told Will that Maddie had followed him down. She swung her legs through the open window, then eased herself down into the room. He put a finger to his lips—an unnecessary warning, he realized—and pointed to where Giles was sleeping. He then pointed to himself, indicating that he would wake the prince.

Maddie looked at the door. Outside, the guards seemed to have fallen silent. Or maybe the thickness of the door masked the sound of their soft conversation. She took a pace toward the door, her hand on the hilt of her saxe, and nodded to Will, indicating that she was ready.

Will took a deep breath. This was going to be the tricky part, he thought, waking Prince Giles without having him make too much noise. He crossed silently to the bed and knelt beside it. He readied his hand above the prince's open mouth.

Just as well he's sleeping on his back, he thought. Things would have been much more difficult if he had been on his side, facing the wall. He placed his mouth close to Giles's ear, and dropped his hand over his mouth, holding him firmly, muffling any sound the prince might make, preventing him from crying out.

He felt the young man's body stiffen in alarm as he came awake, and heard a faint grunt as he tried to speak.

"Don't cry out, Prince Giles," Will whispered in the prince's ear. "We're here to rescue you. Your father sent us. Relax. We're friends."

He could see the prince's eyes, wide and ringed with white, staring up at him. Gradually, as his words sank in, he felt the young man relax.

"Do you understand?" Will continued, keeping his voice low and calm. "We're friends. Don't make a sound."

Giles nodded his head—insofar as he was able to nod under that iron grip. Will saw the alarmed look in his eyes drain away and the prince lay still.

"I'm going to take my hand away," he continued, maintaining a soothing, even tone of voice. "Don't make a sound. All right?"

Again, the prince nodded and Will slowly removed his hand, ready at a moment's notice to replace it. But Giles was silent, apart from his ragged, panicky breathing. Will nodded encouragement. Keeping his face close to Giles's ear, he continued to speak in the same quiet, soothing tone.

"That's good," he said. "Now, here's what we're going to do."

41

HE EASED HIS HAND UNDER GILES'S SHOULDERS, RAISING HIM to a sitting position and turning him so his feet were on the floor.

"We're going out the window," he said, indicating the open window a few meters away. Instantly, he felt Giles's body stiffen and he saw the whites of his eyes widen in fear.

"Don't worry," Will whispered, trying to sound as reassuring as possible while keeping his voice lowered. "We'll have you on a rope and we'll pull you up to the next floor. You won't have to do anything."

The young prince shook his head. "But I can't—" he began, fear causing his voice to rise to a dangerous level. Quickly, Will clamped his hand over the young man's mouth again and shook his head.

"Keep your voice down!" he whispered urgently. "The Baron's men are just outside that door."

He felt the prince breathing rapidly, but some of the tension went out of his body and he looked at Will, motioning for the Ranger to remove his hand. Carefully, Will did as Giles requested, ready in an instant to clamp it back over his mouth if necessary.

"But the height . . ." Giles whispered. "I have no head for heights."

Will patted his shoulder. "Just keep your eyes closed and we'll do all the work," he said. "Now come on."

With his arm around the young man's waist, Will raised him to his feet and urged him toward the open window, where Maddie stood, her hand stretched out to him. Fearfully, Giles stepped across the room until he had taken Maddie's hand. She drew him toward her so that he was leaning against the wall, to one side of the window. Will turned back to the bed and quickly stripped off the quilt. Rolling it into a cylinder, he lay it on the bed and pulled the blankets up over it. He regarded it critically. To a casual glance, it looked as if there were someone asleep in the bed.

"That should do it," he said to himself. Then he joined Maddie and Giles by the window.

"You'll have to go first," Maddie told him. "I can't pull him up by myself."

He nodded, and reached out the window for the dangling rope. As he did so, Giles, thinking he was about to be tied on and forced out the window, pulled away from Maddie's grasp. There was a small table against the wall, with an unlit candle in a candlestick on it. The frightened prince bumped against it and before Maddie could reach it, the pewter candlestick toppled and fell, rolling off the table and onto the floor with a crash that sounded deafening to their highly strained senses.

Instantly, Will flung his cloak over Giles and dragged the

prince down to a crouched position beneath the window. Maddie froze against the wall, pulling her own cloak tight around her.

There was a rattle from the door as the cover to the peephole was flung open. For a moment, a glimmer of light showed from outside the room, only to be snuffed out as someone put their eye to the peephole.

Fortunately, the window wasn't in a direct line with the peephole. It was off to one side. Maddie's heart pounded against her ribs, then she heard the peephole cover closing and a voice from outside the door.

"It's all right. He's still asleep."

They waited for several minutes, making sure the guards were satisfied. Then Will swung himself up onto the window-sill, gripped the rope and started climbing.

Maddie watched the end of the rope jerking in time to his movements. Then it fell slack and she knew he'd reached the window above them. A minute or so later, the rope reappeared, jerking up and down several times as he signaled to her. She leaned out the window, caught the loose end and brought it inside, knotting it quickly around Giles's body, under his arms. Giles whimpered, looking fearfully at the window and sensing the long drop below it.

"Come on," she said, urging him toward the window. But he shook his head and pulled away, muttering indistinctly.

She put her mouth close to his ear and spoke urgently, albeit in a lowered tone. "For pity's sake, get a grip. If you keep making noise, they'll be in here and we'll be captured. Now come on!"

Again, Giles shook his head and tried to pull away from the open window. Finally, Maddie's patience gave out. Quickly, she drew her saxe and slammed the hilt against the side of Giles's head, stunning him. As his knees gave way, she caught him and draped him over the windowsill to prevent him falling to the floor. She tugged fiercely on the rope and felt it tighten as Will began to haul the dazed prince up. She guided his legs and feet out the window and watched as he slowly rose, in a series of small jerks, out of sight.

It seemed like an eternity before the rope dropped outside the window once more. She seized it, slipped the loop around her shoulders, then went out the window and climb-walked up the tower wall to the top floor. She went headfirst over the sill, rolling to her feet and casting the rope to one side. Will was kneeling beside Giles, who was shaking his head blearily.

"What happened?" he asked her.

She shook her head angrily. "He panicked and I had to knock him out." She let go a huge sigh of relief, feeling the tension of the last few minutes releasing as her heart rate slowed. They were out of Giles's chamber, away from his guards. Now it was a simple matter of making their way down to the sixth floor and lowering him to the walkway on the wall.

And if he doesn't go quietly, she thought, I'll knock him senseless again.

Will was heaving Giles to his feet. The Gallican prince shook his head, a puzzled look on his face.

"Are you all right?" Will said, and Giles nodded uncertainly. Will led him to the door, one hand under his elbow. He paused again and laid his ear against the rough wood of the door. There was no sound from outside. "Okay," he said. "It's all clear. Just follow me and stay quiet. If anything—"

He got no further.

The door crashed open and the room was flooded with light

as Baron Lassigny and half a dozen armed men burst in from outside.

"Well, well," said the Baron in a voice thick with sarcasm. "It seems the jongleur has come to sing you to sleep."

His eyes shot to Maddie as she made a belated attempt to draw her saxe. "Don't do it!" he warned her.

Will gestured for her to stop. "Leave it, Maddie," he ordered. Against so many men armed with swords and clubs, their two saxes would be hopelessly overmatched.

As Maddie let the weapon drop back into its sheath, the Baron signaled his men forward.

"Tie them up," he ordered. "They're under arrest."

TO BE CONTINUED